GREENFINGER

Greenfinger

JULIAN RATHBONE

VIKING

ACKNOWLEDGMENTS

It is not done for a fiction writer to admit that his fiction has some basis in reality, or that he has been helped by others in his researches. However, I have had so much help with this book it would be churlish not to acknowledge some of it. So—thanks to Di and Phil, who wrote so often and so copiously throughout their two years in Central America and whose photographs were an inspiration as well as a source of information; to Milan, who talked me into the herbarium at Kew Gardens, and to the eminent botanists I met and talked to there; and to Nick . . . for Greenfinger.

I have read shelves of books, but one must be mentioned: *A Naturalist in Costa Rica* by A. K. Skutch, published by the University of Florida. I think it is better than Gilbert White's *Selborne* and it deserves to be far better known than it is.

VIKING
Viking Penguin Inc., 40 West 23rd Street, New York, New York 10010, U.S.A.
Penguin Books Ltd, Harmondsworth, Middlesex, England
Penguin Books Australia Ltd, Ringwood, Victoria, Australia
Penguin Books Canada Limited, 2801 John Street, Markham, Ontario, Canada L3R 1B4
Penguin Books (N.Z.) Ltd, 182–190 Wairau Road, Auckland 10, New Zealand

Copyright © Julian Rathbone, 1986, 1987
All rights reserved

First published in 1987 by Viking Penguin Inc.
Published simultaneously in Canada

First published in Great Britain in different form by
William Heinemann Ltd. under the title *Zdt.*

Grateful acknowledgment is made for permission to reprint an excerpt from "Love of the Common People" by Ronnie Wilkins and John Hurley. © 1966 Tree Publishing Company, Inc. International copyright secured. All rights reserved.
Used by permission of the publisher.

"La Muralla" is by the Cuban poet Nicolás Guillén.

"Canción de Cuna" is by Valdés.

LIBRARY OF CONGRESS CATALOGING IN PUBLICATION DATA
Rathbone, Julian, 1935–
Greenfinger.
I. Title.
PR6068.A8G7   1987   823'.914   86-40501
ISBN 0-670-81588-8

Printed in the United States of America by
The Book Press, Brattleboro, Vermont
Set in Meridien

. . . a country that is primarily agricultural should not be dependent upon imported foodstuffs. I would search the world for a constellation of perennial plants that together would yield a balanced diet, and I would spare no pains to adapt them and their products to the requirements of each of the major regions of tropical America.

A. K. Skutch
A Naturalist in Costa Rica

Weed: *Any plant growing in the wrong place at the wrong time.*

Part I

1

Costa Rica is noted in Central America for its stability, cleanliness, fairness, democracy, and for the fact that it has had no army since 1949. Yet it has its problems. The population is expanding, not least because of the excellent health service, and the world markets in its principal exports have collapsed. As an ex-president once said, Costa Rica provides the desserts—the bananas, the chocolate, the coffee, and when the West tightens its belt those are the things they cut out.

There is land hunger in the countryside, work hunger in the agglomeration of towns round San José on the central plateau, and hunger for the capital that would create industry. Most disturbing of all, as prices rise, there is real hunger—not so much in the shanty towns, the *tugurios*, or dungheaps, on the peripheries of the towns, but more often in isolated corners near the centres where old apartments collapse as rents are no longer paid and squatters live next to the old and infirm.

Eighteen months ago, as I write this, a man was killed in one of these areas. He was leaving the local branch office of the Communist Party when he realised two men were on the other side of the narrow alley. He turned to get back into the CP office but was cut in two by a short burst from a Heckler and Koch machine-pistol. The assassins snatched a small green satchel which he had been carrying.

The police arrived quickly and were punctilious in the way they carried out their duties. It was established that the dead man was Ignacio Morena, a Nicaraguan botanist. His papers were in order, his presence in Costa Rica properly visaed. He had been researching native strains of *Zea mais*, maize, in the herbarium of the Museo Nacional.

It was assumed that the killers were "Contras," Nicaraguan exiles operating with U.S. support against the legal, democratically

3

elected government of Nicaragua.   Nobody looked deeper than that for a motive.   Why should they?

The green cloth satchel had contained rhizomes, or tubers, that Don Ignacio had found somewhere in the interior.   They were not thought to be significant.   A week later the case was filed.

A circular storm stacked cumulus above a horizon where bruise-coloured cloud base fused with black sea.   Nearer, the crowns of palms thrashed in sudden gusts of wind and the scarlet and purple bougainvillaea shivered and shimmered as fingers of air were pushed through the blossoms.   Fitful sun struck rich white gold from the chrome of cars and a darker glow from bronze-tinted glass.   A rolling bank of dark vapour pushed back the sunbeams, scattered them over the thoroughfares, shanty towns and scrub, leaving almost black the six squat octagonal towers that clustered asymmetrically round a taller pentagon.

The concrete emulates basalt, the window frames are finished in chocolate matt.   Only the giant sign turns slowly to catch the diminished light—A and F in gold, solid thick and round, and for an I a stylised chunky corncob in flashing green: AFI, Associated Foods International, Americas Divisions.

Shallow steps, glossy and dark, climb to toughened glass which soundlessly slips open.   Lit by concealed spots, ferns and ornamental palms gleam.   A fountain tinkles and a tape plays the slow movement from Beethoven's Pastoral, endlessly repeated. Facing the entrance, and framed in giant curtains made from textured wool, a huge bronze slab names the twenty-eight companies from Agrob SA to Zeaprod PLC that make up AFI. Among them GREENFINGER Inc. stands out, its letters larger, and the "I" of "FINGER" again an unopened corncob set as the raised finger of a clenched fist.   Beneath it all, the legend runs, "Who makes two ears of corn, two blades of grass grow where one grew before deserves the lasting gratitude of all mankind."

There is no receptionist, no guard, but each of the black doors has the thin slit that will receive a plastic card.   If the code on the magnetic tape is right they open and take you into galleries where computers and retrieval systems spin, flash and hum, or up to offices clustered at the top of each tower.   There men, mostly men, very few women, sit at huge desks beneath more palms and ferns.   They murmur to each other over cordless phones, tap but-

4

tons on desk consoles, and muse over the green glowing data that pulse across their screens. They do not heed the cloud palaces that form, shift, and tumble, the endless succession of spume-crested rollers, the head-shaking dance of storm-tossed palms, and they hear nothing save each others' voices, laid back and cool, and the ticks and bleeps of shifting displays.

The office of the vice-president is at the top of the Centre Core. Its enormous windows fill three sides of the pentagon and all look out onto the ocean. The vice-president alone of all who worked there did likewise, but only when the surfers included nubile girls. That day the weather was bad. And the news on his desk was bad too.

A large man, approaching sixty, he was happy enough with the toys technology had given him, less happy with the smart-ass snow-snorting technocrats, Uncle Gadgets he called them, Digital Men, who sought to replace him. He tapped out a code. Heard a buzz. Spoke.

"Matt. I've had a word with Jethro about this thing. You should look at it. GF16932/ZM85 will get you in."

Over in Core One Matt Annenburg, tall, neat, with gold-rimmed spectacles, heard his master and obeyed. Figures, words, trickled across his screen. He watched them for a time, then picked up his cordless phone.

Coffee cups clinked, silver chimed.

"What I have to say is this," Annenburg's accent was polished New England. "Zdt has turned out as badly as we thought it might. It makes product, it lasts, it's tough. Product-wise it is three hundred per cent more efficient than straight Zd."

Wind hurled rain on tinted glass. A gesture, no more. Concealed lights brightened, sensitive to the dark cloud that raced in from the ocean. Undistracted, Annenburg went on. "Jethro has ongoing projections which outdo those of six years back."

The woman, thin, middle-aged, tensile, spoke: "Zd is in-house. We can do as much for Zdt."

"No. No point. We have to take it out."

She gave a visual display unit a half-turn towards her. Long and immaculate nails clicked on the keys. Her companion, a man, large and hairy, slowly took off his jacket, released gold

5

cuff-links, and rolled up his shirt sleeves.

"Fine, Matt," he said. "You tell us. Tell us all there is to tell us."

"Sir? Annenburg here. Core Three have put together a scenario relative to Zdt you might be ready to approve."

"Sure they have. They're paid to."

"Right, Mr. Vice-President. It breaks down three ways. First, Nicaragua."

"Why first?"

"The most straightforward, I guess. We take it out."

"Right."

"I mean we really do have to take it out. Right out."

"Fine. Listen Matt. It's your baby. You say that bit of Nic has to go, then it has to go."

"Sir. I think it has to go."

"What else?"

Annenburg pushed back his spectacles so they sat on the bridge of his nose. His hands were sweating. "In Costa Rica we have to take out the source of Zdt. Now that's not quite a straightline project. . . ."

"Someone's on the land."

"Peasant land invasion with support from a government agency, ITCO. And UNAFO's in on it too."

"They can be turned. No problem."

"It may not work out quite so simply. These peasants have been there a long time. Six years. They won't just go. And Costa Rica is not Honduras. It's not Guatemala. . . ."

"Shit Matt. I know what Costa Rica is."

A long pause. Matt sweated on. "I'm not happy. This is a big show."

The voice came again, gravelly, wheezy, from a generation earlier than Annenburg's, a generation that smoked cigars, ate fats, and drank neat spirits.

"Sure it is. If we don't off Zdt the company could lose, worst case base-line projection, thirty million a year. It could be the end of Greenfinger. Work to a budget of three million."

"I meant . . . shouldn't we make it a matter for the Standing Committee?"

Again the long pause. Down below a surfer, staggering along

6

the deserted sidewalk above the heaving sea, struggled to hold on to his board. Great gusts of wind plucked at it.

"Well, no, Matt. I don't think so. It's not that big. I think this is just the sort of show the Standing Committee would like to hear about when a successful outcome has been achieved. And Matt?"

"Sir?"

"That's much the way I'd like it to be as far as I am concerned. From here on in, you're on your own. Of course you must choose and activate a project committee, but keep it small, tight, contained. It'll be your show. Your show, Matt. Let's call the whole project . . . 'Weedkiller.' "

The vice-president shut off the communication system, poured himself scotch, unblended malt. Let's see, he thought to himself, how Uncle Gadget handles Weedkiller. Just let's see if he's got guts and spunk. Let's see if Digital Man has got what it takes.

He rolled the neat spirit over his gums, rinsed it through his teeth, and swallowed. Let's just see.

2

Matt Annenburg, brisk, efficient and frightened, set up his Weed-killer project committee—Maureen Adler from corporation security, Ike Roth, who handled AFI/CIA liaison through an old chum from Cornell, and Jethro Tyler, who had moved about a lot in the Organisation but had started as a microbiologist and could handle the scientific side. They agreed with him that it broke down initially three ways: The Nicaraguan Field Research Station, the Costa Rican bureaucracies, and the United Nations Agriculture and Food Organisation, desk of Middle America.

They decided that Ike Roth would take on board the Nicaraguan angle. For Costa Rica they surfaced a high-definition personality profile of their man there, liked what they saw, flew him up to Florida. It became clear he knew his way round the government agencies and the relevant bureaucracies. And Jethro Tyler knew his way round UNAFO, had worked in the past with the deputy director, who now sat at the Middle America desk, and knew his weaknesses. That took care of the three perceived slices of the Weedkiller operation.

In the week before Christmas Ike Roth met Colonel Jas. Schulz, Jr., in a private sitting-room in the Tegucigalpa Sheraton, Honduras. The colonel was officially on secondment from the Eighty-fifth Airborne to advise the Hondurans on counter-insurgency. In fact his job was to teach insurgency to Nicaraguan contras. Since the recently opened hotel made a speciality of business conferences, the room was equipped with a screen, an overhead projector, and a slide projector. The colonel used the OP and spoke fluently. Part of the preparation for his posting had been a three-week course in MEC, media-enhanced communication.

"First, a satellite pic of the south-west quarter of Nicaragua. As you see, it is almost filled by this football-shaped lake, Lake

8

Nicaragua, emptied to the east by the Río San Juan which flows to the Caribbean and marks the border with Costa Rica for much of the way. The place you are interested in is here.

"In the next picture we focus in and you can see the set-up very clearly. Two composition block buildings, white-washed, corrugated iron roofs. Three glass hothouses. . . ."

"They won't actually be hothouses. Controlled environment units. Humidity and temperature control to force on germination and growth. Probably made in Cuba to Russian design."

"Right. And then filling two hectares split into a grid system of sixty-four blocks, these stands of rice, maize, and beans.

"As far as we can tell it's not defended, not by Nic Regs anyway. But those SOBs all carry guns, usually AKs or ARs, even the kids and the young girls, you can't expect it to be a pushover."

"If I was mounting an operation like this, I'd want air cover, an airstrike followed up by an assault group, and a third section to cover withdrawal. In all I wouldn't take it out with less than one hundred and fifty combat men and I'd want some artillery, mortars anyway. The crops—you want those out too?"

"Sure. Yes."

"I wouldn't use fire. Too much H_2O about. You'll want defoliant, dioxin or one of its improved derivatives, and I'd use it from the air if your operatives don't want to father legless kids.

"So. To summarise. To do this properly, with the right back-up, logistical support, you're talking about battalion strength."

"Colonel, you're putting me on, I guess."

"No sir. No way. I'm giving you the optimum military breakdown. Military optimum is achieved when you take out your objective with no casualties. The more you cut back from optimum, the more casualties you sustain. Take it right down and you risk failure too."

"No way are we going to put in a battalion of trained troops."

"Too right; you're not."

"So give me a bottom-line projection with a sixty-forty chance of achieving objective."

"Given the right equipment, the right training, and above all the right stuff, twenty men could do it. But someone will get hurt, that's for sure, and I don't mean Nics."

"Can you find the . . . right stuff?"

"Sure I can, but I'm not going to."

"No?"

"No. Number one. The shit will hit the fan if we mount an operation out of Costa Rica. Ticoland is very volatile as of now. We're working on it but it's not through yet. And you're in a hurry. If it went wrong and we, the U.S. of A., got tied in, the government could fall and we could end up with an Allende situation. Like in Chile, you know? And another factor. This is all too tied into AFI, and since Guatemala back in the fifties, we don't mount this sort of operation for a specific corporation. That got us a lot of bad press, that did. The way we knocked over a democratically elected government on behalf of United Fruit. So you have to mount this independently."

Ike chewed a nail. "So. Where do I find the right stuff?"

"Try Fritz Steiner. Make contact through the Bay City Bar in San Sal."

"Thanks Colonel."

"My pleasure."

Roth found out who Fritz Steiner was and decided that personal contact was contra-indicated. Steiner was already into areas where AFI would not want to be corporately implicated, and he was in any case not unfastidious personally. Ike went back to the AFI man in San José, and a suitable intermediary was found.

Early in the New Year, then, a small, dapper, dark-haired man with a thin moustache, dressed elegantly in a dark suit, the jacket draped over his shoulder and flashing the peacock-blue silk lining that matched his tie, jigged through the bustling late-morning crowds that thronged downtown San Salvador. He jaywalked across Ruben Darío, dodged a packed bus and a taxi. His open-work black-and-white shoes twinkled up the steps of the huge Metropolitan Cathedral, the scene of the 1979 massacre of students that marked the beginning of the civil war and repression. A tall, fair-haired man, in a short-sleeved dark blue shirt and grey slacks, folded down a newspaper and held out a hand.

"Francisco Franco?"

The dapper little man took the hand, looked up into cold blue eyes, the left one of which was twisted by a deep, irregular scar that ran up to its corner from his cheek.

"I am Fritz Steiner. Have you eaten? No? Do you know San

10

Salvador? Okay. I'll take you to a *típico* restaurant where the *pupusas* are great and on Mondays they have *gallo en chicha*. Fighting cock casserolled with corn."

The two men pushed back into the maelstrom of shoppers, peddlers, businessmen, workers. Everywhere, and never in less than pairs, armed police and soldiers stood on corners or pushed ruthlessly through the densest crowds. Once, near the market, a youth suddenly ran, and two soldiers, white-helmeted, Beretta sub-machine-guns swinging in front of them, clattered in pursuit. The crowds swirled apart in front of them like shoals of fish before sharks.

In the market, beneath flaring lamps or caught in beams of sudden sunlight, small plump ladies in bright shawls prodded live iguanas testing for eggs; towers of caged chickens kept up a steady shrill scream; gaudy parrots looked sullen or screeched; butchers smashed rather than hacked at bloody carcases of goat and pig; huge piles of fruits and vegetables swayed and tottered in baskets on the heads of shoppers and porters.

Out on the other side Steiner, his hand on Franco's elbow, steered them both into a small, dark, but intensely noisy *comedor*. A clothless table was found, briefly wiped. Half-litre beers and *pupusas*, tortilla sandwiches filled with spicy mince, were banged down in front of them. Steiner ordered fighting cock stew.

He leered at Franco. "Not really your sort of place, eh Paco? You're a Tico, aren't you? I guess this is all a bit strong for a Tico. Never mind. The worst that will happen to you is gravy stains on your smart suit. They know me here, don't you Dolly?" He caught the buttocks of a plump, sixteen-year-old *mestiza* girl who was pushing past with plates of piled *pupusas* above her head. She looked at him, head barely above his though he was sitting and she standing, and hate and fear burned in her dark eyes. Steiner leered back at Franco. "María Dolores, a lovely bit of ass." He bit into his *pupusa*, drank beer. "Okay Paco. We'll go on speaking English. You can cope with that? No one speaks mucho English here so we won't be giving any secrets away."

The dapper supposed-Tico nodded, dabbed at his mouth with his bright blue handkerchief, dabbed at his forehead. It was very hot in the teeming *comedor* and the big fans below the ceiling simply pushed the air around, air laden with heat, humidity, food smells, sweat and worse.

11

"Did you realise we were followed here?"

Franco shook his head.

"Out there in the street, on the other side, by that kiosk."

In a gap in the roaring traffic, through clouds of black diesel smoke, Franco saw two men leaning against a wall, smoking. Both wore mirror shades, and both quite clearly had shoulder holsters beneath their loose-fitting jackets.

"They're my minders. They're the real reason I'm safe here. If anything happens to me in here, they'll rub out everyone who works here. Even Dolly. If I get the shits from the *gallo*, they'll firebomb it. You know why I need them?"

"I think so."

"You tell me, Paco."

"You train death squads."

Steiner laughed—a bark rather than a laugh. "Say that in Spanish and I'll have you jailed for a month."

Franco, who had spent much of his life outsmarting bragga-docios, *lazzaroni* and other breeds of street thug to get out of the Mexico City slum where he had been born, and eventually into a promising situation with AFI in San José, smiled blandly.

"If not death squads, then what?"

"Task forces. Groups with a single task."

"*Einsatzgruppen.*"

Steiner leant back, eyes glittering, the grin bending the scar into a line like stylised lightning.

"Paco, I could like you. Sure. *Einsatzgruppen.* Ours here in El Sal are the best. My father was a *Hauptstürmführer*, which is senior to Klaus Barbie. We knew Barbie well and worked with him in Bolivia. We left in 1979 and came here. My father advised the El Sal army. Held rank as lieutenant colonel. Died, naturally, in nineteen eighty-two and I have inherited his position, his knowledge, his techniques."

"And his philosophy?"

"That too, Paco. Ah. The *gallo.*"

The bird, cut into eight pieces in a yellowish stew, was served into shallow bowls with tortillas on the side. The flesh was orangish, brown, stringy, tough, gamey. Steiner tore at a leg with strong white teeth, gestured slowly with the still-linked bones.

"You know, people do not always appreciate the skills, the techniques, the know-how that goes into our work. We do not

12

just drive around the *barrios* with pistols kidnapping people we do not like the look of. There is theory as well as practice. First, in a war, the victorious army drives back the beaten foe, liberates an area of land from the clutch of the enemy. But inevitably a detritus is left behind, like germ-breeding patches on land that has been cleared for planting or building. It is our job, the job the SS did for the Third Reich, to identify where these germ pools are. That requires skill. We look at the records that pre-date our victory, the files, the bank accounts, the police reports, membership lists of clubs and political parties. We speak to the parish priests. We locate the infected areas through these means. Then we infiltrate. And only when we have a sizeable catch do we haul in our net and sanitise the contents.

"Then follows the third phase. Always there are links between germ pools. These must be traced. Some, therefore, will be kept back for interrogation. This must be done skillfully, with intelligence. Barbie was no good in this area, often ruined things by beating prisoners to death with his bare hands. We manage things better here." The three main bones of the leg were now clean. Steiner laid them carefully on the table. "Two years ago the world thought that the FMLN and the FDR were unstoppable, that a second Nicaragua was inevitable. But we have won back the towns, we're winning in the rural areas."

Franco gave up poking at his meat with a fork and also picked up a piece of carcase, learning forward, determined not to be harmed, even by gravy stains.

"I have never," he said, "underestimated the effectiveness of single task groups run on the lines perfected by the SS. Nevertheless. . . ."

"I know what you are going to say. The work you have in mind for a select group of my men is not the same sort of operation. In fact you require a specifically trained *Einsatzkommando*. Let me say all the men I have picked have rural experience. My adjutant is a South African counter-insurgency expert jungle trained by the British in Malaya. My number three is an ex-Green Beret who enjoyed his tour in Vietnam. However, we will need one week of intensive jungle training."

Franco nodded. "That need we have already foreseen. On and near the Pacific coast of Costa Rica we are arranging a training camp for you."

"Good, good. I think I detect the hand of Colonel Schulz in this. Now, we will need a chopper and a good pilot, and a navigator. And arms. Are you listening? Can you remember all this?"

Franco set down the wing he had been gnawing at, wiped his fingers, and leant forward again. Steiner spoke slowly, ticking off the items on his fingers.

"Twenty Armalites with five hundred rounds for each. Two M60s with one thou of tracer for each and one thou conventional. Four RPG7 rocket launchers. They are very effective, easy to come by and their Russian origin always confuses people if they fall into the wrong hands. Two mortars with a hundred rounds for each. . . ."

Steiner's delivery was staccato, clear, not loud. It carried across the tiny space between them in spite of the din inside the *comedor* and from the traffic outside. After each group of items he waited for a nod from Franco before going on to the next. Wiping up the last of the gravy with the last tortilla, he concluded, "One hundred grand, dollars, in advance, the same the day after we do it. Ten grand to any operative hospitalised for more than a week. All medical and funeral expenses. Right Paco, do you have all that?"

Franco nodded.

"Rum?"

"No thank you. I have a lot to remember." He stood. Steiner did not.

"Sure you do. The bill here is yours. Bonus for the proprietor. Usually he lets me eat for free. Can't think why. Pay the lady at the door as you go."

Internal memo. Tyler to Annenburg.

Reference: Weedkiller
Subject: United Nations Agriculture and Food Organisation, Middle America Desk.

1. Roberto González Ortega is retiring prematurely because of chronic ill-health. He needs a clinic and we're subbing him. We're also going to put our muscle into a UNAFO scheme for rehabilitating marijuana fields in Belize, which he is anxious to see launched before he retires.

2. An ambitious Swede called Per Hedborg is about to tour Middle America including a two-night stopover at San José. He's ambitious, wants Roberto's job, and to get it will do what Roberto tells him. He's going on to Belize and I think we could give him an invite to Greenfinger Cay, using the Belize project as an excuse. Some or all of us could meet him there and check him out. This would be the week before Easter.

3. The UNAFO man in San José is Christopher Carter, a Brit agricultural economist. He's new to the game, and anxious to do well. Has recently remarried, and had a baby, so with a previous family claiming maintenance too he's not about to take chances with his job. He works for ITCO, the Costa Rican agency that has the final say on the land where the weed is growing. As of now he is a strong supporter of the peasant squatters on Weedland, but indications are that he will do as Hedborg tells him, who will do what González tells him, who will do what we tell him.

OK, Matt? Ciao. J.T.

The United Nations Agriculture and Food Organisation is housed in an up-ended shoe box by a lake. Alpine scenery floats above the farther shore. It's an open sort of place, busy too. Men and women trot purposefully up and down the concrete steps, past the Henry Moore representing Mother Earth suckling Mankind, in and out the swinging doors, and most have the absorbed, unwatchful simplicity of the innocent. They know why they are there, they know they are doing good, they know that even if they are concerned about position, place, and promotion within the bureaucracies they serve, nevertheless the bureaucracies themselves are a good thing.

Amongst them, having parked his nearly new Saab in one of the more privileged bays, Per Hedborg, a tall, blond, handsome Swede with a neat, fair moustache and big, open blue eyes, walked with even more confidence and springiness than those around him. He wore a neat, narrow-brimmed hat with a feather, a check tweed jacket made from a wool reserved by its Hebridean weaver for the more expensive stores in Europe, and dark slacks. He carried a brief-case ostentatiously made from scarlet plastic—it said, no animal died to make me. He knew where he was going: to Deputy Director Roberto González Ortega—Desk for Middle America, Floor 16.

"So, Per, you're off in what? A week, ten days?" The deputy director, a short, grey-faced man who chain-smoked, peered over half-lens glasses and prodded ineffectually around his desk for a diary.

"Two weeks, sir, to be precise."

"Always you are precise." This was said drily. Always Per Hedborg called the deputy director "sir," just once, at the beginning of every meeting. It was irritating, they had got on well for five years. Shortly, with smoke-induced emphysema already severely incapacitating him, the deputy director would retire and Hedborg would take the desk—unless he did something stupid. González was sure Hedborg had never done anything stupid in his life.

"And this is your preliminary briefing. Well. I have here the files, most recent reports—much of it already familiar to you of course. There are two I should like you to pay particular attention to. One in Costa Rica. One in Belize. The one in Costa Rica has run into something I don't understand too well." With continuing effort he hoisted himself round to the desk, pushed about amongst the files and folders on it, found the one he wanted. "Sant'Simon. You remember?"

"Yes. I remember."

"Simple business. Small-scale. A co-operative coffee farm in the Cordillera de Talamanca, on the west slopes of the Cerro de la Muerte. About thirty families involved. They've been there six years, just now harvesting their second lot of coffee and it's done well. So they are putting in for title. To their land. Our man there is Christopher Carter. English. We pay his salary to work for ITCO, which is the agency that monitors projects of this sort. He's found it viable, recommends ITCO to support the peasants' claim."

He paused, gasped for breath.

Sympathetically Hedborg tried to fill in. "Something's gone wrong?"

"Yes. It's in the folder. Suddenly no one in San José likes it. They want the peasants out. Carter can't see why. He's upset. I can see his point. He says there is an orchestrated campaign

16

against Sant'Simon. . . . Now. Belize."

He pushed one file away, drew in another, sank back into the deep desk chair Per Hedborg could shortly inherit. The ailing Peruvian stubbed out his cigarette, found an aerosol ventilator, emptied his shallow lungs and twice squirted vapour into his rattling tubes. The mauve tinge receded from round his mouth.

"This is important. Lot of land being used to grow marijuana. The owners, smallholders mostly, gave up conventional crops when they found marijuana could do better. They've had problems. American gangsters, Cuban exiles for the most part, buy the stuff, kill the planters and take back their money. The government arrests planters and buyers on a rota and then lets them go again. But given a good reliable market the growers would be happy to get out of it. They'd go back to sugar-cane. So. We have a pilot scheme we're putting together with AFI to grow cane for industrial alcohol. Per, I want this to work. It will please the U.S. drug agencies. It will be very good PR and after the UNESCO fiasco UNAFO could do with that. Matt Annenburg is the AFI executive in charge. You know him."

"Yes. I know him. He's ok."

"I think so. So. I think this one will work. It will look good. UNAFO closes down the marijuana fields in Belize, and moves us a step nearer to solving the coming fossil fuel crisis."

3

At the second meeting of the Weedkiller project committee Maureen Adler, a big woman, lean, tall, dark, and tough, introduced a fourth dimension. She said: "We'll need to put down a sweeper in Costa Rica, in San José. Contingency only, hopefully we won't need him. But one thing I've learnt from the security angle is to take care of contingencies. I'll handle it."

Annenburg was nervous. "It's not part of my perception of Weedkiller that anyone should get hurt. Nor do I think AFI can afford to be exposed on the wrong side of the law."

"Possible exposure is what I'm talking about, Matt. We don't know how things are going to fall out. We don't know who may get in the way, or threaten to blow whistles. In this sort of operation it's always possible that situations can arise where someone has to be stopped. But stopped. Listen, I know what I'm talking about. You let me handle it. I've been here before, I know my way round. Believe me, we need a sweeper."

Matt, who was more frightened of macho women than almost anything else, agreed to let her handle the fourth dimension.

Maureen Adler flew the Concorde to London on a Tuesday, stayed at the Grosvenor House, Park Lane. The next morning a cab took her through cold rain to an address off Baker Street where she had an appointment to see another colonel, though this one was British and retired—Colonel Finchley-Camden of Wolf Hound.

Built in the early nineteenth century as a respectable house for a respectable man, say a pharmacist or a senior clerk in a bank, the office of Wolf Hound was not as big as a town house in Mayfair nor as small as an artisan cottage in Chelsea. It was painted white with a scarlet door. The door knocker was polished brass and in the shape not of the traditional lion but of the head of a wolf or savage dog. Indeed this ambiguity of image existed throughout Wolf Hound. The line drawing on its letter-head resembled a wolf rather than a hound, the glowingly restored Victorian oil painting that hung over the mantel-piece in the ground floor reception room depicted a wolf turning at bay to face hunting dogs—and it was the wolf that was the hero of the picture.

Reception was spotless and orderly. Current copies of *The Field*, *Country Life*, the *Financial Times* and *Design for Safe Living* sat four-square on the mahogany table. Contemporary prints of Peninsular War infantrymen hung in neat gold frames in the alcoves. It was warm: heated by a small simulated log fire that looked very real indeed, set in an Adam grate of polished steel and black iron. The plaster work in the cornices and round the chandelier had the very slightly grey look that reproduction crystal cannot match. Maureen Adler was impressed.

"Come up to my den, Miss Adler, and we'll have a chat."

She was even more impressed with Colonel Finchley-Camden. He was tall, tanned, had silver hair, wore a green jersey with leather shoulder patches over a check shirt and cavalry twills, and he spoke in the slow, easy, entirely confident drawl that only Eton, Sandhurst, and ten centuries at the top can bestow. His "den," in the second-floor front, was less formal than the downstairs room, and was furnished as a bachelor's sitting-room. The armchairs were dark leather, the carpet was from somewhere east of Kars, there were silver trophies, polished but used to hold pencils, pipes and so on. A Sheraton wall table carried drinks in decanters and fresh coffee in a Cona flask. A silver-framed photograph displayed a pale-blond lady surrounded by black Labradors and children dressed in Laura Ashley smocks. Only a large desk, a telephone, a grey filing cabinet and a black Apricot computer suggested that it was a place of work.

"Coffee?"

"Black, no sugar. Thank you."

"No point in beating about the bush. You want a chap to tidy things up for you in . . . where was it? Yes, Costa Rica. That's the jolly little place next to Panama, yes?"

"That's right, Colonel."

"Fine." He drank off his coffee and moved from the armchair to the desk. "As you know, here at Wolf Hound we are basically in the security business. As consultants. Why did you come to us?"

"You were highly recommended. Prima Fuerza in Madrid suggested you could help us."

"Fine, fine. But surely someone nearer your own patch would have done as well. . . ."

"That's disputable, Colonel. And we are very concerned indeed about our profile with regard to this project. We want to keep this angle of the operation as far from home as possible."

Finchley-Camden smiled. Handsome though he was, this was not necessarily a pleasant experience for those who saw it.

"Under the circumstances that's understandable. Well, I think we may have the chap for you."

He unlocked a drawer inside the lid of the desk and pulled out a small flat plastic box much like a TV remote control unit. He dabbed out a sequence of numbers and a small wall safe swung open. Inside, Maureen Adler could see a stack of three-and-a half floppy disks. Finchley-Camden took one, uncased it, and popped it in his Apricot. A display appeared on the screen, he dabbed more numbers on the Apricot keyboard and the display changed.

"I think this might be the chap you need. James 'Dusty,' of course, Miller."

"Yes?" She tried to sound curious rather than excited, tried to manoeuvre herself into a position from which she could see the screen without appearing over-anxious to do so. He made sure she could not.

"Quite an impressive record of mayhem. I came across him in the army, in fact for a time I was his section commander in Cyprus back in the late fifties. Royal Buff Caps. Together we took out a farmhouse. I picked up a gong and he got a reprimand for excessive zeal mopping up afterwards. Then we ran into each other in Borneo. Special Air Service, behind the lines, cloak and dagger stuff, in the jungle. He took out a couple of Indonesian sentries with a rather nasty little trick he'd learnt from a Gurkha who had it, I understand, from a genuine member of the Assassin sect. Sort of Japanese stranglehold with one arm and with the other you twist the chap's head and push at the same time and that way you dislocate the poor chap's cervical vertebrae. Ever since it's been his technique of choice."

"Ever since?"

"Oh yes. Sa'ant Miller has a very considerable track record."

Finchley-Camden had put on gold-framed half lenses to look at the screen. He peered down over them at her, noted the flush that had spread up her cheek-bones to the dark, well-groomed hair about her temples. A big, strong woman, he thought, and very fit. Tennis fit, I should say. Excited now, let's see if we can't give her a thrill. "Do you want to know more?"

"Why not?"

"Next known incident, training with the SAS in the Brecons on the Welsh Borders. They always work in teams of four in the SAS, and the fours naturally split into twos. Miller and his mucker got holed up in a blizzard for a night and cost their team a challenge cup. One of the other pair said their team of four would have won if Miller had not been buggering his fancy boy in an igloo. Two days later he fell out of a tree he had been sharing with Miller and dislocated his neck. No proof of foul play, but everyone knew.

"Then Newry, Ulster, 1973. Four-man patrols in plain clothes. Acting on a tip off went to a pub where they were meant to find a couple of INLA operatives. Two left in the car to cover, Miller and his mucker go in. The car is blown up with an RPG7 rocket, one chap still alive and screaming because his guts are all over the floor. Miller's mucker comes out and is cut down with M60 tracer. Only Miller survived. They'd been set up of course. Ten days later Miller went AWOL, and while he was away his informant was found in the urinal of another pub with a broken neck. Actually she was a woman. Lord knows how Miller got her into the gents. Well, he was right out of order on that one and we had to ask him to leave. Honourable discharge, of course."

"Of course." She thought over what he had said, did some sums. "But he must be getting on a bit now."

"Late forties. But he keeps himself very fit. And of course with experience he had learnt to be thoroughly professional in his approach to his work. And there's another thing. He speaks fair Spanish, has been based in the Canaries for a few years now, where he has quite a nice little number going in the time-sharing racket and so on. So that should help in Costa Rica. They do speak Spanish there, don't they?"

"Yes, they do." She pulled in her legs, straightened her back, made a decision. "How do I get in touch with him?"

"Oh no, dear." Again the smile. "We do that for you. Actually he's just finished a job for a client of ours down in the West Country, so I'll have to wait a couple of days until he gets back to Tenerife before I get in touch. We rather tend to keep away from each other, for obvious reasons, when he's over here. No. The deal is this. You pay us an agent's fee, five grand, pounds, and give us a contact we can pass on to him. After that he's yours. But, let me repeat. He's very professional. Does one thing, and does it well. Don't' try to get him to do odd-jobbing, minding or whatever. And he's not cheap."

"I think he'll do. He sounds the sort of thing we want. But we're not going to take him on hearsay, not even yours. At the very least I want to see him. Myself, preferably; if that's not possible, then a nominee."

"Not possible without our fee on the nail first." He dabbed out the display, retrieved the disk, switched off the Apricot, took off his spectacles and smiled again. "A cheque will do. It'll be invoiced as a consultancy fee, if that's all right. My accountant chappie likes the paperwork to be done properly."

Her cheque-book was cased in snakeskin with a gold clasp. The cheque itself was drawn on a personal account at Chase Manhattan, London. He locked it away in a small, old-fashioned cash-box, and stretched his long legs.

"Sa'ant Miller is staying at the Royal Bath, Bournemouth. He'll be there just tonight, so you'll have to move quickly if you want to see him. And I do mean just so you can look him over. Don't speak to him, don't let him know you're even interested. He's working, he's sensitive when he's working, and you have a pretty neck."

He took her back down to the front door himself, and when he saw it was still raining insisted on calling a taxi for her. This, she thought, is real old-world courtesy.

"Are you over here for long, Miss Adler?" he murmured as he handed her in. "I was wondering, if you're not booked up per-haps we could do a show this evening, take in a spot of sup-per . . . ?"

She smiled back through the open window. "In Bourne-mouth?"

On March twenty-sixth, at 2:15 P.M., in steady cold rain, "Dusty" Miller, ex-Sergeant James Miller of the Royal Buff Caps and the

22

SAS, boarded an Aviaco DC9, flight 1789, at Bournemouth airport, England, bound for Tenerife Sud. He took a window-seat at the rear of the non-smoking section and almost immediately immersed himself in a Spanish textbook on real estate conveyancing. Occasionally he referred to a small dictionary, and occasionally he made notes in a small notebook.

The flight dragged on, above cloud almost the entire way. Children ran up and down the narrow aisle. The Spanish stewardesses played with them, allowed them into the flight deck. Half of the front window had been blocked out with green plastic to protect the crew from the glare of the sun. An hour or so before landing, an F-111 with Spanish markings hurtled soundlessly towards them, passed five hundred feet below, less than a quarter of a mile away on a near collision course at a collision speed in excess of twelve hundred knots.

A small smile lengthened thin lips beneath a close-cropped thin line of a moustache. Miller was forty-five years old but his face looked older. About five foot eight and just on 150 pounds, he was a shade less fit than he would have liked, though he was heavy-boned and well muscled. He was dressed neatly in a grey lightweight suit which contrasted with the informal if expensive leisurewear most of the rest of the passengers wore. His hair, also now just touched with grey beneath the Brylcreem, was cut short in the style inflicted on him when he joined the army cadets at the age of fifteen. Thus he was, in the context of a holiday charter flight, Palmair from Bournemouth to Tenerife, conspicuous, far more conspicuous than he imagined, far more conspicuous than he would have wanted to be.

His eyes drew attention too, especially if one made eye contact, something he usually avoided. They were small, close, grey. They were expressionless like a hawk's or a shark's, save when something deep inside Miller's psyche was touched with excitement— then they smiled. And the only thing that gave Miller that sort of buzz was sudden danger.

He had enjoyed the near miss from the F-111 which no one else had noticed—except the pilots, Miller thought, and they'll be changing their underpants as soon as they can.

He ate and drank nothing on the flight—just a Polo mint on take-off and now another as the steep descent between Gomera and Mount Teide began. At last they broke through the cloud base, and the mountains, dark green on one side, volcanic brown and very high on the other, dipped and swayed above the tilting wing of the DC9. The sea shone like unpolished but damasked gun-metal except where patches of sunlight pierced the cloud and put down pools of blue and green.

An hour or so later Miller unpacked his one large suitcase. He was in a two-bedroom, self-catering apartment in a large complex of chalets, apartments, studios, gardens and swimming pools known as Paraíso del Mar, one of the most financially attractive developments in Playa de las Américas. The apartment was pleasant. The floor was tiled, the furniture gave the impression of Castilian solidity, there was a small but well-equipped kitchenette. The fact that it was exactly duplicated eighty times was, for Miller, an advantage—he could change his address whenever he wanted to, but not his surroundings.

Above all, in a closet in the hall there was a safe. For twelve hundred pesetas, five hundred returnable, reception handed over the short magnetic peg which activated its electronics. He could then set his own six-figure combination and vary it as often as he liked.

In it Miller put the documents which proved he owned fifteen per cent of Paraíso del Mar, the deeds of other properties in Playa de las Américas and the neighbouring resort of Los Cristianos, bonds in Barcelona Textiles and Spanish Nuclear Fuels, fifteen thousand pounds in fifty-pound notes, and one ounce of best quality cocaine. Whenever he travelled he took these with him— except the cocaine which he had bought the night before in the cocktail bar of the Royal Bath Hotel, on his way back through Bournemouth, and the banknotes which he had earned on the trip just finished.

He completed his unpacking—three changes of everything— and in twenty minutes had thus stowed away almost everything he owned. He poured himself a malt scotch and watched the sun sink splendidly behind the island of Gomera. Nearer, the ocean glowed glaucously, palms linked the sea to the sky, and neon signs on discos and hotels blinked and winked. Music, car noises, and an ambulance sirening in the distance. It was warm. Miller liked it.

Later he went out, into the Veronica area of discos, car rental

24

firms, boutiques, bars and restaurants. On the beach, untamed by the moles that protected much of the resort, he watched surfers—Germans, Norwegians, Swedes—who picked up pennies during the day touting for estate agents and discos. The moon was bright above them, directly above them so you could not tell if it was on its back or its front. In a restaurant he ate sea bream and fried bananas and drank rum. He picked up two German girls, took them back to Paraíso del Mar, and when they had all finished gave them the ounce of cocaine.

Then he slept for thirty-six hours. When he woke the Muzak taped into the room was playing a bouncy version of "Fernando's Hideaway."

On the afternoon of March twenty-eighth he found a message pushed under his door. He was to ring a London number, one he knew by heart. He did so from a public phone box which he had to feed with one hundred peseta pieces.

"Finchley-Camden?"

"Here."

"Miller."

"Good chap. First. Your results are in yesterday's paper. Went very well. Good show. Second. We have another for you."

"No. I'm just back. Try someone else. Sir."

"I'm sorry but they've asked specifically for you."

"So?"

"Well, Miller. This may seem rather extraordinary but the fact is they know you bought a white crystalline substance in Bournemouth last Wednesday evening, and took it into Spain where you gave it to two German girls for services rendered."

"I'll break their fucking necks."

"Perhaps. But not yet. In the meantime they seem to have you over a barrel. I really do suggest you do this job. I mean we don't want to have you deported back to Blighty, do we? And Miller?"

"Yes. Sir."

"This job is in Costa Rica. Details later by the usual route."

"Where the fuck is that?"

On his way back to his apartment he bought a copy of the *Daily Telegraph*, always a day late in Tenerife. A retired civil servant had fallen to his death on the cliffs above Durdle Door. Retired from the Ministry of Energy, he had been about to give evidence at a public enquiry into the siting of a nuclear power station on Chesil Beach. The police did not suspect foul play.

And where the fuck is Costa Rica? The rich coast. Presumably they spoke Spanish. If so, after five years in property in Los Cristianos and Playa de las Américas he would be able to cope. Well enough to buy some real estate if nothing else.

It was raining at San José when Miller landed—the volcanoes shrouded in low black cloud, a white mist like cotton wool in the foothills—but here the rain was thick, heavy, warm, the first real squall to mark the end of the dry season, and herald the beginning of the wet which would build up over the next six weeks or so.

Miller was met by Francisco Franco who today wore a light blue raincoat over his sharp suit. He took Miller by the elbow and led him scurrying through and round the sudden puddles, under the rain-tossed palms to his Toyota Corolla in the car park. They drove in silence into San José. Franco spoke only to describe the hotel he was taking Miller to.

"It's the Fortuna. You'll like it. Run by Chinese so it's clean and the food is first-rate—international and Cantonese. Very central, not large. That's what you wanted?"

"Sounds all right. So long as there's a taxi service handy I can rely on."

"I can fix you up with a Hertz rental."

"I don't drive."

Franco, however, drove neatly and well, slotted the Toyota into a gap in front of the hotel, and saw Miller up the steps with his case.

"I'll let you settle in. I'll be back in an hour."

"Give me three."

Miller checked the room and its private bathroom with finicky minuteness, getting to know the positions of everything, furniture, carpets, checking the ease with which the drapes pulled, the shutter blind closed, the amount of weight the shower curtain fixture would support, how easily the taps turned off and on and how hot and cold they ran, whether the bed squeaked, absolutely everything. In half an hour its every feature had become part of his psyche, it had become homeground, his territory, a place he could fight in and have that advantage, a place from which he could escape.

Then he unpacked precisely as he had at Paraíso del Mar, the same things except this time there was no cocaine and less money. There was no safe in the room, which annoyed him, and he took his documents, which represented his accumulated wealth, and two thousand dollars down to reception, booked them into the hotel safe. The Chinese receptionist was cool, efficient, and though young and pretty did not flirt. That pleased him. He bought from her or took as free handouts maps of the city, of Costa Rica, bus and train timetables, the Pan Am and ENTA schedules, the cards of three nearby taxi firms.

Back in his room he stripped, did the Royal Canadian Air Force thirteen-minute exercises, and then had a shower. In the shower he masturbated, briskly, as if to unload a possible source of distraction. He shaved and trimmed his very narrow moustache with an engineer's precision. Before dressing he drank a quarter of a gill of Glenlivet malt, mixed half-and-half with the mineral water supplied by the management. He drank it very slowly and read through the whole of the Costa Rica section in the *Fodor Guide for Central America*, and then went methodically through all the material he had picked up at the desk.

At last he dressed—in check slacks with a crocodile belt, an open-neck plain blue shirt, a dark brown jacket. In the inside pocket he had his wallet, one credit card, and three hundred dollars. No weapon. Miller never carried a weapon unless he knew he was going to need one, and then only for as short a time as possible. His broad, short-fingered but very strong hands were more reliable, and legal too.

Precisely three hours after his arrival the phone buzzed. Franco was in the foyer.

Miller said, *"Dígale que se sube."*

Franco laid on the table four photographs. Two were mugshots, the sort of passport-sized photo one affixes to forms of application, for a job, for a work permit, for a visa. One man, one woman. The other two were larger prints of people photographed unawares in an airport arrival area, outside an office block. He added to them an onion-skin piece of A4 on which four names, places and hours of work, and home addresses had been typed in IBM sans serif.

"None of them is booked yet. There may be others. There may be none."

Miller shrugged. "You know my terms. I stay for ten days at a retainer of two hundred dollars a day plus expenses. If you haven't commissioned me by then I go."

"I don't see . . ."

"I don't care to be too long in a place where I might have to work. Ten days is the limit. I don't mind doing more than one commission but I leave within sixty hours of doing the first."

Franco sighed. "All this has been agreed."

"I like to be sure. One last thing. You pay me five days' retainer now. You don't get in touch with me personally again ever. You send in a sealed envelope details of any further commissions. For these four you simply phone in the letters A, B, C, D and I'll get on with it. Plus of course the twenty grand in cash. Right. I think that's it."

Franco shrugged, counted out ten fifty-dollar notes.

"You have everything you need?"

"Yes." Miller tapped the notes into neatness, folded them into his wallet. "Okay Franco. *Adiós*."

4

An old lady, scanty fluffed white hair, very thin with old bones, saggy skin, dressed in a quilted dressing-gown, raked hot ashes out of a grate and onto ceramic tiles. She then lay down in them and the quilted dressing-gown began to smoulder.

"I'm doing it for you, Kit."

Kit Carter moaned, flung out a hand, pushed the dream of his mother, who had died quite normally of bronchitis and old age the year before, back into the psychic recesses from which it had come, and forced himself up to the surface reality on which consciousness usually floats.

He had a very strong erection, the sort that feels like a telegraph pole. He pulled the girl he was with into him, let her feel it from behind, pushing up between her buttocks. She turned, and he turned with her, onto his back. She pulled herself onto her knees above him but crouched so black hair swung about his face, snagged in his beard.

She eased herself down.

"Gently."

Right down. He was right in.

"Don't do anything. Let me do it."

Her breasts, very small, very white, widely spaced with nipples like tiny walnuts, pressed into his chest; with large hands he held her buttocks, squeezing, kneading, searching the dampness between, finding the solid root of his own sex. She wriggled rhythmically in a tiny spiral motion, pressing herself hard into the bone above his prick. Then she pushed on her hands so the sweat-moistened kissing surfaces of their torsos parted and she ran him in and out of herself more fiercely.

"Kit, Kit, Kit! Kit!"

"Rosa, Rosa, Rosa, Rosa, dearest."

And then his dream broke—the old lady smouldering in her fireplace.

"Kit. You didn't come."

"No. Sorry. But you did?"

"Oh yes. But why . . . ?"

He turned his head, was silent, watched the heavy woven curtains, red, greens, brown, shifting in the late-morning breeze. Outside the traffic from Paseo Colón, two blocks away, was winding up for the pre-lunchtime rush hour. He shifted his head slightly, took in a naïve tapestry of Chilean peasants building a school under the guns of Pinochet's tanks. *El pueblo unido jamás será vencido*—The people united will never be defeated. Too much folk-weave, he thought. Middle-class exiles from Chile go in for it a lot. Liquid dribbled as his prick shrank even more. Fingers slipped over his thigh towards it. He turned on his side to veto their advance.

She sighed. The bed shook as she sat up. He half-turned so he could see her. She was very straight above bent knees splayed out, head dropped forward, white arms raised to hoist up her hair, coil it, fix it with pins.

"Anyway," she said through teeth clenched over the last pin, "I am not your dearest."

"Just now you are."

"No." She shook her head and a lock flopped towards her neck. "That won't do. You have a wife you adore, she will be here in ten days, and when you remember her you don't come with me. I expect," she added, "as the time gets nearer, you will fail yet more disastrously. There. That will do." She swung her legs over the side of the bed, looked back at him. "Perhaps, Kit, this should be the last time. There has to be a last time. Yes," her voice hardened, brooked no dissent, "that was the last time. And very nice too." She kissed a finger, planted it on his lips, stood and pulled around her a thin cotton wrap decorated with blue and lilac flowers. She tied the cotton girdle.

From the bed he looked round the room as the shower hissed, trying to fix in his memory things he would not see again. Yes, a lot of folk-weave and other artefacts from the shanty towns round Santiago. A cork noticeboard on which were pinned letters from political prisoners held without trial. Six long shelves of books—the standard works of Western sociology and anthropology and some of the Marxist and structuralist ones as well— a typewriter, a filing cabinet, raffia mats, cane chairs, lots of cushions, and huge paper flowers.

"Coffee?"

"Of course."

"It's ready."

The fragrance of best Arabica picked three months earlier, not more than fifty miles away, roasted yesterday, and hand ground as he lay in bed and listened to her winding the mill, had heralded it. The shock of its freshness was still a delight, even after five months, a shock that came too with the fruit, the fish from both oceans, even the beefburgers. It was a great country.

He got off the bed, pulled on a long yellow wrap, far too big for Rosa. "How come," he had said on his first morning there, "you have a wrap big enough for me already here?" She had pouted: "It fits most men."

Because he was not the wisest of people and often projected his guilts and hang-ups onto others, he occasionally reacted badly to the garment. At other times, more generous and open, he wore it with pride.

On the table, instead of the usual Spanish-style *magdalenas*, there was a packet of breakfast cereal. Slightly anxious she watched him tip out a handful of tiny squares. Lip-smacking Smalzers, he read. On one side of the packet Disneyesque animals cavorted through a field of stylised maize. Inset in one corner there was a medallion: a clenched fist, the index finger a corncob thrust upwards, and a ribbon. Greenfinger—the Guarantee of Quality. And round the medallion, "Two ears of corn, two blades of grass, where one grew before."

"Do you like them?"

"I don't know. Where did you get them?"

"At the *supermercado* on the corner. I thought they might be what you are really used to."

What my *wife* gives me?

He tilted the box. Made in the U.S.A. "This is Yankee imperialism, you know? Anyway, I think you're meant to eat them with cream."

"Kit. They cost a lot of money. That packet, sixty colones."

Kit Carter sipped coffee, looked across the tiny table at her. She looked back, eyes very dark and shiny, then flinched away. Her tiny ear perfect apart from a gold sleeper, the hair pulled back from it into a neat but by no means severe bun, her long white neck, a pulse just visible in the blueness of a vein. . . .

"Shit Rosa. I don't want to go. I don't want not to come back."

She kept her head turned away, but her voice was steady, light. "Let's have a good feast. A blow-out. Get a little drunk."

"Where?"

"Lobster's Inn."

"Why not?"

An hour or so later they left Rosa's apartment and walked the couple of blocks up to the Paseo Colón. The weather was perfect, almost too perfect. Kit had been in Costa Rica for five months and since it was now mid-March, four of those had been in the dry season. He could scarcely remember the short but torrential downpours that had come every afternoon, nor the occasional tropical storms, huge with much thunder and lightning and great winds storming along the narrow plateau of the Meseta Central. Since December the weather had been uniformly fine, sunny, virtually cloudless, and at nearly four thousand feet above sea level, a perfect temperature in the mid-seventies. His huge Greenpeace umbrella—"Stop Acid Rain"—had remained furled at the back of a closet.

The effects of the long drought were beginning to show. In spite of frequent waterings from massive hoses the larger plants in the many parks had taken on a dusty look, and the same dust, a steady invisible accretion from Volcán Irazú, gusted round the street corners, drifted in the gutters. The weather would soon break, he was now frequently assured by his Tico friends; ochre cumulus piling above the mountains and an increased sultriness in the air towards evening indicated they were right.

Tico, Tica, what do they mean, he had asked, what do the words come from? No one knew—Rica-Tica, Rico-Tico, Costa Ricans, it's what everyone calls us, one colleague in ITCO had said. To other Central Americans it means soppy, sissy, something the opposite of macho. To us it signifies civilised, gentle, generous: all the things most Middle Americans, Ladinos with mixed blood, are not.

Rosa and Kit crossed Colón to look at the windows of two or three clothes shops on the other side. Standing in front of a plate glass window Kit reflected that they made an odd couple.

Not usually an over-observant person, he had not really noticed this before; now, with parting very close, he continued to store up images to remember.

Rosa was small, by Anglo-Saxon standards tiny, less than five feet tall with a heart-shaped face that would have looked elfin but for the great hoops of her gorgeous hair, black, deepest indigo it seemed at times, piled round the back of her head. She always wore simple plain cotton or linen dresses which nevertheless looked very smart, and thin-thonged sandals. One of the things Kit thought he liked about her was that she contrived to look so elegant on what he took to be a very small dress budget.

Kit was dressed in a green, loose-fitting brushed denim jacket, with pleated pockets, and jeans, but expensive ones. His shoes were of faded red leather, made to last forever; he hardly ever wore any others, and they had cost a lot of money.

Now he took in the prices on the dresses she was admiring, coveting. Bleakly he wondered if he ought to buy one for her, and then fortunately had the sensitivity to push back the thought. It had not been that sort of relationship at all, not at all.

An incongruous couple indeed—he over six feet, well built, reddish hair balding but with a luxurious red-and-gold beard, pale blue eyes which, deep-set beneath heavy eyebrows, often looked a little lost. It was a look that appealed to women because of its apparent gentleness, defencelessness. In fact it usually drifted onto his face when he was a little bored or not quite understanding what was going on, or when because of far-sightedness he couldn't read something. But he was only forty, and his father had not worn glasses until he was fifty. . . .

Lobster's Inn was dark after the bright sunlight and crowded with businessmen and a sprinkling of civil servants. There was too a table of American tourists breaking out from their hotel. Still, the head waiter found Rosa and Kit a place tucked away in a timbered alcove. Kit's eyes, refusing to adapt to the gloom, could not cope with the menu and Rosa had to read it for him. He chose *palmitos* salad; she protested, the Costa Rican penchant for the immature heads of the euterpe palm was doing neither the rain forest nor subsistence agriculture any good at all. He was irritated, and insisted. She ordered an exotic mixed affair and laughed when it too, amongst a lot of other fruits and vegetables sliced, diced and grated, had its *palmito* head nestling in the middle.

They had hot Pacific lobsters cooked with spicy sauces and drank rum punches made from Nicaraguan Flor de Caña—the best rum in the world. As Rosa had suggested, they began to get just a little drunk. She chatted brightly, was witty about some of the people she worked with and for at ITCO and elsewhere. She had three posts—sociological adviser to ITCO, consultant to a chain of banana co-operatives in the Valle del Diquis at the southern end of the Pacific coast, and part-time teacher at the Instituto de Antropología Social. It was her work for ITCO that had brought them together, particularly an analysis of kinship at Sant'Simon, a commune of landless peasants farming land without legal tenure.

Suddenly she interrupted herself. "Ugh. I can't stand that man."

"Who?"

"Don't look round, you dummy, he'll know I'm talking about him, and I'd hate that."

"Who then? Do I know him?"

"Charles Darwin Junior."

Kit laughed. "Chas. He's okay. A bit of a clown, but you can have a good time with him."

"*You* can. A man, perhaps. But not a woman. I tell you, Kit, he's a bottom-pinching male chauvinist pig. And he's bad news elsewhere too."

"Because he's an exec for Bullburger Costaricense, SA?"

"Chief exec in San José."

"Really? I didn't know he was that high up."

"You see. The clownish persona. But he's no clown."

"Who's he with?"

"Three Americans. Thin, serious. Botanists I would guess. He's picking their brains on rain forest clearance so he can get yet more pasture for yet more beefburgers."

"Oh, come on, Rosa."

"Listen. In the last twenty years beef production has doubled. But the average Costa Rican, not your Josefino, but your average Tico eats forty per cent less. An American cat eats more."

"Miaow."

"Purr, purr, you mean."

He ordered sundaes, large confections with tropical fruits,

and then went to the lavatory. When he came back she had gone.

He looked round, bewildered, then hurt, especially at the sight of the two sundaes. The restaurant was less full now. Not far away Charles Darwin was shaking hands, slapping the backs of the three thin, bespectacled men he was with.

Darwin was short, fat, and his peripheries were blurred. A frizzed-out halo of thinning hair gave a nimbus to a face half-filled with moonish glasses, a nose that hardly existed, lips made indefinable by spittle. Generally he wore brownish check flannel shirts with button-down collars and buttoned sleeves, and indistinct ties, knotted once, and run up and down for weeks on end. Only his hands were solid—short-fingered, podgy-palmed, but strong.

He almost slapped the buttocks of the last of his guests, sent him on his way into the bright street, then turned to Kit.

"The lady's not for ices." He shrugged, beamed. "She split. I'll split her banana split with you. And a quarter of Flor de Caña while we can."

"While we can?"

Darwin sank into what had been Rosa's place. For all his blurred edges waiters moved at his command, and a quarter litre of the rum appeared on the table with ice, sliced limes, fresh glasses.

"While we can?" Kit repeated.

"Uncle Ron has spoken. No more, no not ever will anyone who likes to be liked by Uncle Ron ever again buy anything from Nasty Nics. Nicaragua. Nix to the Nics."

"Fuck Uncle Ron." Kit poured, not too exactly, Flower of the Cane. "Cheers."

"Ciao."

Darwin leant back, put his palms on the table, titled his chair, her chair, allowed his stomach to inflate so it stretched the buttons on his shirt.

"So, she split. Well, you've been batting some time. Rosa Portillo. Fine piece of ass. No doubt God can make something neater than a lady's ass, no doubt God never did. And of all the ass he ever made Rosa's must be one of the neatest. Not that I ever got to it. I tried, old chum, I tried. But it always seemed to slip out of my grasp. And now she's split on you. Why?"

He spooned deep into Rosa's ice. Kit, angry but helpless, admitted the truth.

"Because my wife is coming out. Will be here in just over a week."

Darwin chimed his/her spoon on the edge of the tall glass. "Uh-uh. Well, well." Suddenly he was bereft of words. He had been outclassed by this Limey in the sport of pussy hunting, for Limey had had good pussy then slipped it just in time before wife turned up. That, for Darwin, was that. He was not going to pursue a conversation on a subject where he could not demonstrate expertise surpassing that of everyone else present. He changed the subject.

"Río Remedios. Those guys I was with are on the research team there. You know. You must have heard of them. Checking out the rain forest canopy with modern engineering, up-to-date technology."

"Yes. I've heard of them."

"Well, you would have had to I think. I mean up the valley from them you have this co-operative running. Sant'Simon."

"I don't run co-operatives."

"You know what I mean. And I have to tell you this, Kit. I was going to anyway, but now the opportunity is here, I'll tell you now." Darwin scraped out the bottom of Rosa's ice, drank rum. "Bullburger has an interest in that team of very deeply dedicated scientists, in fact not to put too fine a point on it, we own them."

"I thought they came from Milton University, Iowa."

"Sure they do."

Darwin let this rest. The implication was that Bullburger, the fastest fast-food chain in the West, owned Milton University. Probably, Kit thought, they do.

"Anyway, they tell me your co-operative—okay, UNAFO and ITCO's co-operative at Sant'Simon is polluting the Río Remedios. Lot of shit coming down. Especially in the dry season. When there's not too much water to dilute it. And I mean shit."

Carter waited. From four, five sources already he had heard similar stories and always the pay-off line was the same. Darwin duly provided it.

"Sant'Simon should go, you know. Sant'Simon will go."

He grinned across the small table like a Cheshire Cat, but a Cheshire Cat that was not about to fade.

Part II

PART II

5

Well. I have this fantastic Spanish lawyer here in Tenerife, called Jesús María Batista y Galdós, and he has asked me to put on tape my whole account of all the dreadful things that happened in Costa Rica and the tragedies, grievous tragedies ending in the not very wholesome predicament I am now in. I am to be entirely honest, which will not be difficult since I have never told a lie in my life, and I must leave nothing out at all, and this won't be difficult either as I am, I think, a very frank and straightforward sort of person, with no hang-ups—unless an irresistible urge to love and to be loved, coupled with a terrible rage against the haters of this world, be counted a hang-up.

He asked me to write it all but shit man I said I can't do that. So he gave me this dinky recorder and lots of cassettes and he and his firm will edit, translate, and transcribe and then I'll have to swear it is my sworn deposition, and being as, since, he will have done mucho good editing and cut out mucho of the shit I am now putting in, it will please the *Juez de Primera Instancia*, and all the other judges too if necessary and I'll be let off with a caution.

Not, I have to say, that I am in any sort of hurry to split from here where I am indeed very comfortable and a lot better cared for than in may other places I have been. Certainly it's better than the Church of England home I was once in. They call this a house of correction, where I am *mantenida bajo custodia*, like on remand, but I get two good meals a day, food I like, the company of the other ladies here for many hours a day, and, of course, they all love Zena. I have fourteen willing and happy babysitters: problem is, I can't get out!

Anyway, back to the long chain of events which brought me to this dire situation.

My name is Esther Somers. I keep my name, even though

married. I am a black working-class lady. Kit used to say: the only way you can't feel guilty of exploiting someone in Britain today is by being black, working-class and a lady. He should have added gay. And that's why he went for me. He said. That is bullshit. He went for me because I am five feet seven inches tall, weigh eight stone ten pounds, have a body like a black birch tree, a mind like an IBM computer, and because I love fucking. He said all that too, and it was truer than the bit about the black working-class lady, though there was a little truth in that too. The poor silly shit was your actual prototype, genuyne, paid-up, Christ-I-am-guilty liberal humanist.

Kit, Christopher Carter, went to a nice fee-paying school where they walloped him if he was naughty much like my Daddy used to wallop us before he got put away. Then a college at Cambridge University where an unlikely talent for speaking foreign languages brought him by degrees—oh, dear me, yes, by many degrees—to being a lecturer at Hume University, Christbourne. Where he was my moral tutor. Moral!

Ooops. I expect you heard. That woke up Zena, so that meant a feed—she still likes a bit of nipple even at eight, no nearly nine months, and then, well, the old routine, some solids and a bit from a beaker, I've never given her a bottle, no way, no rubber in her mouth thank you, not even a comforter, then change her nappy which had a nice little humper in it, smelly but nice and firm. Finally down the corridor to play with María Victoria de los Angeles who the fuzz is trying to prove is on the game and also involved in my spot of bother, so I can now get right back to these my memoirs. I must remember Don Jesús María and try to push on. Where was I? Kit. Poor Kit.

Well. There he was at Hume University, Christbourne. He had tenure. Fifteen grand a year. Sterling. A lovely wife and two lovely children. No. He didn't. I'll tell no lies. His wife was a ratbag and his two children, both boys, were evil. They used to shoot sparrows with their airguns and they were racially prejudiced.

"Daddy, did you go out with your black last night? She gave you curried goat—I can smell it on you."

I get a little angry when I think of that little lot. I hit one of them once. Hard. I told you I hate haters.

40

Kit and I went out for a bit, he and his family split and made a shitty mess of it. She had been a lecturer in French at Hume but now wanted a meal ticket for life.

He had had enough of teaching, was bored, so took early retirement and a golden handshake, three years' salary, and went to Reading University to get an M.Sc. in agricultural economics. He did a couple of lousy jobs for cowboy consultancy firms but ended up with this nice number in San José, Costa Rica, attached to ITCO, paid by UNAFO.

Only trouble was, by the time he landed that juicy little plum, I mean it might have been El Salvador or Chile, I was eight months gone with this juicy little plum, I mean my lovely Zena. . . .

It's now nine-thirty, Zena is again clean, fed and asleep, so I maybe have three, four hours ahead of me. I'll tell it as straight as I can. My head's quite clear. I have to say María Victoria de los Angeles is a nice girl and her boyfriend is nice, came to see her today, and as a consequence we all have a little dope, *ganja*, in here tonight, but nevertheless I will do my best, I will try not to be prolix. That was what Kit used to write on my Galdós Special Subject essays: *try not to be so prolix*. It's what he said when I told him Zena was on the way, but it was just his joke, our joke, really he was very happy. Shit. Now I am going to cry.

Don Jesús María Batista y Galdós. Are you related to Spain's greatest novelist since Cervantes? Maybe you are, he was after all like you Canarian. He was pretty prolix too.

I flew out to Costa Rica on March twenty-seventh. It was a bitch of a journey. Dawn from Heathrow to Miami. Night-stop. Reached San José two in the afternoon on the twenty-eighth. Zena perfect almost the whole way but screamed up a storm in the Miami hotel where some not very nice ex-Cuban gangsters were having a conference and complained of the noise she made. I didn't like the landing at San José. Too many volcanoes around, the *meseta* is not so wide and very built up. Steep descent, set Zena off again so Kit's first sight of her for five months she was screaming up another storm.

You know, Don Jesús, one thing a young mother finds the total pits? I'll tell you. It's the "Hasn't your mother . . . ?" syndrome. Addressed to baby for Mother to overhear. Poor Kit

41

started right in with that: "Hasn't your mummy been treating you right? Did your mummy not change you in the plane, then? Is your mummy's little baby hungry?"

Well, I was very glad to see him, very glad, mind-bendingly over the moon, but all that took the edge off of it. Still, once we were clear of the customs and immigration and all the bullshit, and were sitting up in Kit's Daihatsu luxury jeep for the trip into town, I hoisted up my shirt, plugged myself in, and she shut up. Mind, even then he didn't look one hundred per cent delighted with our behaviour and I reckoned rightly I was soon to discover he was going to oppose public breast-feeding. Tough, Mac, I said to myself, 'cos as long as she wants it, that's the way it's going to be.

The drive into town was not as great as I'd hoped. Mind, the Daihatsu was fine—you sit real high up, and it has class and comfort, I liked that. But all you hear about Costa Rica's beautiful *meseta* isn't so true of the airport road. But airport roads never are that great, are they? Look at the one you have in Tenerife. Half-finished motorways through shanty towns, though I could see back up in the hills it looked prettier, lots of garden-like small holdings, shrubs with scattered white buds under palms—yes, your actual coffee. Kit said soon it would all come into bloom at once, especially once the rain really started and while the full bloom only lasts a day, it's a grand sight.

Shame about the shanty towns, I said, because tell you the truth I was still a bit sore with him, and all his letters had been so full of what a wonderful place Costa Rica is, I wanted to pull him down a notch.

But always the unreconstructed teacher he now told me commiseration was not in order, the *tugurios*, dung-heaps, shanty-town slums were not always as bad as they looked. Mostly they were the newest migrants off the land, not so much starving as looking for a better life in town. Which for the most part they found since they were the peasants with enough get up and go to do something. The serious urban poverty was in pockets where inner urban decay had set in.

Well, this quick rundown of the sociology of the urban agglomeration round San José took his mind off the breast-feeding and let me give the town the once-over as we penetrated the environs and got to the centre. And San José I have to say I like. Although it's set out on a grid system it's bumpy, up and down, and that breaks up the geometry, and then it's got these lovely parks. Kit made a slight detour to take in the Parque Nacional, the Teatro Nacional which is gorgeous, and the Parque Central, before dropping down a bit towards where his, our apartment was, not far from the Pacífico railway station.

And the apartment was fine too. Of course he'd made an effort to get it nice for us, he had had a cleaning lady in, and there were lovely fresh flowers everywhere, gorgeous scents, fantastic blooms. He told me the names of some of them, but I've forgotten. And fruits too. Oranges and bananas ripened right there, they had a fantastic flavour, and *nísperos*, sort of sharp and scented at the same time, papayas, and . . . Poor Don Jesús. You don't want to know what I think of Tico fruit.

Just the two rooms he had, living room and bedroom but both large, a dinky bathroom, and a kitchen just big enough for two to eat in but no oven. There was a fridge though and a small freezer and I was glad to see Kit had bought the Braun food blender I'd asked for, for the baby's solids, and of course in the bedroom a cot too which was really great, being made out of wood and the ends painted up in the peasant designs they use on the ox carts out in the *meseta*. Kit said there's nothing Indian about these, there aren't any Indians in Ticoland, or ethnic, they were invented when the tourist trade first started sixty, seventy years ago. Who cares? They're pretty.

Of course old habits die hard and most of the walls of the living room were lined with Kit's books. He left a lot behind, they're in store now in Christbourne, I suppose I'll give them to the Spanish Department, but all his agri stuff he'd taken out with him at phenomenal expense, plus a whole lot more he'd bought in San José. Mind you, he was on to a good thing, was pulling down more than he made as a full-time lecturer in England. Stereo, TV, video, even an answering machine on the phone. Somehow, sometime I'm going to have to see to all that, if the landlord hasn't thieved it already, oh shit I might cry again.

Don Jesús, you told me to say how much I loved Kit, that that is going to be a great help with *Los Jueces*, if I can convince them of that. Listen, Jesús, I adored that man. But those first days in Ticoland weren't so easy. After five months you remember what you want to remember about a guy and forget a lot else. And in five months a guy can change, especially when he's forty-plus— I mean a bit more hair goes from the crown of his head, his tummy gets a touch slacker, he gets perhaps a touch more staid in his ways. And a baby just eight months old is a hell of a shock, I mean she was less than three months when he went and a lot happens in those months. Well, that's what I put it all down to then, that and I expect he'd found changes in me too, things he'd want to get used to.

So, after we'd had some fruit and coffee, and I'd seen the flat, and he'd tried to erect Zena's baby-walker I'd packed flat in one of my cases, and given up, and I'd done it for him, and she was quite happy scooting about this new lovely place, the walker ran a treat on those terrazo composition floors though the folksy rugs he had, from Chile he told me, snagged it up a bit, I wanted, well I wanted him. You know?

And I expected him to want me.

There's a lot I loved about Kit. His kindness, gentleness, understanding, even his slowness at times, he could be slow, intellectually slow I mean, but he always got there in the end, or beyond there if you're with me—he had real understanding of lots of things. But I loved other things too. He had strong long thighs with curly gingery hair. A broad chest ditto. A tummy with a deep black tummy button and a lovely prick. There I've said it, Don Jesús, but you asked for it. And a lovely hard bum so he could clench my finger tips. . . . And so after an hour or so that's what I wanted and I made up to him in the bedroom, snuggling at him from behind, getting his shirt up and his pants down, and well, really I was very hot and ready to go and it seemed like he was too.

But then something went thud in the living room and Zena began to bawl and we found she'd pulled the phone down on her head.

It was understandable that that put Kit off and we had another session of "Poor baby, did your mummy?" and we left it at that until we had eaten and had a drink or two. We stayed in that evening, though I would have liked to go out, and got Zena to sleep. Then we played some new records I hadn't heard, Quilapayún and Los Chalkakis, I should have rumbled all that Chilean stuff, and I played the new Bruce Springsteen tape I had brought from the U.K., *Born in the U.S.A.* And then we tried again. And as soon as he got his prick half-way in he came and that was that. What's more he went sulky and broody about it and I had to do my mothering bit to cheer him up. He cheered up, but that's all he got up, and though I tried not to show it I was well pissed off. After five months, more really because we'd only done it a few times after Zena was born before he had to go, I was ready for it, loved him, and, let vanity have its say, I've a lovely body and most often I love doing it. With the right man, I mean. So it was a touch demeaning to find the right man was not interested, not any more.

Later that night, still in bed, he began to tell me how he was very worried about this trouble one of his projects had run into at work, a place called the Co-operativo de Sant'Simon, and at my prompting, and because he planned to take me there in two days' time, he told me all about it.

When he had, I half believed it was the main source of his trouble, but I have to say too I half suspected there was something, someone else.

Still that's not important. But Sant'Simon is—and I'll tell you about that, and our trip there, which turned out to be quite a business. You'll see how important it is when I tell it, and more important really than not managing to swing together straight down the line first chance we had.

6

Right. Kit was now fully trained as a Spanish-speaking agricultural economist, Ph.D., M.Sc., and employed by the UNAFO, the United Nations Agriculture and Food Organisation, to work for ITCO, the Instituto de Tierras y Colonización, Costa Rica. What this ITCO does is first of all vet, and then support, both legally and financially, land-using schemes initiated by peasants. A team of agricultural economists is part of all that, they have to assess the viability of the projects, whether they'll make good use of the land, make a profit on their cash crops, is the infrastructure serving them, roads, and markets, and where coffee is concerned a *beneficio* which is a processor ready to handle the crop for a fair price, and a whole bagful of factors come into it.

This Sant'Simon co-op had, according to Kit, got their act together very well. Up in the mountains above San José, about eighty kilometres down the Inter-American Highway, and only ten kilometres or so off it, it had running water from mountain streams and subsisted on beans and maize while the coffee bushes matured. Sure the coffee market is in tatters, but there's still no cash crop in Costa Rica does so well per capita for the workers.

Being as . . . since Sant'Simon was high up, and they really knew their business, most having worked as day-labourers on the big Cafesa *haciendas*, they were producing a very high-quality coffee, plus enough beans and maize and salads and fruit to feed themselves and some livestock, so basically the coffee was the bonus, the accumulating capital to build into a school, put down a deposit to the electricity generating board, keep them in clothes, and get them to San José for the big football matches. They even had their own team in their own strip. All this Kit told me and I saw it myself soon enough.

What they still lacked and could only be got with ITCO backing, was title to the land, and since this was just the sort of project ITCO had learnt was most viable, Kit thought it would go right ahead. But now, just in five or six weeks, it was falling apart. Everyone was suddenly against it. Over the top it all was, too many things suddenly to be found all wrong at once.

First the environmentalists, who are big in Costa Rica, which has a large middle class, said the valley they were at the top of was one of the last unspoilt ones in the area. Sant'Simon would pollute the water, hunt the monkeys and stun-bomb the fish— peasants always did. Then a guy called Miguel Saavedra from Education, who Kit thought was okay, turned in a report saying the school was no good. And Electricity said it would be too expensive to lay on power for the use it would get. And one of the big coffee *haciendas* said it had an option on the land anyway, and the Health weren't so sure about the purity of the water, and the owner of the nearest *beneficio* said he was overcommitted and couldn't handle the crop.

"What does all this add up to?" I asked.

"Conspiracy," Kit said. "Conspiracy to close Sant'Simon and get the peasants off the land."

"Why?"

And he couldn't tell me, couldn't guess. It just didn't add up. It was government policy to support projects like this. Sometimes he wondered if it wasn't him they were after, some Tico with clout wanted his job for his nephew or whatever. This seemed not likely to me. Kit had a tendency to paranoia. Something to do with his mother sending him to a private boarding school when he was only seven where he got walloped. At all events he was certainly hung up about mama.

I said maybe Sant'Simon just wasn't as good as he reckoned, maybe all these reports were right. In that case, he said, I'm a fucking awful agricultural economist. Which I may be. Seeing the paranoia was taking a twist another way, I tried, like with tact, to shut off that line of conversation.

But he went on. "Anyway, my boss from UNAFO, a chap called Per Hedborg, is coming out next week. He'll have a look at it. He's great—if he says I'm wrong then I'll believe him, no one else. But I think he'll say I'm right. And you'll see too. Wait till you've met the *pueblo*."

He actually used the word. You know, Don Jesús, that word can have an emotive charge. So I said, Okay, I'll see the place

47

and meet *el pueblo*, and we went to sleep at last. For five minutes that was, before Zena woke up again and I had to feed her.

And again, you know, he was more all over her than he had been over me and left me thinking perhaps I am not the radiantly lovely being I think I am. Paranoia can touch the best of us.

And I wondered again when we were trying to sleep, if up amongst that *pueblo* there wasn't the reason he was acting so offish, the nooky that had kept him happy while I was away.

Next morning he got up and went to work and left me to my own devices which I liked mucho. First Zena of course was up to her devices too but I must say she had settled in just fine already, I mean only crying when she was hungry or sleepy, what more can you want? So I gave her the nipple for twenty minutes or so, both tanks, and some of the baby food Kit had bought— Caribbean Sunrise Breakfast, start your kiddie on the Greenfinger path to health and happiness.

Then I put her in the Snugli and hoisted her onto my back— this is tricky on your own until you get the knack—got together a traveller's cheque, passport and so on for myself, I like to have my own money and I've saved up a lot, nearly two thousand pounds sterling, a little from a bequest from my dear aunt in Brixton, but most saved from five years in part-time jobs like Tesco cashout in Christbourne while I worked for my degree. Upper second in French and Spanish, Kit said it would have been a first but I never would bother to master the snotty sort of English they expected me to speak and write. Anyway I went out with two grand all my own, and that's how I was able to get here from Costa Rica so quick. Also I took a fistful of *colones* Kit said was for housekeeping, and I and Zena ventured forth to sample the delights of San José.

Delights they truly were. The air was like, yes, champagne. The sun was warm, but cooling breezes gusted on the corners. Everywhere people smiled and wagged fingers at the coffee-coloured cherub peering over my shoulder: "*¡Qué rica, la nena! ¿Cómo se llama? ¡Zená! Preciosa,*" and sometimes smiled at me too. Well truly I was innocent: they took me for her nursemaid, I mean she's that much paler than me, I mean I am black but black as you know, so they read me as the servant, smiled at both of us and ripped me off every time I bought anything.

You see what I knew, because Kit had told me, but what I forgot is blacks are looked down on in San José. Although we Jamaicans built the railroad and farmed their banana plantations from 1870 onwards, they did not allow a nigger up the railroad from the coast until 1947. They even changed the driver on the train for the last twenty miles. So, they placed me as some gringo's nigra servant and they treated me nice. With his *bambino* on her back. Fine.

Well all this I pieced together later but there and then I had a ball. I found a nice little market, fish, fruit, and veg, and some meat and I put together a feast for his lordship's return. I was ashamed though. There were fruits and vegetables I've never seen even in Brixton market, yet back in Kingston where my Nan brought up my mother, she would of known what was what.

One vendor offered me a slice of like red juicy butter off a fruit he had on his stall. It was sweet. Fragrant. Oh yes. Sweet and fragrant. So I bought a couple and damn near found I had no *colones* left. Mamey fruit. Heavenly. Heav-en-ly. But dear Kit told me off when he saw what I bought.

What the hell. I pushed together a king of a supper for him. Avocado, papaya, sweet potato, chops . . . goat, yeah, and soaked them in coconut juice, not the milk, but the liquor you get soaking grated coconut in water and then squeezing it off, three king prawns each with a *salsa picante* I put together myself from fresh red chillis, coriander, tomato using the Braun blender. Not served in that order but with the mamey fruit to finish off.

And again he could not get it up.

Bad day at the office or the fact I'd blown half a week's housekeeping on one meal? Bad day at the office, he said.

Next day we went to Sant'Simon. We left eight o'clock in the morning in the Daihatsu because Kit said there might be rain in the afternoon and visibility would become nix in the mountains, but also he had business in Cartago.

The first bit was disappointing. The *meseta* is becoming very overcrowded, you know, and because of land prices development hugs the road which is being rebuilt, repaired, got up and put down elsewhere as they try to make a motorway of it, so although the views up into the mountains are fine, and from the highest point at Ochomoyo there's a great view of Volcán Irazú, the ambience is somewhat spoiled by the RECOPE oil finery, and lower down they still don't look like they've got everything straight yet from the floods and ashes and lava from when Irazú blew its top twenty years ago. Cartago too for the most part had that unfinished look, but Kit dropped me in a real neat church which he thought might interest me while he went off to the local ITCO office.

Generally speaking God doesn't do a lot for me, he's had too many haters on his side, so I moved through this church at first a bit sceptical that I wasn't wasting my time. But it was airy and bright and new, with sparkling mosaics. Most people were moving one way so I fell in with them, and thus we came to a small room to the left of the big altar, the walls hung with like little gold charms of legs, hands, feet and letters too, well, I've been to Lourdes out of interest only, and knew these to be votive for supposed acts of healing and that made me feel a bit sick and oppressed, I don't hold with mumbo-jumbo.

Then on down narrow steps to like an underground grotto with natural rock, a pool of water that looked black beneath the lights, and above it the reason Kit had told me to go, because there she was, Nuestra Señora de los Angeles, the patron, no, *matron* saint of Ticoland, and for all their lofty disdain of the Jamaicans who built their railroad, under her crown and robes, and jewels and all, she is a spade, as black as I am. So I murmured to her, "Lay on five," and gave her a wink. She winked back. A miracle. But not one arch-hater Karol Wojtyla will allow to be authenticated. Zena gave one of her crows and I could feel her bumping her *café con leche* fists on my shoulders, so she'd seen it too.

The road up out of Cartago is great, and worth getting up early for though it was now pushing eleven o'clock. The hillsides are steep and mostly cleared to Alpine meadows of lush long grass where great fat ochre cows graze on fields of carrots, onions, potatoes, you name it, everything grows on those steep hills, even at the end of the dry season it was lush and rich and green on account of the countless streams and rivulets, even the fenceposts sprouted leaves. Mind you the highway itself is a bit horrendous what with hairpin bends and coaches, trucks, tankers, jeeps and diesel fumes.

Shortly it gets too steep even for these farmers and you get up into the cloud forest—great trees, the oaks of Costa Rica, huge, up to one hundred and fifty feet high, and each one with its hanging gardens of mistletoes, weird drapes of moss, giant ferns with elephant ear leaves five feet across, and everywhere you are in cool cloud, visibility rarely more than a hundred metres, and deep thickets of bamboo beneath the trees. Eerie.

But then you break out above that, and through the trees you can see blankets of white mist lying in long fingers down the valleys below us, especially on the eastern Caribbean side, and in front of us a dark massif rose treeless above the forest with the road always snaking closer and closer to it, and the oaks beginning to thin out and become smaller. This massif is el Cerro de la Muerte, the Mountain of Death, and it is in a valley on its western flank that Sant'Simon lay, the beginning of the wild Cordillera de Talamanca. I should like to say that I shuddered with prescience when I heard the name, but I did not.

Truth to say we were very cheerful and at ease with each other right then—whatever bothered Kit down in San José he had left there: we joked, laughed, and he really loved telling me about everything we passed, he'd done the trip four times before, and truly it really was great having him there to point out and explain all that was worth seeing. I began to feel it was like old times and soon we would be as jolly as we always had been, except when his wife was bugging him, at Christbourne.

"How long now before we get there?" I asked.

"Forty minutes. Less."

"Okay," I said, "then we can stop and let me feed Zena and change her, else the first experience your friends will have of her she'll be screaming up a storm."

We did just that in a neat village called Ojo de Agua where there was a spring, an eye of water, where we queued with truck drivers and got in just ahead of a coachload of Yankee tourists, then sat at a nice rustic café and ate tortillas with spicy tomato dip and drank that marvellous coffee, and watched the world go by—most of it on a cloud of diesel fumes.

I fed Zena and Kit went a bit pink and looked the other way as if I was with someone else, but I joshed him about it and he even stared down a redneck truck driver who looked like he was contemplating some rudery. And then something really lovely happened—right there.

There was an edge of shrubs with delicate orange and pink trumpet-shaped flowers and, dipping their needle-like beaks, their wings whirring so fast they were like a mist, four or five green humming-birds. That had a strange effect on me, that sudden beauty, so I relaxed, let my back go and positively wallowed in it all, the trees, and flowers, the sun hot now though patchy and spilling blobs of gold on that big mountain still beyond. I must have smiled or something because Kit covered my hand with his and we found space to kiss, so Zena came off the nipple and smiled up at us and then wham back onto it she went.

He said, "I wish Trevor Everton was here."

"You want another man here just now?"

He laughed, kissed me again. "No. But Trevor is a great naturalist and he could tell us all about those flowers and those birds. You'd love him. We may meet him at Sant'Simon. He goes up there once or twice a week."

"Where does he live then?"

"During the wettest part of the wet season he has a flat in San José. But for four or five months a year he bivouacs out in the forest and collects plants, studies the wild life, that sort of thing."

"All on his own?"

"All on his own. And this season he's studying the riparian habitat by the river two or three miles below Sant'Simon. He comes up every now and then to buy tortillas and beans off them and have a chat, then he disappears again."

Well, certainly, we did get to meet this Trevor Everton and in most dramatic circumstances. He was a really nice guy, really nice, and I owe him my life, and, more important, Zena's.

Three, four miles on from Ojo de Agua and really out now onto mountain upland, shrub and savannah, the *páramo*, we suddenly turned right and west down an unsignposted dirt track. Perhaps half a mile more of open country, then suddenly the road dipped between two rocks and Kit pulled up. He took me by the hand and we walked out onto one of these boulders. He told me to shut my eyes, move six paces more and then he said open up and look.

It was unbelievable. In front and below us a steep narrow valley, filled with trees, dropped away steeply, the crowns of the trees were all you could see, many of them huge, and here and there either in blossom, whites, pale ochres, pinks, or new leaf and old leaf brownish, rising and falling, and rising again on and down until they merged into a long wide belt of greeny blues and bluey greens yet misty too, which seemed to tilt up the way flat land does seen from a distance and a very high altitude, tilt up to the ocean: a silvery white, sand or surf or both—we were twenty miles away—briefly emerald then purest sapphire to an amethyst horizon, also unnaturally high from where we were. The splendour, the size, the perfection of it all were beyond description, and to cap it all, stacked high in the sky, great piles and layers of cloud, shadowed and sunstruck.

The buzzing and rushing in my ears, the effect of the height we were at, receded a little and through it I now detected the magical fairy sound of mountain streams still near their springs, and as a burden the slower chime of a cow or goat bell.

Although the road now descended quite quickly the *páramo* remained in patches for six or more kilometres before it finally gave way to the montane forest of yuccas and those giant oaks again. On it and under, the trees were often quite large, often as much as a *manzana*—you see how much I learned, Don Jesús? A *manzana* is three-quarters of a hectare—where the ground was unbroken and fairly flat, quite large patches of tall strong grasses, maybe six feet tall or more, a lovely fresh green except where some were in male flower with nodding russet blooms, and when the breeze blew over it it was like the passing of a spirit as the heads rose and fell in natural unison, truly a lovely sight.

"What is that stuff?" I asked.

"Wild maize," Kit answered. "Our friends really find it very useful, though of course the cobs are nothing like as big as the cultivated varieties."

Well, he was wrong of course. There's no such thing as wild maize, this probably being a strain, as Trevor Everton pointed out later, surviving from pre-Columbian times. And believe me, Don Jesús, there's a lot more to say about it, but all in due course, at the right time.

And just then we saw the first of them, of "our friends" as they truly came to be in the all-too-brief-a-time I knew them, an old man in a big wide-brimmed straw hat, leading a donkey down the winding white road, laden with great bundles of the stuff. He raised his stick in salute as we passed.

"Mostly they use it for fodder, and it's done very well as such. I've never seen better-fed oxen, goats, donkeys as we'll see at Sant'Simon."

The roofs of two wooden structures below us came into view, shaded by giant yuccas. As we dropped round a bend or two towards them I could see they were set back off the track in a sort of lay-by which had been cut back into the bank so these sheds were perched about eight feet above the surface. I also noticed how a track circled off the road just above them and came round behind them.

"And what are those for?"

"*Recibidores.*"

"Receivers?"

Kit laughed. "Yes. Just that." He swung the jeep into the lay-by and turned off the engine, leant forward over the wheel and explained. Always the pedagogue my Kit, and truly I loved him for it. You get nowhere without education. "This is as far down the valley as ordinary lorries can easily get. During the coffee harvest our friends haul the beans in ox carts up to the *recibidores* and all the truck driver has to do is back up to that hatch, open it, pull down the chute inside, and down come the cherries."

"Cherries?"

"The coffee beans are inside scarlet fruits, very pretty they are, which look quite like cherries. The thing is they have to be processed quite quickly before the outer flesh ferments. The truck takes them to the *beneficio*, the processing plant, which is near Cartago. In point of fact, when I first looked into Sant'Simon to see if it was viable, this was the weak point, I thought, and I nearly damned it on that account."

"Why?"

He set the engine going, engaged four-wheel drive.

"We're still nearly three hundred metres above the highest point the coffee will grow. The road gets steeper, more difficult. The coffee harvest is in the wet season, often at the very wettest time, and this road should become a river, and ox carts would churn the hell out of it. Then I came out and saw what they had done."

"Which was?"

"I'll show you." He let out the clutch, and we moved off, but slowly—partly because the track was now only just wide enough

54

for the jeep and there were horrendous bends every hundred yards or so, but also so he could explain what the co-operative had done.

"They first came here seven years ago. It was a land invasion but they had a little cash, compensation for dismissal, tools and some livestock because they had been farming for themselves too. No one interfered. It was a bad time. Recession. Oil crisis. Coffee markets collapsed. The authorities were happy to leave a group of sacked agriworkers who seemed eager to fend for themselves to their own devices. Hundreds were coming onto the *meseta*, into the *tugurios*, every month.

"Anyway. Coffee bushes take five years to mature, before they fruit properly. During that time they farmed at little more than subsistence level, no point in doing more, the markets for corn, beans, even livestock are too far away. They put the rest of their energy into preparing for the first coffee harvest. And that was mainly making this road serviceable. Well. It doesn't look much, but actually it's little short of a miracle."

He pulled into another lay-by, put there, he said, so ox carts could cross, like sidings on a one-track railway. He switched off the engine again, turned to face me. I wanted to kiss him. I always did when he got like this—enthusiastic, excited about something. His eyes gleamed, sometimes, especially when describing other people's efforts, heroism, became tearful. Don Jesús María, I loved him. I really did. You tell the *juez*—it's true.

Anyway. They'd metalled two miles of road with rock they broke themselves and gravelled the top. More important than that they had ditched it, and run piped gullies under it, experimenting each wet season while their coffee bushes grew, to get it right, so the water ran down the sides or under it and left it dry.

"When I saw that, and learned how it had been done, well then I knew Sant'Simon had to work." He set the jeep going again. One more bend and we came to our first view of it all.

It was beautiful. No, Don Jesús, it really was. That bend took us round the shoulder of the mountain and a wide steep basin opened up in front of us. Because we were on the shoulder, on the edge, and because they had cut down the trees on the outer edge of the road, perhaps just so the incoming traveller could see the view, there, momentarily, it all was.

The basin was fan-shaped, broad at the top, narrowing and levelling as it dropped. It was rimmed with untouched forest—giant trees whose long, slender, grey and silvery trunks were exposed by the clearance so you could see their elegant, soaring thinness climbing to their spreading crowns, and it was filled with terraced coffee bushes, neatly spaced so they made sweeping criss-crossing rows, glossy dark green and just on the point of flowering so the buds looked like pearls, millions of pearls, scattered over the green. Here and there larger trees—ingas, a lovely frondy legume, and cecrops—had been planted or allowed to stay to fix nitrogen and provide shade. And through it all one could trace no less than three rivulets, tumbling, cascading, rushing from the watershed we had left above us, swirling along concreted channels, in and out of pipes, and then left to run free again until they met near the base of the fan to form the Río Remedios.

Around this confluence there nestled beneath a shifting veil of blueish smoke a village of some thirty dwellings, loosely circled by a patchwork of tiny fields, sheds and barns.

All this spread so clear before us was the vision of a moment, for the track quickly sank into forest again and when it came out to skirt and then plunge through the coffee itself glimpses of the village were less frequent and less complete until suddenly we were there.

Our visit was expected and our progress had been marked, and I can scarcely describe our welcome and the excitement of the next few hours. The people of Sant'Simon knew too well of their predicament and looked on Kit as their protector, but it was not just that, they had to fuss me too, *la bella negrita*, and of course Zena was instantly idolised, petted, caressed, cooed at, passed from arm to arm and, bless my lovely little Zena, she took it all with scarcely a cry, but laughed and gurgled and blew through her lips at them and gave the high squawk she does when excited and that made all laugh and throw up their hands, and "little parrot" they called her, *lorita preciosa*, and they had presents ready for her, a rattle made from woven maize leaves with a little silver bell beside, and a tiny leather waistcoat stamped with a sun pattern and fringed with tassles.

7

They . . . Don Jesús, I'm sure you're wondering why I am going
on like this about Sant'Simon, and I have to tell you this: what I
did, that put me in this dire predicament, was done as much for
them as it was for any other reason, so you'd better tell that to
the judge.

They were not as I had expected. What had I expected? Some
city person's pastoral dream. They were all ages. Most of the
old looked twenty years older than they were, had wrinkled faces,
the lines etched with grime, stubbly beards, not only the men,
and not a lot of teeth. Their skins were weather brown, their
knuckles lumpy, their clothes baggy and makeshift and they
smelled. Their children, the ones about Kit's age down to mine,
were fat for the most part, had teeth usually not their own and
they often did not fit, big hammy hands made for work, bellies
made fat by beans, tortillas and sour cassava beer, and they wore
shirts, dresses and jeans whose buttons were stretched to pop-
ping. And their children went from rangy adolescents in acrylic
sweatshirts and jeans down through even rangier brats who were
sly and mischievous, the girls in dirty white dresses, the boys in
cut-down hand-me-downs, and so to black-haired, dark-eyed
babies all overweight, and all in need of a wash.

Eighteen times in an hour I was told Zena was too thin, would
be lost to us if I didn't fatten her up, and once I had to grab her
back from a granny who was giving her goat's milk from her
own grandchild's bottle.

In two days I got to know a lot of names and played with a lot
of kids, and gossiped with a lot of ladies, and in the one night
talked and talked and maybe some of all that I'll tell you later
but right now I'll just mention Manuel and Minerva whose
houseguests we were to be for a day and a night and a day.

Manuel was like a leader of the commune—which it was, more

than a co-operative, only communes don't have leaders so that's wrong. But they do have experts, specialists—like Umberto who grew broomcorn on his patch and made brooms for all; Ipolito who made coffins and kept the burial ground clear of tall weeds with his *machete*, still mercifully after seven years a small area; Conchita, a refugee from Guatemala and a forest-dwelling Indian who knew the lore of the forest, what would ease a fever, prevent pregnancy, soothe a bee sting. What Manuel was an expert in was the authorities.

He was small, stooped, thin, had large clear brown eyes, white hair shaved to half an inch, looked like an alert eighty-year-old but was sixty-five. His first experience of the authorities befell him in 1934 when he was only fourteen. His parents were *campesinos* who had been evicted off of a smallholding. Daddy worked for a coffee *hacienda* whose owner gave him no wages but just the use of a plot of land to farm as he liked. But when he got knocked over by one of the first buses on the *meseta* and had his hip broken, he couldn't work no more, so they lost their smallholding. As Manuel explained, his father and mother had had a lot of children to provide labour to keep the land which was not theirs productive enough to actually raise some cash. Peasants who have tenure under reasonable terms have very small families. A good piece of land that three or four people can work and live comfortable off is the best contraceptive in the world.

Anyway, without that land, the family was now in desperate straits and Manuel knew there was work down on the Caribbean amongst the blacks at Puerto Limón, on the banana plantations. So he stowed away on the train and got down there, aged thirteen or fourteen, and got there just in time for the great 1934 strike against UFCO—la Frutera, alias el Pulpo. The strikers lived on turtle eggs, fish and bananas, and won great concessions. On paper. Then el Pulpo reneged. The strikers rioted. This was the excuse the bosses wanted: police and army moved in and smashed them with great violence and brutality, as witnessed to by two outer fingers of Manuel's left hand which were twisted up like a diseased claw on a pigeon.

For the rest of his life he fought the bosses and educated himself so he knew why things are as they are, and how they should be changed. He met Ché in Costa Rica in 1948 and went to Cuba with him. Later he was in Nicaragua with the Sandinistas.

But now, he said, he was old and happy to end his days at Sant'Simon.

Minerva, who lived with him, never had he married, was fifty years old and a widow, with six children, two on the commune, and twenty-five grandchildren, five on the commune. She was a barrel of a woman, five feet high and five feet round, with a halo of white hair showing under the rim of her straw hat which she never took off. Miguelito, her cheekiest grandchild, told me why—she had a bald patch like a priest's.

When all the fuss of our arrival was over she took me into the cabin she shared with Manuel, and with her daughter and daughter-in-law set about preparing a feast, while Manuel and some of the other men took Kit round the commune and showed him the work that had been done in the month since he'd last been there, showed him the accounts of the coffee harvest and discussed with him how they planned to spend the large cash profit. They were also to discuss these troubles they now seemed to have run into. I was definitely not approving of this arrangement—it seemed to me the ladies should go along in all that sort of thing too, and I said so, but Minerva said, "Don't you worry my girl, we'll get our say and in the meantime there'll be no food for any of us if we don't get on with it."

So, we got on with it—Minerva, Carmen, Rebecca and I. I must say a word about this Rebecca because she was a black like me, or anyway mulatto, octaroon or whatever other whitey name you want to give us to classify us racially and thus sow envy and contempt where there should be love, harmony and solidarity. She was small, pert, lively, quite dark but with some Oriental in her too, lot of Chinese labour brought into Central America in the late nineteenth century, all of which though common enough elsewhere is unusual in Ticoland.

Like Conchita the Indian lady from Guatemala, Rebecca was a refugee, but in her case from Honduras, she having come with her parents fleeing oppression, to Costa Rica, where the refugee agency at Heredia asked Sant'Simon to take them on. And she had married Minerva's son and was two months gone with her first and when I asked knew nothing at all of morning sickness after two occasions, thanks to an infusion of Conchita's.

The four of us then repaired to Minerva's cabin and began to prepare an evening meal of some substance. The cabin had just two rooms, one small where Minerva and Manuel slept on a low bed with a *palliasse* filled with dry straw and herbs, and another quite large, say fifteen by twelve feet. The floor was trodden earth strewn with grasses and herbs which kept it fresh; the walls were clay and wattle fixed to a frame of timbers known to be termite-proof; and the roof, on a sloped frame of close-spaced rough-hewn laths, was a thick thatch, part woven, part pinned down with wooden pegs, of palm and plantain leaves, recently repaired ahead of the rainy season.

Most of the Sant'Simon cabins were less secure against the elements, being simple planks nailed across timber frames, which planks shrank and warped with sun and rain. Only those used by the elderly arthritic were wattle which take longer to build as mud has to be puddled, then allowed to set in thin layers, processes only possible in the short dry season. Now, however, they were experimenting with a Mex technique of sun-baking clay and straw bricks in moulds. Again a long process, but hoped to be more lasting than clay and wattle.

Both outside and inside of Minerva's cabin were painted first with a solution of cow dung which acted as binder, insulator and, so I was told, insect repellent, though this last I found not easy to credit being as all known dung attracts insects and there were plenty there. Finally it was limed.

Plenty insects, in spite of the smoke and in spite of the lizards, up to a foot long, that lived in the thatch and other interstices, and made a specialty of the cockroaches. The smoke came from Minerva's two fires, one a trough of smouldering charcoal set in a raised sort of table on which heavy iron pans constantly simmered, and another in an old oil drum, one end of which was intact, leaving a round steel *plancha* or *comal* on which she cooked her tortillas. Above the former was a sort of window. Sometimes the smoke went out of it, more often it billowed back into the room, the walls of which, although it could have been no more than six years old and perhaps less, were already blackened. But I have to say once the fires were burning slow and hot, there was much less smoke.

We bustled about, dividing our labour according to our special gifts and inclinations, having first left Zena on the verandah in the capable if not overly clean or tender hands of Miguelito and his sister Encarnación. Carmen, Minerva's daughter, who was in appearance all that name suggests, still having on her the bloom hard work and childbearing will shortly render coarse, but lacking all her namesake's vice, washed and rewashed beans already soaked, black, black-eyed, red and brown, chopped garlic, onions, tomatoes.

Then she went out, and took me with her, and her third and latest, nearly a year old, called by everybody Chico, on her hip. We set off down the little lanes that separated the cabins, each decorated with geraniums and other flowers I could not name, set in emptied cans, and so across the rills—once by a bridge big enough to take an ox cart, and once on stepping stones, and so into the edges of the fields, plots really, of maize, beans, fruit trees, cassava, and so on that surrounded the settlement. Another delight I should mention in the settlement was four, no five I think large macaws, mainly bright blue, that were tame and swooped about us adding colour and *alegría* to the scene.

On the edges of the fields she, and I to her instruction, plucked chilli peppers and sweet ones too, coriander, mint, and so forth, and salads. The maize fields had, all but two, been recently burnt off to kill the weeds grown four feet and higher in the short months since the cobs were picked and the plants died, to return as ashes the nutrients of stalks and leaves. But two plots had standing maize already in flower and some even in cob above an undergrowth of beans, melons, pumpkins and other squashes. There was significance in this unseasonal growth I was yet to understand, though others knew it well enough.

Out there in the fields I felt a need to answer a call of nature that would not be denied and quite without embarrassment she took me in amongst this corn where we squatted and wiped ourselves with the green leaves of the undergrowth. This could seem a dirty business but was not—all that was solid was taken up by dung beetles et al. in less than three hours. As we turned for home the sky, which had been overcast an hour or so, thickened and heavy drops of warm rain splashed about us. By the time we were indoors it was fairly rattling down, but a short squall only.

Nothing put off by this rain on the way, Carmen showed me the school and the church, the first a one-room cabin already in use with books, toys, a globe, a blackboard, and all other things necessary bought from the proceeds of the first year's coffee harvest. Most adults could read and write, and three of the women very well—Ticoland has good primary education for all but the most remote areas—and these three took it in turn to teach. It was hoped they'd now be able to hire a math teacher who could do music too, to come in three times a week from the nearest large village down the highway. The inspector from the education ministry had been very impressed, he said, though now it seemed he was singing a different tune to a different fiddle.

The church was but a floor and a roof—they were waiting, Carmen said, to see how the bricks turned out, for they wanted a proper building worthy to shelter the Body of Christ. That was their excuse for not getting on with it, anyway. A priest came in most Sundays, and already the open but roofed space was being appropriately decorated for Palm Sunday, the day following.

Back in Minerva's cabin Rebecca had caught, killed, plucked and dressed two hens judged to be old and poor layers and in this was shown how signally Kit and I were honoured for though there was much livestock in the settlement, little was eaten and only on special occasions. The cows drew ploughs and gave milk, the goats likewise kept for milk, the donkeys and oxen for fetching and carrying to and from the highway, and the hens for eggs. In previous years the men had hunted for parrots, monkeys, small deer, and the pig-like rodents of the forest, but now desisted out of respect and fear of the bourgeois environmentalists in San José. Even the pigs they rarely ate themselves but took to Cartago market.

This task of preparing the fowl now done, Rebecca shared with Carmen the task of washing and chopping the herbs and verdure we had gathered while Doña Minerva undertook to teach me the skill of how to make tortillas.

For all Minerva boasted she and the other ladies were the equal of the men in the commune, I took leave to doubt it, and doubt if Middle American *campesinas* will ever take their rightful place alongside the gentlemen as long as they remain slaves to the tortilla.

It's a business.

First the cobs are taken from the store, a sort of tall deep wardrobe made from rough-hewn slats set a half inch or so apart so air will circulate and keep down mould and fungi, and these are washed and set in pans to simmer some hours in a solution of charcoal-ash or lime—this loosens the outer case of the grain. Then they are washed and washed again to get rid of the ash or lime—the stage of the process at which I entered it. Now the grains are milled through a sieve with a hand-turned blade—much like an old Moulinex my auntie in Brixton used, which was a slow laborious job involving frequent cleansing of sodden husks that had got left behind from the inside of the sieve.

The result is a yellowish mess which now has to be squeezed, and kneaded and squeezed, and kneaded and patted, and kneaded until it sticks together enough to hold its shape. At this point I was thankful Zena demanded more than Miguelito and Encarnación could provide, and after changing her (her disposable nappies much admired and envied by all), I fed her, and thus was able to watch for a time the tedious process without having to take part.

When at last the dough adheres, it is shaped into balls like a tennis ball or smaller, patted flat, and then pressed thin in a press. Meanwhile the charcoal in the oil drum is blown up to a fiercer heat, so the improvised *comal* that was once its top becomes near red hot, and the tortillas, three at a time, are dropped on its surface. In a minute or so blisters begin to appear and then Minerva stoops to flick them over with finger and thumb which she sucks frequently to keep them cool and then wipes on her plastic apron, not too clean. There's a history to this apron. It was cut from a bag of Agrob fertiliser, chemical, two or three hundred-weight of which they had had to buy when they found some seed from Zeaprod would not respond to green manure.

This last part of the process of tortilla-making is of course mercifully short compared with the rest, but the whole business is frankly a downright nonsense, and, forgive me Don Jesús, not only a symptom of the servitude of women but one of the means by which it is maintained—it is not possible to make twenty tortillas thus in under two hours, and a large family will eat twice as many in a day. On that afternoon, expecting ten grown-ups and numerous children for supper, Minerva hoped to make a full hundred, but settled in the end for sixty.

I must though close my digression on the tortilla with the observation that broiled fresh and eaten soon they are delicious and wholesome, especially served with a simple filling such as Carmen had prepared of green tomatoes and green peppers fried in a little sunflower oil. As my foster-parents in Milton Keynes would say, they are decidedly "moreish" which is why wherever there is abundance of corn the people are fat, and when you see pictures of the poor souls in Nicaragua, Honduras, and Guatemala, where all look thin, you know they lack sufficient of this, the very simplest staple of the poor. Either that or the ladies are sufficiently liberated to fight Yankee imperialism and have no time to make them.

Towards dusk, which is sudden, especially under an overcast sky, the men returned with my Kit amongst them, anxiously searching me out to be sure Zena and I had survived so long amongst these untutored primitives. He forgets I started life ten to a room under Westway, Notting Hill, before the filth body-searched my Dad on sus and found dope in his dreadlocks. Then I went to a Church of England home which was not fun at all, and then to my aunt in Brixton who had five of her own. Believe me the children of Sant'Simon were a world better off than I until my primary school teacher spotted me as a high flyer and I was took, taken in by my ever-loving foster-parents Benjamin and Nova Travis of Milton Keynes.

Now there was a lot of bustle and invitations and arguments as to who was staying in Minerva's cabin for supper and who was not, the outcome of it all being six more people than there was properly room for, or ten more than there was food for, stayed, but then their wives and families came too to add their tortillas and stews to the meal.

Somehow, under one swaying paraffin lamp, all were accommodated by taking down the curtain into Minerva's bedroom, and all fed, and what you know already, and in spite of all it was a whizz of a feast. To drink there was a weak sour beer made from cassava and three bottles of Flor de Caña that Kit had brought went the rounds, each with a tiny thimble-sized measure, so no one got too much at once, and most of the men began to smoke— their own home-grown, home-dried, home-rolled, and I cannot say I recommend it, but it was all part of their aim to be as self-sufficient as possible.

Can you see it Don Jesús? I can, and smell it too, that tiny room, some standing against the walls, others squashed up round the small table, yet more knees up to their chins on the floor, and chaos of tin plates, tin spoons, mugs, ends of tortilla and chicken bones, fruit rinds and pips and slopped bean stew—old faces smiling toothless, young smiling with faultless if occasionally slipping dentures, lined faces, stubbled faces, shining faces, knotted hands, strong arms, sweaty armpits—children's faces at the window and peering round the door jambs.

There was much talk everywhere but I sat near Manuel and Kit who were together at the one small table and the subject narrowed to what was in everyone's minds—why this sudden hostility to the co-operative on the part of all the authorities, which now threatened their bid to get legal and lasting tenure to the land. Apart from what Kit had to report from San José and ITCO in particular, there had been local aggravation too—the Rural Guards harassing people who went up to the highway to sell produce by the roadside, a boy who had been run all the way down to Cartago on a charge of illegal hunting . . . with a sling! and had to hitch a lift back, of inspectors coming with test tubes and chemicals to examine the water which bubbled out of the flanks of el Cerro de la Muerte, of how bacteria had been found, but then a dead donkey higher up the stream too, that no one knew how it got there and certainly it was none of theirs.

Well, I said, filth is filth the world over and they take an unrational dislike to you there's nothing you can do, no way, except sit on your butt and wait for them to go away. But my friend Carmen disagreed—she said the Tico police are not filth, just burros, donkeys, and if they persecute you it's because they been told to.

As I say, for many near them the discussion shrank away to what was said by Kit and Manuel. And I soon recognised Kit was on his super-rational kick trying to get the children to see that life is difficult, complex, interrelated and so on. When he gets—*shit*, got—like that (Don Jesús, it's no use, for me he is still alive) he used to put his hands flat on the table in front of him, put his head on one side and tilt it either to the ceiling or at the table and not even look at you if you interrupted or queried, when he would always say, "Good point, Esther, let's deal with that one," or "Interesting question, Esther, let's examine its relevance." We once reckoned up I'd had over fifty official tutorials with him, excluding the unofficial pillow talk, and I knew the routine. Mostly I have to say I loved it. Yes really. Such certainty, based on such scrupulous arguments, such common sense, such knowledge was a very welcome thing to me after my past filled with doubt, superstition and prejudice.

Anyway his view was that they were mistaken to look for conspiracy or plot, they were the victims of an unfortunate conjunction—the co-op had peaked in several spheres, broken barriers in several areas, all at one and the same time and so drawn the attention of several different agencies at once. There was nothing sinister in this—all they had to do was hold on, cope with each apparent attack in turn, do what was asked of them, and sit it out. Now that all this contradicted what he had said to me, those first nights in his flat in San José, when he had talked of conspiracy, did not surprise me. Kit was a great one for seeing irrational paranoia in himself and in others and a great one for arguing himself and others out of it.

And nothing, no end of skids on the banana skins of life, would ever convince him this is basically an irrational approach. His wife screwed him for every penny she could get, young kids died in cold water in the South Atlantic fighting for Las Malvinas, the police state in the U.K. broke the miners' strike: none of these things were going to happen, and to think they might was paranoia. Before they happened. He never learnt that as the poet said the light at the end of the tunnel is often the light of the oncoming train.

Manuel's line was that the commune was a danger, a threat.

"How can such a simple thing be a threat to anyone?" asked Ipolito, he who made coffins.

"Consider," said Manuel—unlike Kit he always found the eyes of whoever had spoken, and spoke back directly—"it was once the case that this was so—that all farmed enough to feed their families and enough to sell for cash to buy those necessaries they could not grow or make."

"So my grandfather told me."

"He had his own patch of land?"

"He did. On the *meseta*. Not ten kilometres from San José. Six *manzanas*—three for coffee, three for wheat and beans."

"What happened?"

Ipolito said that the big *haciendas* held down the price of coffee, yet because they were competing for the good land on the *meseta* the price of land went up. So Grandfather sold up and bought

66

three times the acreage in Valle del General. Trouble was the land there was poor and needed fertilisers, and his sons had to get what work they could on the new Pacific Coast banana plantations.

Manuel spread his good hand and smiled. "Thus or in like fashion all good land is concentrated in the hands of a few and we, who once owned our land, have to hire ourselves out as wage-labourers." He went on, "The landowners do not want corn and beans. They want cash. They grow coffee, bananas, raise beef. Soon there is not enough food, so to prevent trouble the landowners buy food and sell it to us at prices they set. They get rich. The Yankee farmer who unloads his food surplus on us also gets rich. The Yankee people get cheap coffee and cheap beef and cheap bananas. And we stay poor . . . until we can grow our own food on our own land and a little coffee just as we used to. And that's what we are doing here. . . ."

But Kit shook his head and rubbed the tobacco smoke out of his eyes. He said that Manuel had made it too simple, that there were structures, processes, mediations which came into the equation. For instance it was not the landowners who bought the cheap food from abroad but the government, and much of it came as aid. . . .

"*Ayuda!*" Manuel made the word sound like a donkey bray. "It is not help—it is usury. We borrow money from the IMF, the world capitalist bank, to buy food we could grow ourselves, and pay huge interest on it, which has to be paid for by exports of coffee and so on, and now they are ripping up our forests to grow oranges. With that money we could industrialise, but no, it is used to pay the interest on those loans. Thus again," he banged the table, not loudly, but enough to hold back Kit's comments, "the Yankees are protected, and the Japanese and the Germans, and their industries, and their markets for manufactured goods."

An old codger interrupted. Carmen told me he had been a soldier in the days when Ticoland had soldiers. He said Manuel was talking too quickly and not to the point, not explaining why the authorities wanted to close down Sant'Simon.

Manuel rubbed his chewed-up left hand across his brow, then took a thimbleful of rum Conchita offered him since he could not pour it himself, and he knocked it back.

"You are right, Don Patricio." He shrugged, spread his good hand again. "I don't know. Don Cristóbal"—he meant my Kit—"says no conspiracy. But it feels like one. Don Cristóbal says there are many structures, many agencies, many ministries, many banks. They all live well off us, the poor and the landless. It is we who are their wealth. Perhaps they do not say if Sant'Simon works, and is repeated again and again until all over Central America the *campesinos* farm as we do, we will lose our nice office jobs, our salaries, our privileges—but perhaps they *feel* it. . . . Perhaps they say to themselves, it's best we discourage this sort of thing before it spreads."

Now at last Kit had to butt in. He said this was mystification plain and simple. Organisations like UNAFO and ITCO exist to help projects like Sant'Simon, Manuel should not paint things so black and white, there was no real evidence for what he was saying, no reality lay behind it.

Manuel shrugged, sat back, head dropped towards his chest which was pushed up like a pigeon's the way old men's are, who have worked hard and gone frail. His eyes looked tired. "I don't know, Don Cristóbal, I just don't know."

A depression, a listlessness born of fatigue, food, drink, and incomprehension in the face of . . . what? settled over the group around him and I was relieved when Minerva brought Zena to me. I gathered my little cherub to me, and wrapped a shawl round her and round my shoulders, and stepped over and round the little crowd and so out into the rain-fresh but warm and happy night.

The moon, three-quarters nearly, hung exactly on her back, not tilted at all in these latitudes, above the black Cerro above us, and thus like a silver bark began her stately voyage across the sky towards the Pacific and a thousand thousand stars accompanied her. The rills burbled and tinkled and flashed back her light, and amongst the strange white blossoms that opened with the dark, giant moths floated, disturbing their spicy scents. There were fireflies and glow-worms.

Presently from Minerva's cabin, a hundred yards behind me, there was a guitar, and improvised marimbas. Then singing. I knew the song. The words are by Nicolás Guillén, the Cuban mulatto poet. I suppose Manuel had taught it to them. I danced to it a little, swung round and back and forth and nursed my darling, and crooned the words to her too.

Para hacer esta muralla	To make this wall
Traíganme todas las manos	We must all join hands
Los negros sus manos negras	Blacks with their black hands
Los blancos sus blancas manos	Whites with their white hands
Una muralla que vaya	A wall that will go
Desde la playa hasta el monte	From the beach to the mountain
Desde el monte hasta la playa	The mountain to the sea
Que vaya sobre el horizonte.	Which stretches to the horizon.

Then the rhythm quickens and my step with it and Zena comes off the nipple and beams her four-toothed smile, pearls in the moonlight, and flaps her tiny fists and chortles.

Tún, tún, ¿Quién es?	Knock, knock, Who is there?
Una rosa y un clavel	A rose and a carnation
Abre la muralla.	Open the wall.
Tún, tún, ¿Quién es?	Knock, knock, Who is there?
El sable del coronel	The colonel's sabre
Cierra la muralla.	Close up the wall.
Tún, tún, ¿Quién es?	Knock, knock, who is there?
Le paloma y el laurel	The dove and the bay
Abre la muralla.	Open the wall.
Tún, tún, ¿Quién es?	Knock, knock, Who is there?
El gusano y el ciempiés	The worm and the centipede
Cierra la muralla.	Close up the wall.
Tún, tún, ¿Quién es?	Knock, knock, Who is there?
Al corazón del amigo	To the heart of the friend
Abre la muralla.	Open the wall.
Al veneno y al puñal	To poison and the dagger
Cierra la muralla.	Close up the wall.
Al Pay Say y la Hierbabuena	To the CP and apple-mint
Abre la muralla.	Open the wall.
Al diente de la serpiente	To the serpent's tooth
Cierra la muralla.	Close up the wall.
Al corazón del amigo	To a friend's heart
Abre la muralla.	Open the wall.
Al ruiseñor en la flor.	To the nightingale in the flower.
Hacemos esta muralla	Let us make this wall
Juntando todas las manos	By all joining hands
Los negros sus manos negras	The blacks with their black hands
Los blancos sus blancas manos	The whites with their white hands.

Then slow:

Al ruiseñor en la flor.   To the nightingale in the flower.

Then a huge shout:

¡ABRE LA MURALLA!   OPEN THE WALL!

Part III

Part III

8

Miller spent much of his first morning in San José in a taxi. He travelled from the Fortuna Hotel to both Pacific and Atlantic railway stations twice and, using the stopwatch facility in his Casio digital, timed the journey in ordinary traffic and in the rush hour. He did the same for the journey to the airport but made that trip only once. He taxied to the hospital complex in Parque Carrillo just six blocks from the Fortuna, checked out the casualty department, noted that it was open twenty-four hours a day, and timed the walk back.

He had lunch, a chilli burger and tamarind milk shake, at the Billy Boy Soda and spent the afternoon checking out the addresses Francisco had given him, but made no attempt yet to identify his putative targets. Again he timed his progress round San José, sometimes on foot, sometimes by taxi. If he noticed the parks, or the architecture of the larger buildings varying from neo-colonial to neo-modern, and giving an ambience not unlike one of the tidier Mediterranean ports, say Alicante or Genoa, it was only to assess their potential as landmarks or impediments to his free movement about the place. The volcanoes, seen occasionally between blocks in the morning, for the most part hidden by cloud in the afternoon, were dismissed as irrelevant, though the rain that came in the afternoon and swallowed up the taxis was not.

He dined off a two-pound T-bone steak at La Hacienda, drank milk again, and went to bed early, after running through the Royal Canadian Air Force routines twice. He slept well.

The next day was more difficult. Boredom threatened—and it was a threat. If Miller was bored he slept badly; if he was bored he was tempted into debauchery—heavy drinking, looking for whores, activities that drew attention. Worst of all, if he was really bored a yet more dangerous attraction presented itself.

Miller had few resources. He could not read fiction. The impossibilities that surrounded the ways people who followed his trade in novels irritated him as did the unreality of the sexual encounters. Non-fiction he read only for a purpose: to improve his knowledge of Spanish conveyancing and fiscal law, or of new technologies as they became available to the police in countries where he was likely to work. He was untouched by the fantasy worlds of cinema or TV. He would as soon count the bricks in a wall as listen to music. What relieved boredom best for Miller was the sudden taste of adrenaline, the brightness of enhanced vision and hearing that it brought, the responses to the stimulus of danger. The most dangerous temptation of all, then, was to exercise his trade at random, for no purpose, with no hope of reward, just for the hell of it: to follow a man into a urinal and take him out there, to walk out of an elevator leaving the operator slumped on her stool, flop-headed, with staring eyes.

On his second evening he went to a soccer match. The modern stadium at the end of the Paseo Colón was about three-quarters full for the play-off between the semifinalists of the Cup—Puerto Limón and to Alajuela. Most of the Puerto Limón team were black, as were almost all their supporters who had come up on the long and spectacular train ride from the Caribbean coast. It was their great-grandfathers, brought in from Jamaica, who had built the line a century ago and died by the hundreds doing it. The history books say Minor Keith built it, but they are wrong. He borrowed the money and virtually pawned Costa Rica to the European banks in the process, employed engineers and hired labour. He did not build it, though his manic energy kept what was essentially a crazy project going until it was finished. Of course it paid off in the end—not carrying coffee to the Atlantic to cut out the Pacific sea route, but as a system of branch lines through the banana plantations he just happened to own.

In 1899 he needed more capital and amalgamated his Tropical Trading and Transport Company with Boston Fruit to form United Fruit, "Manita Yunai," la Frutera, el Pulpo.

Miller knew nothing of this and would have cared less. He did not like the blacks around him—sharply dressed for their visit to the capital they had been excluded from for half a century. But they knew it all. And they showed it. Speaking English, not in the way West Indians of the late twentieth century do, but with an odd, almost Welsh-like purity of accent derived from their nineteenth-century ancestors, they abused the white team from Alajuela. Their accents may have been oddly refined, their vocabulary was not.

Miller, who enjoyed football when played well, that is with cynical exploitation of the rules, sided privately against them. He was not, he believed, racially prejudiced. During his army career he had worked with Gurkhas and Fijians, and had fought and learnt to respect as worthy foes, that is as threats to his own well-being, Cypriots, Indonesians, Arabs and Micks. Nevertheless he did feel all these breeds had their place in the order of things, and it was below his. It should be added that in this order women of all breeds came right at the bottom of the heap. He recognised superiors, but very few. Officers from the middle or upper classes who were also good at being soldiers. Colonel Finchley-Camden, late of the Royal Buff Caps and SAS, now of Wolf Hound Security, was one. To Miller such men were gods.

Thus, on the dark terrace, with all eyes focused on the brilliant floodlit Astro turf surrounded by advertisements for Mustang jeans, Sinco Cola, Greenfinger—*ahora comida para los niños, Ropa Interior de la Princesa Di* (for football is as much a craze with Ticas as Ticos)—with all absorbed in the shifting pattern of play as both sides probed each other's skills, Miller studied the pattern of tropical flowers on the shirt in front of him, the way the black skin on the neck bulged slightly over the collar, the pimples and tight black curls just visible beneath the narrow brim of the pork-pie hat, picked his spot and estimated his chances of slipping away through the crowd before anyone took in what had happened.

The thought made the adrenaline flow but not enough, like the first sip of a dry martini to a deprived alcoholic. Then one of the Puerto Limón players brought down the Alajuela striker, racing through on a sudden break, and pandemonium broke out: car horns, bells, chants, flares, drums—the ideal moment, but half of Miller's mind was now on the game and he waited to see how the free kick would turn out. His attention was also caught by a vicious off-the-ball foul an Alajuela player had got away with while everyone else's attention was elsewhere. It was skilful, Miller could see that, would fill the nigger who had suffered an elbow thrust fiercely into his solar plexus with bile, resentment and a sense of injustice. Later this would boil over into retalia-

75

tion and result in the wrong person being sent off.

Miller relaxed, aware that the game would not be without interest. The man in front of him shuddered a little and said to his neighbour, "I just felt footsteps on my grave."

9

It was the sort of room Per Hedborg most hated because it reminded him so much of his own childhood home. His father had been a specialist in piles in Uppsala, where he had built up a very lucrative practice—Per's life-style would not have been possible on his UNAFO salary alone. His father's taste in interior decoration had been solid, had owed nothing at all to the style we still call Swedish.

Just so the large villa the deputy director for Middle America, Don Roberto González Ortega, rented. In the dining room the wallpaper was practically bas-relief, so raised were the acanthus patterns; huge, richly moulded gilt frames enclosed tiny oils of Alpine meadows; a "peasant" sideboard, black, carried crystal decanters and silver. They ate off a polished round table, which left them—Per Hedborg, Deputy Director Roberto González and his wife Isabel—oddly distanced from each other.

A maid, anonymous in black and lace, served supermarket consommé spiked with sherry. Doña Isabel, thin, angular, aquiline, dressed in black with jet beads that chinked when she moved, watched her brief progress with the tiny tureen, and with one finger waved her away.

"My husband, Mr. Hedborg, continues to speak of you in the very highest way."

All three shared English—but not completely. In fact they would have done better in Spanish, but English is the official language of UNAFO.

Hedborg acknowledged the compliment with a dip of his fair head, first to her and then to the deputy director, who sat slumped and frail in a chair with arms—not a match with the rest of the dining-room furniture. The hand that raised his spoon shook. He lowered it, tried again, and this time made it.

"As you know, Per, I am sure you will take my place when I

go in three months' time. It is my wish you should. Unfortunately it is not in my power to make the decision. However, they may listen to me."

Hedborg maintained modest politeness. "It's very kind of you, sir. But surely someone from the area would be more appropriate."

"I don't think so. If he, or she, came from one of the countries concerned they would always be open to allegations of bias. Someone from the South Cone like myself, or Spain, would have only the advantage of language which in your case does not arise. Your Spanish is as good as mine."

"Hardly."

"Good enough."

Hedborg knew this to be the case. He sipped his wine. Austrian white from Rust which, since it had not been sweetened with engine coolant, was acid to taste. He concealed his grimace and finished his soup.

Deputy Director González suffered a quite nasty fit of coughing as the plates were changed. Veal with a thin madeira sauce followed.

"There is," said Doña Isabel, " a clinic not far from here. It is . . . very expensive. The prognosis is good, but very, very expensive."

Hedborg was interested. "Really? I mean really *very* expensive?"

Doña Isabel announced the fees with smug glee: "One thousand and five hundred dollars a week. Medicaments are extra. But it will be worth it. They virtually guarantee that after six months he will not want to smoke ever again, and they hope to stabilise, possibly ameliorate, the emphysema."

Hedborg attempted restrained heartiness.

"Why, that's splendid. Surely, sir, you need not then retire. I mean the Organisation will give you six months' leave of absence. . . ."

"No, no. My wife is pleased to be optimistic. If the cure works that will be fine—I shall enjoy a more pleasant and possibly longer retirement. But if it does not, then I shall have been wrong to ask for leave of absence."

Hedborg returned to his veal. It was overcooked. He thought: fifteen hundred dollars a week is more than the deputy director's salary. And certainly more than his retirement pension. Of course there would be a golden handshake for leaving early, perhaps as much as three years' salary in a tax-free lump sum. That would be where the money was coming from.

They discussed the recent visit of the Vienna State Opera and the gossip about the rows between the charismatic Lorin Maazel and his employees. The maid cleared the dishes and served zabaglioni in modern Venetian glass. Too stiff, thought Hedborg, she has used gelatine.

"You leave tomorrow, Mr. Hedborg?"

"The day after."

"I hope there will not be too many problems."

He laughed, frankly, almost boyishly. "Always, Doña Isabel, there are problems."

Roberto looked up, over his half-moon lenses, tapped the side of his dish with his spoon.

"There is something, Per, that has come up. Not in your briefing but you should keep an eye on it. United Brands are planning to pull out of bananas on the Pacific coast of Costa Rica. A bad hurricane season in May will give them an excuse. Really it is the U.S. government tariff that is causing the problem. There will be a vacuum. Citrus could fill it and none of us like that. But I have a contact in AFI who tells me a subsidiary is interested in fish-farming in the area. If you get time, look into it. They'll mention it when you visit Greenfinger Cay off Belize. We must keep AFI happy if we possibly can and fish-farming will be better nutritionally, more labour-intensive, and less damaging ecologically than citrus. Mind you they'll probably . . . want to trade . . . one for . . . the other."

This, the lengthiest speech he had made so far, left him gasping and purple round the corners of his mouth. He delved into his dinner-jacket pocket for his aerosol ventilator, and with some difficulty and drama contrived to make it work.

"Excuse me. Please excuse me."

"We will have coffee and liqueurs in here, María," his wife said to the maid, and then to Hedborg, "I am sure you will not mind. My husband does not like to move without necessity."

With the coffee the maid served Spanish biscuits—extremely rich shortcake, far more crumbly than the Scottish varieties, and better. The firm that made them in Navarra, was, Hedborg knew, owned by Greenfinger. It crossed his mind: were they a small present, harmless entirely in itself, brought to the villa by an AFI visitor?

"That co-operative. Sant'Simon. I'm afraid we may have to see that go."

Hedborg waited. Roberto González pulled himself up in his chair, tried to force the crumbs of the biscuit into a manageable ball, did not look up. He went on. "It is not, after all, a project we have any actual interest in. It is simply a matter of making sure Christopher Carter does not feel we are overriding his professional opinion, assessment."

"Or," Hedborg interjected, "of convincing him that there are good reasons to do so."

"Quite. I'll tell you, and you will use your discretion as to how far you go with Carter. Bear in mind his file shows he had radical opinions while a lecturer at Hume University, Christbourne. You may alienate him further if you pass on what I am about to tell you." He pulled out a cigarette packet, nervously tore at the wrapping, flicked his lighter. His nicotine-stained fingers held the cigarette at his mouth only momentarily and he did not seem to inhale; nevertheless he puffed at it ten times in a minute and when it was gone, he lit another. "I've heard from a reliable source that the CIA is against it. They suspect an outbreak of *foquismo*, you know?"

Hedborg knew. *Foquismo* is the revolutionary strategy of planting small, often only two or three, even just one cadre in peasant villages, co-operatives and so on, to work alongside the peasants, indistinguishable from them, and gradually teach them and lead them into revolutionary praxis. A network of such *focos*, focal points, across a given area can transform an apparently docile region into an area that will support strikes, land invasions, even shelter guerrillas.

"It doesn't seem too likely. Sant'Simon is very isolated. The nearest peasant communities of any size are thirty kilometres back up the highway towards Cartago, or another fifty or so southeast into Valle del General."

"That's what I said. But it was pointed out to me that in Costa Rica rural areas are far more advanced than in its neighbours. Communications are reliable and good. The standard of literacy is much higher. They are one culture: the intellectual and the peasant share a Hispanic background. There is not the gulf that exists between the Indian peasant and the Ladino or *mestizo* Spanish-speaking petty bourgeois of Honduras or Guatemala. They mix more easily. This makes a different sort of *foquismo* possible. So I was told."

The cognac at least was exemplary. Reluctantly Hedborg refused a second thimbleful. His pied-à-terre, a service flatlet, was back in town ten kilometres away. The local police were incorruptible and ruthless with drivers who drank more than the very low minimum allowed. He did not intend to spend the next ten days in a rehabilitation center.

The deputy director concluded by promoting, as he had before, the AFI/UNAFO project in Belize of persuading farmers to give up marijuana and return to sugar-cane and other crops from which industrial alcohol could be distilled.

Ten minutes later Hedborg got into his Saab outside the front door. Doña Isabel came down the steps after him although he felt all that was necessary had been done in the way of farewells. He let down his window. She stooped a little—an unusual posture for her.

"I do hope you have a very successful trip, Mr. Hedborg. A great deal hangs on it you know. My husband really is very anxious that he should feel able to recommend you without reservation for his post." She straightened, the silks of her dress rustled, jet beads clicked, and he sensed she was looking out across the roof of his car at the small moonlit lawn, the black laurels, not out of any interest in what she might see, but to avoid eye contact. "He would not like to know I have said this to you, but I think it is true to say his health, recovery, in a way depends on it. He has given much of his life to the Organisation. A very good law practice . . . He should not, I think, be asked to give life itself."

"Of course not, Doña Isabel, of course not."

She turned and he heard her evening shoes rattling the gravel, tapping on the steps, saw her silhouetted in the door. She did not look back. The maid closed the door.

Hedborg set the Saab going, turned onto the road and followed it along the side of the silvery lake towards the lights of the town. There was, he reflected, an equation. The Middle American Desk at UNAFO plus an enormously expensive clinic for the reformation of hardened smokers, minus . . . other factors. He wanted promotion, he wanted the Desk. Apart from the prestige, and the power, he assured himself he would make a better go of it than his sick predecessor. To get it he would have to countenance a certain amount of wheeling and dealing, trade off one thing against another. But all of UNAFO's work was compromised thus, was bound to be. Too many powerful interests were concerned for it to be otherwise. The thing was to keep it going, for, in the long run, Hedborg believed, it did good, and very little harm, for the harm it countenanced would happen anyway, whereas the good, very probably, would not.

10

On the morning that Esther and Kit made their trip from San José via Cartago to Sant'Simon, Fritz Steiner rounded off the training of his *Einsatzkommando* with a storming route march from the Pacific coast through what he called jungle, back to their base camp ten miles inland. He let the white South African exile—an ex-counter-terrorist-sergeant called Coetzee—lead the men while he followed behind with flash grenades and a machine-pistol. Occasionally he lobbed the former into the end of the column, occasionally he sprayed the canopy above them with live rounds. The exercise was meant to simulate their withdrawal from Nicaragua after destroying their designated target—an agricultural field station.

Their base camp for this training lay a quarter of a mile or so west of a quite large clearing that had been made in the forest to accommodate helicopters supplying the Milton University, Iowa, Canopy Research team, whose camp lay to the east of the clearing. The two parties kept apart from each other and neither knew what the other was up to, which was fine with both parties. The frequent rattle of small arms, pop of grenades, and occasionally the bang of something bigger alarmed the academics even though they had been assured by Francisco Franco that it was all okay, and anyway none of their business. They just got on with their exploration of the lowland Pacific rain forest canopy using a complicated and hi-tech system of ropes, pulleys, platforms and travelling cradles a hundred feet or more above the ground. All this in conscious plagiarism of a similar enterprise being conducted under the auspices of the Organisation for Tropical Studies of the University of Costa Rica at Finca La Selva in the Caribbean lowland. And they were in a hurry to get on—the wet season, with the likelihood of hurricanes, would close the camp in a few days.

While his men barbecued the parrots they had shot on the way and drank cans of Aguila Dorada beer, Steiner went over the previous twenty-four hours with his two NCOs, the second being an ex-U.S. Marine Polack called Grabowski. Grabowski suggested that some of the men doubted Steiner's ability in the jungle. Angrily Steiner insisted that he would spend his last night before their airlift back to San José and forty-eight hours of pre-battle debauch in the Playboy Complex by going on a private walkabout. He would, he said, bring back trophies that would demonstrate his expertise. He said he would walk up to a distant crag he pointed out to them, light a fire there whose smoke they would see, and return by midday the following day.

He took with him a pocket altimeter, a compass, a pair of strong binoculars with night-vision enhancement facility, some chocolate, a nylon hammock, an ex-SS dagger that had been his father's, a machete, half a litre of rum, and his own Heckler and Koch machine-pistol with two thirty-round magazines. It was the weapon he always favoured—its lightness and smallness made it an extension of himself, not only an extra limb but an extension of his personality. What it lacked in accuracy was made up in rate of fire and calibre: the 9-mm parabellum was a stopper—it didn't matter where you hit a target, it ceased to be a threat once one of those heavy slugs had smashed its way in. Anyway Fritz Steiner was never too concerned about accuracy—he rarely met occasions when it was important for, say, one person out of two or three together to be taken out and the others left unhurt.

He wore a light cotton shirt and trousers in combat greenish-brown, a webbing belt and backpack, snake-proof boots, an Aussie bushwhacker hat.

He left the camp at about 2 P.M. just when the first drops of rain started—but it was not a bother. On the forest floor it fell as a hazy drizzle of tiny warm droplets. Movement was not difficult so long as he made no attempts to keep to a straight line. There was little vegetation, simply a deep litter of fast-rotting fallen tree limbs, leaves, fungi that gave off a warm rich smell. He gave the Canopy Research Station a wide berth and headed for the river, reckoning that if he could cross it and then keep it on his left for a couple of miles he would soon locate the lower slopes of the now invisible crag.

After half an hour or so he could hear swiftly running water and progress became more difficult. The ground was more broken, dropped steeply at times, and as a result there were more frequent clear breaks in the canopy—where sunlight got through there was a thick ground vegetation of creepers, bamboo-like thickets, saplings, ferns and so on and he had to use the machete most of the time. He was now less protected from the rain and he was soon drenched. At times he felt an exhilarating panic that released itself in a frenzy as he slashed about him with the heavy blade.

Although the river was running rapidly there had not been enough rain to make crossing a problem. He soon found a spot above a small waterfall where gravelly shallows, worn lichen-covered boulders and a fallen tree trunk combined to make a natural bridge. He crossed, and in the middle caught sight again of the crag he was aiming for. Already it was satisfactorily nearer. As he watched, the rain cloud briefly caressed the trees on its top, lifted again, and a glorious rainbow curved down over it as the sun, now dipping out of the vertical towards the Pacific behind him, caught the rain. Steiner was interested only in his objective. He was equally oblivious of the beauties of huge butterflies, dragonflies, humming-birds, orioles and warblers which haunted the stream, and the flowers that blossomed in amazing abundance at its edge.

He was unaware too that he had been seen. Less than thirty yards away, a little higher up the stream and sitting at the foot of a jacaranda whose giant panicles of lavender flowers provided a royal pavilion some eighty feet above him, there sat a small neat gentleman about forty years old, with the impedimenta of a botanising naturalist around him. This gentleman kept very still once he had seen that the tall, fair German carried not only a machete but what looked like a very large pistol, and only moved when Steiner penetrated the riverside curtain on the farther shore and disappeared. Then he shook his head a little, stood up, and he too backed off into the forest but on the northern side of the stream.

Steiner pushed on. He took another compass bearing and the slopes too indicated which way he should go. He reckoned he had about two and a half hours of daylight left. If he was to eat and be comfortable he should not walk for more than an hour and a half. It was now very difficult ground to cover, the slopes were at times almost precipitous and again, because it was a west-facing slope and the afternoon sun penetrated the canopy, there was thick ground cover. Yet the creepers and bushes gave him handholds to haul himself up with.

In the time he had allowed himself he did not reach the peak, but he did get to a shoulder some three hundred feet below it, from which, thanks to a fallen giant that had brought down some of its lesser neighbours with it, he could see the sinuous sweep of the valley curling below him round bluffs and crags up to a fan-shaped slope which rose to an escarpment above a small settlement of thatched houses. This surprised him. The 1:250,000 map he had did not indicate its presence.

At all events he was satisfied with his position. His altimeter registered four and a half thousand feet, the sun, now below the cloud, was very hot, the rain here had stopped though curtains of it drifted over the settlement, which must have been three miles away, his clothes were drying out; all that remained was to find food and light the fire that would tell his men he had made it.

A troop of white-faced monkeys careered opportunely through the canopy above him, swinging, gibbering, shouting. A short, sharp burst aimed into the centre of the group brought down two and turned the group's screeches to screams, which very quickly receded. They were gone almost before the echoes of his shots had died away. He found one of the capuchins he had shot, quite a young one he judged, little bigger than a rabbit, though he was no expert and dying animals always look smaller and more frail than when they are fully alive. The heavy bullet had smashed out one shoulder-blade, taking a quarter of the monkey's body with it. It died as he picked it up by a hind leg.

He unwrapped a foolproof chemical firestarter, pulled the string that ignited one corner, and heaped on the driest leaves, twigs and branches he could find. There was soon a lot of smoke and some heat. He skinned and cleaned those parts of the carcase that were not too badly damaged and thrust them into the hottest part of the fire. The rest he swung over his head in a wide arc and tossed into the thickets below. He cleaned his SS dagger. He put up his hammock between two saplings and drank a quarter of a litre of neat rum. Lower than him the sun magnificently touched the Pacific horizon thirty miles away and he calculated he had half an hour of reasonable light left. It was not enough. The legs and torso were burnt or raw. Angrily he kicked the fire apart. The sun became a thin slice of watermelon, then was gone. Quickly he ate half his chocolate and drank the rest of the rum.

He was physically exhausted now, pleased with his prowess as a jungle survivor, and quite definitely drunk. He climbed into the hammock and was asleep before the last light had gone, before the big white flowers, whose existence he had not noted, opened and spilled their scent, before the giant moths descended on them, before the animals of the night—insects, reptiles, birds, bats and marsupials—began to scurry and flit around him, before the orange moon, three-quarters full, rose above el Cerro de la Muerte.

The same mountain delayed the dawn and Steiner awoke in a bank of cold mist or cloud, awoke stiff, aching, thirsty and with an early morning erection that did not fully collapse even after he had urinated. He had not brought water with him. In a rain forest you expect to find water. He ate the last chocolate, felt yet more thirsty, and then suddenly a touch frightened. The forest in the pre-dawn moment was eerily silent and the mist was so thick he could not see the canopy above him. He cursed, picked up his Heckler and Koch, loosed off ten rounds into the blank above him. Bird cries and flapping wings continued after the deafening, echoing clatter had gone, and he could hear leaves and branches rustle and creak. He smoked, mastery had been reasserted, he felt better. Slowly he packed up his gear, waited for the mist to lift. All he had to do now was pick his way back to the camp, downhill all the way, confident that he could survive in the jungle and lead men to and out of battle through it.

The mist brightened, was momentarily tinted with rose and gold, then in a space of a few minutes it was gone—had become ascending cloud above the nearly horizontal shafts of sunlight that flooded across the valley beneath it, and touched Steiner's high crag. It was already penetratingly hot and it set the birds going, the parrots and parakeets gliding and flapping, the monkeys swinging and swooping, the insects rustling, chirping, hopping, crawling. The snakes let their tongues flicker like black lightning and Steiner felt better, even better than when he had loosed off random shots from his machine-pistol. He felt better but thirsty still.

He scanned the valley both above and below the crag, saw

how it narrowed higher up and how the track of the river ox-
bowed into him before circling back up through cataracts and
waterfalls towards the settlement he had seen the previous evening. To reach it he would have to cover only half as much
forested hillside if he headed north-east rather than the way he
had come. He calculated that once he had hit the river and
quenched his thirst, he had only to follow its course back down
to where he had crossed it to find his way back to base—and he
was not expected for six hours, until one o'clock. Plenty of time.

This, though, was the steep side and the going even more difficult than the ascent. From the air rain forest often looks gently
undulating, only the deeper watercourses and valleys clearly
marked. This is because the giant trees reach for the sunlight
and then stop—those in valleys and declivities grow taller than
those perched on ridges. Some of the slopes were again almost
precipitous and after two nasty skids he had to deviate, double
back. This annoyed him.

Occasionally he crossed rivulets but he ignored them. He had
set himself a target, the river, which he would reach before he
slaked his now quite troublesome thirst. Dimly he recalled a
parable, legend, tale or whatever, which had been a favourite of
his grandfather, a Lutheran pastor. Something to do with a man
called Gideon, who chose a very successful *Einsatzkommando* from
those of his men who rejected easy ways of quenching their thirst.
All together it took him an hour and a half, and when finally he
slashed his way through the riparian screen he was quite a lot
higher up the river than he had intended.

For a moment he stood on the edge of the chuckling stream
and blinked in the sudden hot glare of unbroken sunshine. Wary,
head pushed forward, he glanced both up- and downstream before completely breaking cover, then un-Gideonlike he lay on his
stomach and drank, scooping the delicious, cold water into his
mouth. Satiated, he clambered over rocks and through shallows
to the edge of the basin he was in, and peered over the edge.

The drop, waterfalls and rapids, looked difficult but at the bottom the valley floor was relatively flat for a mile as the river
meandered towards the crag and made its ox-bow round it. The
other side of the valley closed in beyond it, forming what might
well be a short gorge—the distance and density of vegetation made
it impossible to be sure. But first, if he could get down this first

drop there would be a comparatively easy stretch. He looked about for the best way of tackling the descent and saw, with some relief, a small splash of white paint on a dark smooth boulder, and then another beyond. A track, or at any rate a negotiable route, had been marked out; he began to follow it.

And then he saw her, by chance and against the odds because though the river was wider below and the ground flatter, and he was above it, the giant trees, some of them a hundred and fifty feet high, obscured all but occasional glimpses of the water itself. Nevertheless, from where he was, he could see about sixty yards of linked pools, and water broken by boulders, and leaping, striding, occasionally wading, a tall, lean black woman with a bundle on her back.

Fumblingly he undid his binocular case, spread himself flat on a boulder, and brought her into focus.

They were good glasses. She had a bright red scarf over her head. In profile he caught her face—large eyes, straight nose, high cheekbones, wide mouth the colour of the flesh of a Santa Rosa plum, her skin almost as dark as the skin of the plum, a long straight neck. Then a tiny fist reached up for the gold ring in her ear. A baby. In a blue corduroy sling on her back. The sight of the baby, paler than the woman, gave an extra jolt to Steiner's already blood-thudding excitement.

She wore an emerald green blouse tied above her waist, beneath her breasts, and no bra. She turned further and he could see the flat firmness of her stomach, the depth of her navel, then denim jeans cut very short above thighs like ebony pillars. She turned away again and the tiny brass studs flashed on both sides of her bottom. Her legs were very long, very smooth, glistened with sweat or water splashes.

Again she turned back and this time waved; he could see her mouth open in a shout or call he could not hear above the rush and clatter of the waterfalls, and for a moment he thought she had seen him, but she was waving to someone roughly on her level. It was a man, emerging from the forest into the space behind her. He was tall, red or fair-haired but thinning on the crown. Check shirt, jeans, boots, carrying a stick. Quite a stout one and he was well-built. But a stick! A stick only! Steiner heard a rattling laugh grating up out of his own chest and realised that the grip he had taken on the glasses had become painful. He twisted a little, felt the breech and retractable butt of his machine-pistol pressing into his groin.

The man, making heavier weather of the pools and the boulders than the girl, in spite of the baby on her back, joined her, took her hand. They moved on and a huge swag of yellow blossom, the crown of a forest giant just below Steiner, cut them off from his sight.

He housed his glasses and, confident that the noise of the river would cover his pursuit, began to lope, spring, jump, clamber and even, where it was possible, run. A black elation throbbed in his chest, forced sweat from hands, head and groin, yet co-ordinated his legs and arms, torso, back and brain into a machine that could suddenly deal with the awkward ground as readily as if he were a cat or a baboon.

Nevertheless, it was a full twenty minutes before he came up with them.

They had found a small pool, no more than sixty feet wide at its widest and surrounded by large, flat, smooth boulders with patches of shingle here and there between them. It was, apart from the entrance and exit of the river, almost entirely enclosed by dense vegetation, much of it in blossom, and, apart from the very middle, mostly shaded by the crowns of the trees around. The river was quieter on this stretch, and Steiner, having placed their position from their shouts and the baby's cries, approached more slowly, silently. Again there were birds everywhere, dragonflies, butterflies, and not far off the chatter of monkeys.

They were on the far side now, the north-western bank of the pool, and had found one of the few substantial patches of direct, ground-level sunlight. Snaking into a position on the farthest bank from them Steiner pulled himself into a sitting position between the twin trunks of a leguminous sapling that had broken out of one seed. Their pinnate leaves almost covered him, he was in darkness, the woman and man in eye-searingly bright light with sparkling water between. When raised, their voices carried.

The woman was standing with her back to the man. She shrugged and wriggled and the straps of the baby-sling fell from her waist and loops slipped down her long bare arms. The man took the freed sling and turned the baby to face him. The woman turned, unzipped the pouch and lifted the baby out, held her in the air above her head, body horizontal against the sky, chubby arms and legs spread like a flying squirrel. She had nothing on but a disposable nappy and she gurgled with glee. Her mother now set her down on the shingle, delved in a small knapsack the man had been carrying, and pulled out half a tortilla, which she gave to the baby. The man and the woman then sat on either side of the baby and looked across the pool, straight at Steiner, or so he thought. But the myriad sunlit insects and birds that hovered, swooped, hung in shifting clusters between them, held their attention.

For him this hiatus after the pursuit now quickly shifted into boredom; the need to push the scenario on was prompted not by a physical desire that had faded, but a desire of the will. At this cold moment he decided he would rape the woman, humiliate the man, and murder all three. Without taking his eyes from them and with a minimum of movement he too got out of most of what he was carrying or was strapped to him, keeping only the SS dagger and the Heckler and Koch.

When he was almost ready her laugh suddenly belled across the water, the first sound he had clearly heard. She stood, pulled down her denim shorts, stepped out of them, while her shoulders and arms shed her blouse. For a moment she stood thus, entirely naked, arms stretched to the sky, legs astride the man, her back to Steiner. Sun struck gold across her shoulders, down her back, across her bottom.

The man remonstrated, half stood but she pushed him backwards and fell on him, pulling at his trousers and shoes. He resisted for a moment, gave in, assisted. She fell on him, they twisted, turned, the yellow body of the man now beneath and then above and at last beside the loveliness of the black one, then suddenly she pushed herself up onto her haunches, back straight and spat in the man's face.

She turned and, hardly pausing to weigh up the depth of the water, whether or not there were weeds, snakes, who knows what, launched herself into an almost perfect shallow dive. The insects and birds were swirling away even before her body shattered the surface to fling priceless treasures in the air. Lilac-coloured blossoms dropped from above.

Her head broke the surface in the middle of the pool and a shake of short black curls scattered a dynamic tiara around her. She twisted, faced back towards the man, trod water, yet drifted with the current towards the ridge of large boulders that marked the end of the pool. Her feet found the bottom and, up to her breasts in water, she stayed her ground.

Above her the man stood, alarm across his face then a sort of shame as momentarily his hands flitted across his pink and quite untumescent sex.

"I'm sorry," he called. "I'm truly sorry. Ezzie, I really am."

"Fuck you, Carter." Her high, angry voice was like a baroque trumpet. Parakeets and macaws attempted mimicry.

"I'm sorry Ezzie. I just . . . I feel . . . too exposed here. Besides, the baby . . ."

"The baby is just fine, Carter." And indeed she was—temporarily distracted from her tortilla by the commotion but by no means anything other than entertained, she chortled.

"You know what I think, Carter? This is the fourth time, and you know what I think?"

She thrust water with a great sweep of her hand so it sprayed in a fine rainbowed arc across him. Some drops scattered onto the baby who looked up, alert, ready now to cry, but remembered too that it still had tortilla in its hand, so did not.

"You know what I think, Carter? I think you have had nooky here in Ticoland and it's psyching you. Am I right? Shit. Sheeit. I *am* right. You fucking bastard, you . . ." She began to wade towards him, stumbled, so that in spite of everything he flung out a hand to save her and then. . . .

Two seconds of mind-shattering Pandemonium—literally that, the sound of the Capital of Hell let loose, then cut off as if the lid had been put back on. Chips of rock flew, missiles whined and the incredible clatter went on to bounce around the crags.

Steiner, mirror shades over his eyes, brown cotton clothes smeared with mud and rotten stuff, picked his way towards them across the boulders behind her. The Heckler and Koch swung like a cybernetic limb attached to his right arm, his left hand clutched his groin. Esther lost grace, clambered as ungainly as a seal out of the pool and onto the shingle to scoop up the baby who was now howling like a machine that has slipped a cog and is running at ten times its normal speed, sheering teeth from other cogs as it runs. The mother sank to her haunches, knees splayed, and pushed a still wet nipple into a mouth that instantly latched on. The scream dropped into a heaving, fast-repeated sob. The man too had scrambled back to the baby—both he and the woman were now crouched protectively round the child. Large-eyed, pale in spite of the strong colours of their complexions, momentarily petrified with shock and terror, they stared up at Steiner.

During thirty seconds the noises of the forest rebuilt themselves. Birds recovered the power to call and sing, monkeys tentatively checked with each other that all was well. The rush and trickle of the water reasserted itself. Steiner weighed up the position. He could not rape the girl while the baby was at her breast, so the baby would have to go first.

He moved towards the family, the muzzle of the machine-pistol shifting from woman to man. He rather thought that of the two the woman was the more dangerous—until he had got the baby off her. A plan formed: he would seize the baby by one leg and throw it as he had the monkey carcase the night before, in a high turning arc to crash into the river below. He would make the man tie the woman's arms behind her. He would shoot the man in the knees. He would rape the girl. Then he would kill both with his knife. Slowly.

He moved in, his right foot touched the shingle.

11

Don Jesús María Batista y Galdós. *Licenciado* Don Jesús. Jesus.
Listen. Suddenly everything here is shitty. The boss nun, whatever she's called—Mother Jailer—has flipped her lid. All right.
So we had a little dope in here last night, but Jesus, Jesús, she's
doing a berserk, actually berserking. Listen, you hophead. She.
Has. Taken. Zena. From. Me. *Se me llevó Zena.* Now. You
will get this tape at about 9 A.M. right? If I do not have Zena
back in this room with me by 1 P.M. I will tear the fucking head
off of the next nun, or wardress, or whatever, that gets within
reach. I mean it Don Jesús. I really mean it.

Do you know what the fucking bitch said? Perhaps she thought
my Spanish wasn't up to it, but the mouthful I gave her back
pretty damn quick disabused her on that score, I can tell you.
She told me, Don Jesús, that while she could just about see how
a woman might kill a man, and yet be a good mother, though of
course that did not mean she condoned murder, she could not
see how a woman could be a good mother and smoke dope.
Listen Don Jesús. I'm near breaking point. I took a grip on
myself at the time, I had just fed Zena and changed her, she's a
treasure, so she's okay for a few hours, but if I don't get her back
by 1 P.M. I . . . I don't know what I'll do.

Don Jesús. You come up and tell that bitch that I am not a
murderer until proved guilty, and like you said before, that I am
entitled to all rights save those to come and go as I please. And
if there's a fine here on Spanish soil for smoking one-tenth of a
gram of *ganja,* then I'll pay it. But you get my baby back, right?

And. Another thing. I wasn't going to mention this like because you're a man and men aren't supposed to get involved in
this scene, even liberated ones like poor Kit steered clear, but
Don Jesús, you have to know this, I am actually now having my
period. Right? Do I have to say that in Spanish? *Tengo las
reglas.*

94

Now this is a personal disaster because I would like to have been pregnant. It occurs to me *you* would have liked me to be pregnant as that would have been an added proof of my love for Kit. But that's by the way. Don Jesús. You wear a wedding ring, you must know what I am talking about. The darling sweet Mother Superior whose head I am going to pull off if she doesn't give me back my baby, has given me a packet of sanitary towels the sort you wear suspended from an elastic cord. You will have to do something about this. If the lover of María Victoria de los Angeles can smuggle in dope, then you can smuggle in a packet of Tampax. Regular, it's not heavy. I mean my period's not heavy, I don't need Super. I'm under the weather, I suppose. So. A packet of Regular Tampax, right? Charge it.

I suppose I had better get on with my story now. It'll pass the time. But don't expect . . . oh, *shit. Give me back my baby.* Sorry.

Not long after they'd sung "La Muralla" and one or two more like it the guests left and we got some sleep on rugs put on the floor. Now it was empty I could see under the paraffin lamp just how rich and varied the wild life was. The place was just crawling. Minerva said the lizards kept down the spiders and the roaches. There would have been an awful lot of spiders and roaches without the lizards. I didn't sleep much. It was hot and smelly and Minerva and Manuel snored like hippos on the other side of a partition of dried leaves. The moonlight was so bright it was oppressive. Zena slept, then began to cough and whimper, she was cutting her second bottom tooth, so I cuddled her for a bit.

The sounds changed. The quality of light shifted. I went out onto the step. The valley was filled with mist and the moon, like an orange, was just dipping into it. Behind me, over the mountain, the sky looked grey. Dawn on its way, and it would be quick. The air was fresh and clean after the cabin and I could hear the streams and river. Way down below, a couple of birds, hawks or eagles, swung and soared above the crowns of the few trees that came through the mist. Kit came out behind me and I said I'd like to go down the river, and he said okay and got the sling.

Kit had been down a mile or two before, he knew where we could go and where not. He pointed out white marks on some of the rocks, said that guy Trevor Everton, the botanist he'd told me about before, put them there.

The sun came up and the mist lifted. It was all very pretty.
After an hour or more we came to a nice spot, sort of shingly
and warm with a pool and I wanted to make love but Kit didn't
so I had a swim instead.

Jesús. I don't want to go on with this, and I want my baby,
and what happened next was not nice.

This fucking German came out of the forest with a machine-
gun and nearly shot us up. He had mirrored shades so I couldn't
see his eyes but he had a scar zigzagged from the corner of one
eye to his mouth. And it was very clear what he was going to
do, that he had it in mind to perform on me what Kit didn't seem
up to. . . .

Jesús. I'm not going on with this. Not till I get Zena back.
But I tell you what I will do. I'll hunger-strike. Yet. I'll hunger-
strike till that bitch brings baby back.

Wow! Jesús, she's back. Whoopee. She got herself back, the
sweet little darling. She woke up almost as soon as they got her
downstairs, or wherever, and blew her top. She screamed and
hollered and screamed. And those nuns tried everything—they
played with her, cuddled her, cradled her, left her, they went to
the *farmacia* and got a bottle and formula. My baby's never had
rubber in her mouth before, nor will she ever again. One of the
trainee screws, I mean novices, told me all this. The boss nun
wanted to leave her, said she'd get tired and stop. But after an
hour the others couldn't stand it anymore and rebelled. First
battle my little girl has won against the haters of the world. And
not the last.

Anyway, all is now, however temporarily, fine and dandy again,
and I'll get on with my story. I've fed and cleaned her and she's
in the little cot they found for her, and smiling and rosy and cosy
as if nothing happened. She sleeps well when I do this story-
telling, bless the little mite, I expect she likes the sound of my
voice. No Tampax however yet.

Where was I? Oh yes. Mother-naked on a rock nursing my
little girl and about to be raped by a Kraut psycho with a gun. I
crouched over her closer and closer, tried to wrap myself round
her so of course she began to squirm and wiggle as well as sob.
I could feel the wetness of her face, from her eyes, nose and mouth

streaking against my boobs and my tummy, and a fierceness boiled up with my panic. You know, Don Jesús, how I feel about my Zena. Kit too was the same. As the Kraut stepped off the last of the flat stones and onto the shingle above us, my lover positively snarled and moved forward into a crouch, peering up at him, even straight into the small black muzzle of the gun, seeing our reflections in those mirror shades.

Like that the three of us were turned in on ourselves, an enclosed field of energy, bad energy, lust, fear, hate, deafened by the storm of blood in our ears and the rush of the river as it tipped over the edge of the pool, tunnel vision concentrated on the twitch of muscle, or flicker of eye movement that might signal resolve translating into action. So we missed the eddy of foliage behind the Kraut, the soft footfall on the rock and saw him only when he was already there, a short, neat, dapper figure in pale-blue cotton shirt and trousers, canvas trainers, and holding a short-barrelled shotgun. The first Kraut knew of him was the heavy prod of this in the small of his back and the shift in our expressions. "The gun on the floor please, and the knife," said our saviour, "or I blow a hole out of you." Kit scrambled forward and took the machine-gun as it fell. "Now go back where you came from. Quickly."

And, you know, he did. Just like that. He scampered off over the rocks and down the side of the waterfall as fast as he could go, not to be seen again, not that day.

Well. Our saviour, you might have guessed, was Trevor Everton, the field botanist Kit had spoken of, and he was a really nice person. Polite, precise, but not pushy. Gentle and careful. Quiet. Neat's the word. Real neat. And right there in the rain forest he offered us . . . tea!

Certainly we, poor Kit and me, we needed something. We were holding on to each other and to the baby, and half crying, and laughing even, and I had this very serious attack of the shakes, just could not get over it. But I did in the end if only because something had to be done to stop Zena's sobs.

Trev Ev now found something terribly interesting to look at through the small binoculars he carried while Kit and I got dressed, and then Kit and he did this terribly British bit: "I say old chap, awfully handsome of you to come along and sort things out." "Not at all, old chap, a chap has to do the right thing." It wasn't quite like that, but near enough to give me the giggles which they put down to hysterical reaction, and tea was mentioned again.

I didn't believe in this tea, and nor did Kit, he said when we talked about it later, but this Trevor had it all laid on. Carrying his shotgun in one hand and the Kraut's machine-gun in the other, he led us through the river screen, all ferns and saplings and green, green, green, and into the rain forest proper and it was eerie, like a submerged cathedral, it was so wet. Sodden underfoot, and sodden in the air, but hot too, especially where there was a hole in the canopy and these shafts of white sunlight came streaming down through the hot haze and made all the flat leaves and fronds they hit burn white and silver. And elsewhere what Trevor called sunflakes scattered like daisies on the litter, and if you stood barebacked for any length of time under one of these you'd feel the sunflake burning a hole like through a magnifying glass. And the trees, all tall, tall, and with great bladed buttresses supporting them because the soil had no depth, and it all echoed the way an engulfed cathedral should, echoed with cries and songs of birds—intermittent now into the hot and somnolent stage of the day, and other cries and calls too.

Not much grew on the broken and sloping ground, just mulch and rotting trunks and limbs of trees, until you looked and were lucky and saw a patch of pearls, new-grown fungi, and always ants, and spiders, and centipedes and millipedes, and beetles and bugs that heaved and rustled and scampered and scurried through it all.

It wasn't far, ten minutes from the river, and Trev's bivouac was, you've guessed it, neat. Between two immature trees, about twelve feet apart, he had fixed a ridge pole and collected branches and leaves to form a tent. With the canopy above it was just about waterproof. Inside he had slung a hammock and neatly stacked round it were the very few things he needed: plant-drying presses with two wick-burning paraffin stoves, polythene bags for the dried specimens, and insect-proof boxes for the bags, a Calor gas camping stove, a small saucepan, a small bag of beans, and a few tins, three changes of clothing, a couple of spoons and, oh dear, he said, only one mug. Still, it's quite big, you can share.

The tea came out of a caddy and was, he said, two of Darjeeling to one of Earl Grey. No milk, but he had a slice of lime. It was okay, you know?

I looked round, sensed the stillness and the mystery and gave sort of a shudder. Maybe the Kraut had followed us, was lurking. I asked, don't you get lonely? He smiled. He didn't laugh a lot, but you often saw that shy, private smile. Not really. He used to come with a couple of companions but they always got edgy with each other, so in the end he tried it alone. He had a Walkman and a load of Ludwig van B. I could see it all. Him lying in his hammock, the submerged cathedral all round him and the Ninth blasting away in his ears. I once saw a piece of graffiti in the big park in Madrid. It read, "The Gardeners of the Retiro live like Gods." So, I reckon, did Trevor Everton.

Dangerous, though, Kit suggested. Not really, said Trev Ev. Safer than Central Park or Paddington. The worst you can expect is falling branches. They're self-pruning and they come from a long way up and you hear them coming. Not so funny at night in a storm but then I'm not usually here in the stormy part of the year, he said. In fact he was about to pack up in a week or so.

Snakes?

"No problem. Not many poisonous. They keep out of your way if they can." He had this funny, clipped way of talking. "Actually that's why I have that bit of nastiness." He pointed at the shotgun. "But I've never used it, not sure I know how, and I don't usually carry it."

But he'd been carrying it that day because he had seen the Kraut the evening before. "He didn't see me. I kept an eye on him. He was quite horrible. Shot two lovely white-faced monkeys with that thing, made a terrible din wherever he went, and was, oh just messy. Didn't like him. Not one bit. So I decided to keep an eye on him while he was in this neck of the woods and there you are."

"God, we were lucky," said Kit.

"Not really. Don't believe in luck."

"Where did he come from?"

Trev Ev thought he knew. Below the waterfalls, in the lowland forest, there was an American group researching the canopy with ropes and wires and lifts, all flown in in helicopters. Not, said Trev, his scene at all. Still the chaps there were all very decent and lent him things occasionally, and sometimes he just went down there for a chat. Anyway four days ago there had been an awful racket going on there, or not far off. Shooting. Grenades. The Americans said twenty men had been dropped in. Some private army training. Common enough in Central America. Trev reckoned our Kraut was one of them, in which case he wasn't too bothered about a return visit since they were meant to be leaving that day or the next.

By then we had finished our tea and were feeling better. Trev said he would come up to Sant'Simon with us. The commune sold him beans and fresh fruit, and he couldn't resist Minerva's tortillas. He tidied up, of course, and the machine-gun, machine-pistol, Kit said it should be called, was a problem. Kit didn't want it. Trevor neither. In the end he wrapped it in the oily cloth he used to keep his shotgun in and put both together under the head end of his hammock. Then he took us back up the river.

That was quite a different experience, you know? I mean compared with when Kit and I came down. That Trevor knew everything and, maybe because he didn't have too much chance to talk, he would not stop. No way could we stop him, nor did we want to.

First of all he told us how to find him if ever we wanted to call in again and really it was quite simple: follow the white paint marks down the river until you come to a diamond shape, turn right by a big palm, not so common just there, sweep round the top of a gully, drop down, a fallen sotacaballo or riverwood tree showed the way, following the direction its crown pointed and a hundred yards beyond it there you were.

He told us how his white marks were not really to set out an easy path but marked off divisions in his study of the plant life so he could scientifically compare how species grew differently at different points in the river's progress, at different times of the year. His main study was the riverweed family which streams out from the rocks like the bright green hair of water nymphs, but he knew it all. What I had took, taken, to be humming-birds were pygmy kingfishers, so Kit asked about fish, and Trev said there were plenty and more since the commune had stopped bombing the pools, so Kit asked Trev if he thought the commune was an environmental hazard.

"Oh no," said Trev, and I quote, but first he sat down, for

100

which I was grateful, because it was all uphill, and still no breakfast. "Their presence will change the forest below them," he
said. "But it's not a major intrusion. It's not like clear felling,
it's not even like selective felling. And there's far too much of
both going on all over the country. Okay they cleared some
recently established second-growth cloud forest to plant the coffee and some virgin forest went where the settlement and fields
are, but I doubt if they took out anything irreplaceable. Anyway
it's done now so it's no use beefing about it."

"No danger to all this down here, because of their presence up
there?"

"Danger, no. Look. Forest is not static, unchanging, no matter what some ecologists say. Three very dry years or very wet
could radically alter its character. So could the volcanoes blowing their heads off. Sant'Simon isn't going to do anything like
that, nothing on that scale. One or two species might do mar-
ginally better because they're there, one or two a little worse.
You've got to remember that within limits ecospheres are self-
adjusting. Listen. If the conservationists are trying to put the
boot in tell them from me they're talking rot, especially since
your people have stopped shooting the birds and animals and
bombing the pools. I like Sant'Simon. I want it to stay. Hey.
Now just look at that."

That was a tropical otter. It was stretched out on a great boulder and a broad trickle of water showed how it had just emerged.
It licked its slick pelage. It yawned. Stretched. Then the warm
air shifted between us, its squat head came up, and its whiskers
rose sharp and erect. Then it slid off the rock and was gone.

It went on, all the things we would not have seen without
Trev. A pair of chestnut-coloured birds, small, with black-and-
white striped waistcoats, fluttered in the tangled vines along the
riverbank. Riverside Wrens Trev said they were and he told us
how he had once seen them chasing off a big black snake that
threatened their young, hanging in a globular nest over the stream.
Then there were torrent flycatchers with bobbing tails and a flock
of Louisiana water thrushes on their way back north, and best of
all migrating moths, *Urania fulgens*, black like scraps of burnt paper unless the sun caught them and then they flashed green and
gold. Suddenly he took me by the elbow and pushed the glasses
into my hand.

"Look at that rock with the yellow lichen. Focus. Track along the bank and what do you see?"

"My God," I cried, "Tyrannosaurus Rex."

It was a lizard, about two feet long but sitting up on its back legs, and it had a splendid crest, which it raised and lowered. In front it had two little arms and hands just like old T. Rex in the Natural History Museum back home. But it had another trick too, for suddenly it ran off still on its hind legs, with its long tail stuck up behind to balance it, straight for the river, and you won't believe this Don Jesús, he actually ran across the water, walked on the water just like JC, your namesake.

"Basilisk," said Trevor. "He won't be liked by your coffee-growing friends, he eats the cherries. Talking of which, can you smell anything?"

We were now at the bottom of the last waterfall below the village and plantation. There was a lot to smell, but then I caught what he was on about. You know how a bramble flower smells like the spirit of blackberries, and raspberry and apple blossom works the same way—that was what this was to coffee, yet it was something else again. Actually its coffeeness was very elusive, you might not have guessed coffee had you not known. Anyway it was a heavenly scent and I guessed right.

And poor Kit. He couldn't catch it at all. Some smells are like that, or some people are. He can't, *could not*, tune in to freesias either.

"I think you've hit precisely the right day to be in Sant'Simon."

We climbed the little cliff, in places it was almost that, but never really difficult, and thus as we got onto the plateau below the coffee groves, spread like a fan across the slopes above us, we could see what he meant. Where the day before the budding blossom had looked like pearls scattered on the dark and glossy green, today they were fully out, snowballs of purest white, right round the amphitheatre in terraced rows, each shrub a rounded cupola of gorgeous blossom. Precisely the right day, because the next the glory would have diminished as each flower became touched with brown in its centre, a stain spreading outwards, as they withered.

"It will be a great shame if there's no one here to collect that harvest when it comes," Trevor remarked.

"Oh, there'll be someone here, all right," said Kit. "It won't be the first time something like this has happened. Peasants invade unused land, get their act together, and then, just as five or six years' work, unpaid, are beginning to pay off some prick discovers Philip the Fourth gave just that bit of land to his family in perpetuity. Part of the trouble is it's such good coffee. The higher it's grown the better, and this is about as high as it will grow."

"I suppose you're right," said Trevor. He smiled his shy, coy smile. "I had a more romantic theory."

"Really?"

"You see, about fifteen months ago I came up here to get some tortillas and beans and I met an old chum. Don Ignacio Morena. A Nicaraguan botanist. It's a small world, the botanical one. After fifteen years in Central America, I know most of the locals. I'd forgotten all about it until the other day when they told me about the trouble they're having. Then I thought, well, Don Ignacio is definitely a Sandinista, and Manuel belongs to the same clan. . . . It could be a connection that annoyed someone in San José."

"I don't think it can be anything like that. I'm not really too worried. My boss at UNAFO arrives the day after tomorrow and he's a good guy. And has clout. He'll get it sorted."

As he finished, a cloud of children closed round us, pulling at us, trying to get Zena down, prattling and laughing. They'd been worried about us, especially after someone had heard gunfire, banging up the valley from below. They carried us off into the village and gave us the breakfast we had missed—*moros y cristianos*, black beans and white rice. It's what real Ticas and Ticos go to work on. I tried to joke: I am a Moor, but they didn't get it, didn't see it that way.

Listen Jesús. That night, back in Kit's flat in San José. After we'd got Zena asleep, Kit really got his act together at last. You know what I mean. It seemed he felt okay now he'd told me he had ass before I came out. I forgive him. Forgave? Nothing to forgive. For Christ's sake the poor guy had been on his own for so long—in a way I was glad he'd gone out and had a nice time with a nice girl, I wouldn't have wanted him going with no whores. I wouldn't let him tell me who she was or what she was like, not my business, especially when he assured me, honour-bound and cross his heart, that it was all over and okay, and no bad feelings on either side.

Hell, I expect I'd have done the same if I hadn't had Zena to cope with all through that time. Coping with a little mite from nought to eight months, on your own after the first three, takes your mind off of things like that.

Anyway, normal service was resumed and very nice too. And, you know what? I reckoned the lady he'd been with had got him to understand things about a lady's parts I'd never been able to teach him. That's a bonus, I thought then, certainly nothing to grumble about.

Later I learnt more about her. Possibly she's a saint. Was.

The point I'm making, Jesús, was Kit and I were not just man and wife, we were lovers too. So tell that to the judge, right? Oh hell. I loved that man, so now I'm going to have a little weep again. And Jesús? Don't forget the Tampax.

Part IV

12

The next morning Kit Carter got up first and bustled about the little kitchen that had been his own territory for nearly six months, but which already looked and even smelled different since Esther's arrival. Spices, garlic, fruit, oil. He had not cooked much and never elaborately, preferring to eat out, and latterly at Rosa's. He did not resent the change, indeed not, but a little irritation there was when for the second time he could not find where she had put something.

He got together two Greenfinger breakfasts, one of adult corn-flakes, the other of baby food, and milk and coffee on a tray and took it into the bedroom. Already she was sitting up and feeding Zena. She was, both were, entirely beautiful. Lovely. Esther cooed and chuckled at the baby, *café au lait* cradled in the crook of her chocolate arm, attached like a loving leech to her long breast, but coming off the nipple as he came in, leaving it long, uptilted, and plum red with a bead of milk on the end. Zena flashed him the most entrancing smile he had ever seen on a human face, then, wham, she almost threw herself back on.

He remembered with a glow of gratitude and pride their love-making the night before, how at one point Esther had said why don't you fondle my tits, and he had said because they seem to belong to Zena, and she had said shit man, my tits are mine, and I say who fondles them.

"Have you got hers there?" she now asked.

"Yes. All ready."

"And you got time to give it her?"

"Yes, indeed. Nearly an hour before I need go."

"Then madam will be ready for you quite soon. Come on, my love, second tank."

And she gently but firmly moved Zena across to the other breast, cutting short a whimper as she did.

Kit adored the breast-feeding, was amazed that it had continued so long after the three months they had all been together following Zena's birth. Ticos or others who objected could shove it. His first wife had had none of it, and he now partly blamed the thread of spite that ran through his two sons' make-up on that: Zena was an unbelievably happy baby, sociable, trusting, smiling, laughing, captivating. "Never will she ever believe the world has gone finally wrong, no matter what it does to her," he had said on the evening of the second day after their reunion, "always after a start in life like that, she will believe there is bliss at the end of the road." And the thought had set off in his mind the idea that maybe that's not so good—perhaps that's why peasants across the world put up with so much, seem somehow to lack the ambition and drive to do something. After a long spell, sometimes, he had read, as much as five years on the breast, they were filled with love and content and above all certainty that goodness would arrive in the end if only they sat around and waited long enough. So he mused as he pottered about the flat and waited for the second tank to be emptied.

For ten seconds or so he peered down into the street below and saw a short, compact man appearing shorter than he was, foreshortened by the height, looking up . . . at him? Then the man turned away, into the small grocery store where Kit and now Esther bought their milk and bread and eggs. For a moment Kit was puzzled—something about the man was outrageously familiar: he placed it. It was *Englishness*. Not just the clothes, since they were neither expensive nor distinctive, so much as the way they were worn. A little ill-fitting. A little mismatching. The Dutch perhaps willfully achieve a similar denial of style, no one else. The man was Dutch or English.

Kit turned back to scoop up his baby, put her in the high tubular-framed chair, rather ugly, made by United Special Steels in Jamestown, Pennsylvania, that had cost a lot more than he thought it should in one of San José's three baby shops, strapped her in, put on a plastic bib, and began to feed her Greenfinger 5. Ingredients: skimmed milk, maize, millet, rice, oats and wheat, maltodextrin, vitamins C, E, Ca-D-pantothenate, nicotinamide, B_1, B_2, B_3, A_1; folic acid . . . just about everything appropriate you could think of. The miracle ingredient of course was taken for granted: labour. Energy per 100g $-$ 415kcal $=$ 1795kJ, he read—

but he suspected more energy per 100g than that had gone into its production.

And all the time he adored the perfect roundness of the back of his baby's head, and how it sloped into a high narrow forehead and dropped down to a perfect little heart-shaped face. The birth had been perfect, of course. Esther had made sure of that.

Now he spooned in the food and continued to muse: the women in Life before Esther, Mother, sisters, first wife, had all been very middle-, indeed upper-middle-class. Privileged. Educated. And all, he now knew, had the embittered mentalities of slaves, even freed slaves. Aristotle was right, he usually was. Freed does not equal liberated. Basically, for all they read Jane Austen and George Eliot (as indeed did Esther, and their Spanish equivalents), knew about the Royal Academy (which Esther would not have given a fart for), and knew, or remembered from their mothers, how to manage servants (Esther had learned in various jobs how to manage masters), *basically* the only purpose of their lives was the support, sustenance, maintenance and general propping up of their professional, academic, banking or whatever fathers, husbands and sons.

His mother particularly had suffered. Very intelligent, and sensitive too, but hopelessly insecure, always seeking the acceptance and approval of father, husband and finally son, she had stunted herself, and, through her possessiveness, him too. He recognized this was so, even if only because he still dreamed of her so often after her death. But he had no real understanding of how deeply he had been wounded by her, wounded by her need to soothe her own wounds.

Whereas Esther: born without any privilege whatever had had to make her own way, and, no doubt helped by her aunt in Brixton whom Kit had met and recognised as intelligent, kind, but tough, had early decided she was no one's servant, but no one's. She had, however, a goal. Perfection. Whatever she did she did right: Spanish, childbirth and childrearing, and also, he thought, and sensed just a touch of threat, her relationship with him. But, thought Kit, she has learnt something else on the way: the art of happiness, which now she is passing on to this divine daughter.

Half an hour later, dressed in neat shoes, smart grey slacks, and white sleeveless shirt, dangling his thin document case from its finger strap and swinging his furled giant Greenpeace Stop the

Acid Rain umbrella, Kit Carter strode purposefully through the fresh but busy early morning streets and boulevards of San José.

Behind him came the man, not so short, but very compact, absurdly dressed in brown jacket, blue shirt, check trousers, all topped off with a borsalino with a small feather, who had earlier looked up at him from the street. As always "Dusty" Miller kept a time check, using the stopwatch facility on his Casio digital.

Kit shared an office in an ITCO annexe, the third floor of a block not far from the Tourist Board Office. It was only ten minutes from his flat and always he walked, threading his way through a thousand men and women all like him heading for offices and agencies, and stopping at "sodas" for a coffee and pastry or toasted sandwich on the way.

In 1948 the parents of these functionaries sacked the army and defused the Communist threat by instituting a genuine welfare state, and they now provided the large and efficient bureaucracy needed to service it. For a time it worked. But coffee prices slumped and with fair labour laws their bananas now come dearer than those of their neighbours. There is no oil. To raise foreign currency more and more land is used for cash crops, and aid is needed to buy food they could have grown themselves. Prices rise, wages do not. Social services have been cut.

Polarisation between left and right is, after all, taking place. Once the police force was a joke—those who had pistols in their holsters invariably shot themselves in the feet whenever they tried to use them. Now there are American advisers and the stock-piles of IS equipment, CS gas, the shields and batons steadily grow while the shrill Voice fills the airwaves with attacks on Cuba and Nicaragua.

Kit understood most of this and he believed his job was doing something to slow down the descent of pleasant, decent Ticoland into the hell of Guatemala or Honduras, the civil war of El Salvador, the beleaguered poverty of Nicaragua. Wherever landless peasants made a go of farming virgin or unused land, the strains on the social fabric were reduced, and the Instituto de Tierras y Colonización vetted such schemes, then assisted the peasants in the long and often tortuous legal business of gaining tenure.

As far as he was concerned Sant'Simon was a model of its kind. He had said so and so had the experts and inspectors from all the other relevant agencies and ministries. At first. But then from December onwards it had begun to go awry. Every formally presented report had found something wrong and it now seemed very likely that ITCO would not support a claim for tenure. If it did not, then the peasants, Manuel and Minerva, Ipolito and Umberto, Carmen, Conchita and Miguelito, and all the others would have to go. And quickly too. Back into the *tugurios*, the dungheaps, the shanty towns that are filling up the interstices between San José and the towns nearby.

He trotted up the steps between a boutique and a "soda" and then the stairs that angled round the lift shaft to the third floor and so to his corner in the open-plan office he shared with eight other officials, three secretaries and ten clerks. Once settled in he began to look through the correspondence that had arrived ahead of him.

Near the top was a large manila envelope. Printed across the flap, beneath the Costa Rican arms (three volcanoes set between two oceans with a sailing ship in each) the legend "Instituto de Antropología Social." His pulse quickened. He opened it, drew out a ringbound pamphlet, a print-out from an IBM word processor. A slip on the front carried his name, typed, and the instruction: for your information only, no action required. The title was *Close Kinship in the Sant'Simon Co-operative*, and the author was Rosa Portillo Bazán, doctor of Social Anthropology, University of Santiago, Chile.

He read it with mounting distress and anger. The first part was already familiar. It traced the interrelatedness, complete with elaborate family trees, of the whole community. Nearly one-third came from only three extended families who originated in neighbouring settlements in the Valle del General.

The rest was new to him. Comparisons were made with similar studies carried out in Puerto Rico and Chile and the conclusion was reached that there was a strong probability that the ills related to inbreeding would appear at Sant'Simon. Studies made by the Institute of Genetic Health and the Ministry of Education were cited.

Kit was familiar with them. That from the Institute of Genetic Health drew attention to two cases of Down's syndrome. Although only one postdated the formation of the co-operative two cases of genetic dysfunction indicated a statistical risk and future births should be carefully monitored.

The report from the Ministry of Education was the work of Miguel Saavedra with whom Kit had been friendly during his first three months in San José. No longer. Saavedra had claimed that the attainment of the children was low. He suspected the effects of inbreeding and was not prepared to endorse the educational viability of the community until a proper study had been made of its interrelatedness.

On first reading Saavedra's report Rosa had derided it. The whole cast of her training, the whole thrust of her personality led her to accept the evidence that shows that environment determines ninety per cent of how we turn out. It was because she had refused to compromise on this that she had lost her post in Santiago after the 1973 coup, had been imprisoned and tortured before making her way into exile.

Kit now felt bewildered and angry at what looked like betrayal. The next note he read was as bad. The meeting of the Action and Forward Planning Committee which had on its agenda Sant'Simon's claim for tenure had been moved forward a week to Thursday, April fourth. Kit felt sure he knew why. Per Hedborg, UNAFO's assistant deputy director for Middle America, was due to arrive in San José on the next day, Tuesday. He would thus now have only one full working day before the meeting in which to make his own assessment of the Sant'Simon project and influence the outcome.

Kit had planned to take his boss, whom privately he rated very highly, almost as a surrogate "good" father, first to Sant'Simon itself, and then to see as many members of the committee as they had time to meet. Without knowing Hedborg's Central America schedule he had hoped there would be time to do this. Now he knew there would not be.

He flicked through the rest of his papers and found nothing pressing. He composed and saw typed a minute strongly protesting the rearrangement of the committee meeting, and sent it to the committee secretary, copies to all other members including the junior minister from Agriculture who would chair it.

Then, because he knew her timetable, he set off to cover the few blocks that would take him past the amazing and really very beautiful Teatro Nacional and the Parque Central to the Instituto de Antropología Social.

13

Rosa had a tiny office, little more than a closet, but at least it was not open-plan. He knocked on her door, she called for him to come in, and he did. She was standing behind her desk, on which there was a cardboard box, and reaching up to a shelf of books. In that position, slightly on tip-toe and stretching up, head turned over her shoulder to the door, she froze for a moment, like a bird about to fly. The colour drained from her face and then flooded back. Without verbalising the thought, he registered that she looked very tired with purple patches round her eyes. She was even thinner and she had changed her hair. Before she had left it long, and wound it into a bun. Now it was shorter and set into a lolling bouffant style which made her seem yet more femininely vulnerable.

"Kit! What do you want?" Her arms came down, her hands finding the desk top for support.

"This." He dropped the report in front of her, purposely using more force than was necessary, letting it smack the surface. "What's going on? Eh?"

She sat down, fumbled in a small soft leather bag for Lucky Strikes and the small gold lighter he had given her at Los Reyes, the Epiphany, when many Hispanics exchange gifts rather than at Christmas. She breathed out smoke from a mouth painted a darkish red that matched her fingernails. Dimly he was becoming aware of how entirely different she was from Esther, something he had not properly registered before. It now seemed to him she was more overtly, conventionally a woman, in a stereotyped way. To him, at that moment, she lacked the freshness, spontaneity, and confidence of his wife.

"Nothing is going on."

"It must be. What you have written here is absolutely contrary to your previously stated position on the matter."

"Do you have to be so pompous?"

He ignored this. "And, as I understood it, contrary to your whole approach to the relationship between environment and heredity."

Her eyes flashed and she smoked her cigarette furiously. Two gold bangles chimed on her sparrow-like wrist. He realised she was becoming angry and he was pleased.

"Listen, Kit. I was asked by the Institute of Genetic Health to provide a detailed breakdown of kinship at Sant'Simon. That is what I did. Scientifically and objectively."

"But that's not all. There was absolutely no need to bring in references to Chilean and Puerto Rican studies made under regimes whose ideology depends on convincing themselves and everyone else that the exploited poor are racially and genetically inferior to the rich. Come on, Rosa, you know how often we've talked about such things. And why did you have to refer them to that bastard's, Saavedra's, report?"

"Miguel's not a bastard. Kit, you take everything too personally. That committee has to build up a rounded but complex picture of the place. They should not consider each report in isolation. I was indicating to them, as is the form, where my report fitted in and reminding them that my investigation had been suggested in the first place by Miguel. Really, Kit, he is not a bastard. Nor am I. Listen. I'm planning to leave very soon. I have a position to go to in Paris. And maybe I can find something at UNESCO. Let's not part like this. Come and have a drink. For old time's sake."

But Kit twisted away abruptly. "I don't want a drink. I want to know why you are doing this to me."

The anger returned. "I. Am. Not. Doing. Anything. To. You."

"Yes, you are. Even if you don't think you are. Listen, Rosa, you know what Sant'Simon means to me. You know how I want these people to have the chance they deserve."

"Yes, I do. And also you know that I still think of you as I always have. As a very dear and loving friend, and honestly, my sweet, I would not do anything in the world to harm you, or even trouble you. Unless . . ."

"Unless?"

"Unless . . . someone else, or something . . . Unless I was forced to."

She bit her lip, turned her head away. Kit interpreted this as a sign the façade she had always maintained was crumbling, that she was on the point of revealing the passion he had always wanted her to feel. In fact she was aware she had come perilously close to saying more than was wise for quite different reasons. She turned back, looked at him through the smoke from dark eyes which were beginning to fill.

"Please say you believe me, Kit. I would not for the world hurt you. You cannot believe I would."

"But that's just it." His voice rose, almost to a shout. "That's just what I can believe."

She was shocked. "But why?"

"Oh come on. I used you badly. I didn't tell you I was married until we had been to bed. And then kept it going almost right up to when Esther was due. . . ."

"You bastard!" Anger washed away the tenderness like a tidal wave. "Do you think I wrote that report out of . . . out of . . . sexual jealousy? Is that what you think?"

"It seems pretty—"

"Get out. Go on, get out. *¡Coño!*"

Shaken, but still sure he had got it right, he left, followed the stairs and passages out into the bright sunlight. He paused for a moment, realised he was actually shaking, his heart pounding. After all, he needed a drink. Tables set beneath a green awning behind potted bays on the other side of the road promised relief. He was already ducking under the awning when he saw too late Charles Darwin sitting alone with what looked like rum punch in front of him.

"Hi. Lover. Come and sit with Daddy. Name your poison." As ever waiters moved at his command.

"Beer."

"*Uno demi-litro de cerveza de qualitad, chico.*"

"Your Spanish is awful."

"Sure. But I get by. How's tricks? The lady wife settled in? And the *muchacha*? Great. But you are keeping her hidden from us. The word has gone round the water-holes of this little old town that Kit Carter has a fine, beautiful hunk of a woman at home, *una negrita*, but he never lets her out. Why not, we all ask. Some hazard one guess, others another." He sipped his punch, sat back, chubby hands loosely clasped over his strained check shirt, eyes genial behind the round glasses, his nimbus of gingerish hair catching the light. "Some say Kit Carter is the very modern model of the ancient jealous husband beloved of Plautus and the other guy whose name begins with 'T.' Terence. And keeps her locked in her room behind bars. The more agile of the *flâneurs* amongst us are going in for pitons and alpine rope. The more guileful have hired locksmiths. But I guess they're all wrong." He leant forward and touched his tiny nose with a chubby finger tip. "I reckon you don't let her out because you're afraid that in this very small town she'll get the whisper that you had ass, and very nice ass, on the side until she turned up."

"Fuck you, Chas."

"I wish someone would. Particularly I wish the fine grade-A ass in question would. You know, I often sit here about now and have a tipple, it's not far from the coalface where I hew for the tiny pittance Bullburger pays me, the service is good and the rum punches well up to par. How's the beer?"

"Fine."

"Fine. But really I like to see her come out of the Instituto, and sometimes I make my presence known and offer her a drink. Never does she accept. Which brings me, deviously, round to the sixty-four trillion-dollar question—comrade, what the hell are you doing here?"

"Business."

"Oh *sure*."

"Really. Look." Kit showed the American the ringbound report. Darwin lifted the cover, ruffled through it, paused over the last page.

"She's put the boot in."

"Yes. But how do you know?"

Darwin grunted a short laugh, pushed the report back, and grinned again. "You wouldn't have brought it round with you if you were just calling to say what happy reading it makes. So. *Why* did she put in the boot?"

Kit shrugged, looked petulant.

"I would guess old chum, you think she acted out of spite. You and La Bella Negrita. Am I right, or am I right?"

Kit looked abashed. Put like that it sounded cheap.

"Wrong, my friend. Ab-so-lute-ly wrong. Doña Rosa is not that sort of girl, no way. A. She has class. B. At her job she

116

is truly professional. Moreover she is cool. You know all this. So why? Because what the report says is the truth."

"But it's not."

"So you say. You would, wouldn't you? But she says she wrote the truth? Or did she give another reason for slamming Sant'Simon?"

"No. No, she said it was the truth . . . except . . . ."

"Except?" Darwin looked at his squared-off nails, glanced quickly over his shoulder, exposing the loose fat that hung beneath his ear and chin.

"She said . . . ," Kit searched his memory, and adjusted it. "She said she would not do something, something she felt she ought not to do, unless she was being forced to."

"But she didn't say she had been forced in this case."

"No." Kit felt bewildered. "Should she have?"

"Hell, no."

They drank and were silent for a moment.

Then suddenly Darwin made a circle of thumb and forefinger and blew a howling wolf whistle. Across the street, Rosa, walking away, black hair bobbing above the cotton dress, her bag swinging from her shoulder, ignored it. Kit felt a pang of compassion, regret, love.

"Well. We won't see her around much longer."

The rum punch stopped at Darwin's lips.

"No?"

"No. She's packing up. Leaving. Going to Paris. France. She has a chance of something at UNESCO."

"Really. Really?" Darwin sank back again and nodded his head knowingly, adopted a vaudeville German accent. "Very interesting. But not possible. Can't allow that, old chum."

Kit returned home later in the day, still in a bad temper. He almost ignored Esther, with Zena on her hip. They had been watching from the window for him and had opened the door before he could use his key. He threw down his document case and the huge Greenpeace umbrella. A tropical rainstorm had swept in from the Caribbean, through the volcanoes and across the city, just as he stepped into the street from the ITCO annexe.

He went to the answering machine.

"This has been turned off.'

"Sure it has."

"But why?"

"Listen honey. I'm in all day. I can take your calls."

"Not all day."

"If I'm out half an hour and someone rings, if it's urgent they'll ring again. Anyway, I can switch it back on if I go out."

"I'd rather you just left it on all the time."

"What's the big deal? Are you afraid I'll take a private call? Is that what it is?"

He sensed again anger in the woman he was talking to, but this time sharper, more violent and positive, less bitter and despairing than Rosa's. He dreaded Esther's rage storms. He suspected they were calculated to intimidate by promising limitless escalation, and he may have been right.

"No. No, of course not." He turned away to conceal doubt. If Rosa had written that report out of spite, she would be capable of trying to make contact with Esther, and although he had admitted an affair to Esther, he was definitely not keen that she and Rosa should have a cosy, or perhaps not so cosy, chat about it.

"Don't you want to know if there were any calls?"

"Yes. Yes, of course I do. I'm sorry."

"Okay." The baby, sensing strain in the air, began to whimper. Esther sat on the sofa, unbuttoned the scarlet blouse she was wearing and plugged herself in. "The master had one call. From his boss, Per Hedborg. Ringing from Mexico City. He tried your office but you were out. Knowing you had an answering machine at home he rang here. He was surprised when I answered, but very charming, very charming indeed. If his looks match his manners I shall enjoy tomorrow evening."

"Tomorrow evening?"

"Do his looks match his manners?"

He realised he was being ribbed for his earlier surliness. "Yes. I rather think they do. But. Tomorrow evening?"

"That's right. An invitation has been received by Mr. Kit Carter and Ms. Esther Somers to dine with Per Hedborg at the Playboy Grill tomorrow at nine. On behalf of both, Ms. Esther Somers has accepted."

"This is crazy."

"No, honey."

"But it is. In the first place, why the Playboy? It's an awful place. American businessmen, CIA area supervisors, American generals use it. And of course American tourists. Why doesn't he stay at the Gran Hotel? And in the second place what about Zena?"

"I explained about her. He was very understanding and accommodating. In fact relaxed. Bring her along, he said. You have to wear your black tie and I shall put on Ossie. And I'll buy something really cute for Zena. One other thing. He has to fly on to Belize on Wednesday evening."

"Oh shit. Did he say why?"

"No. Does it matter? He said he'd spend tomorrow afternoon with you, if you'll meet him at the airport at eleven forty-five, and you are to fix up whatever schedule you can through Wednesday until four o'clock seeing people who might help with Sant'Simon."

14

"Ossie," Don Jesús, is the genuine article. An Ossie Clark evening dress circa swinging '68 and it is utterly fabulous. Black crêpe de Chine skirt, slit in the front to half-way up my thighs with red buttons above it, moves like a Rolls-Royce and exposes a lot if you let it, a top of cream and red and black pattern with cleavage to a tie at the high waist. It's all in the sleeves, on the shoulders. We got it at a Hume University CND jumble sale for fifty pence. Boy, was it the thing to wear to the Playboy! Next morning I found a toddlers' boutique off the Calle Central and bought a dress for Zena, a brilliant peacock-blue cotton with a load of white broderie anglaise, it cost thirty quid! An investment, is the way I looked at it. This Hedborg is about to move up to be Middle America deputy director for UNAFO, and the whole pyramid beneath has the opportunity of fighting it out for a step up—the two assistant deputy directors for his job, the four regional co-ordinators for that post, the eight field officers (one of them Kit) for . . . As Kit says, said, at his age and having burnt his boats in academia, he has to push hard now in this new career if he's to get anywhere. . . . Shit. I cannot always remember the bastard's dead.

By the way. Thanks for the Tampax. And listen. I've had a letter from Benjamin and Nova Travis, my foster-parents from Milton Keynes, via the consulate, and they're threatening to come out and help me, so they say. But what I reckon, Don Jesús, is they're after Zena, who they pretend is their grandchild, so just keep them away from me if you can.

"Back to our evening at the svelte, swinging, with-it Playboy. First of all it is a very elegant place, a modernistic complex of hotel, bars, restaurants, casinos, saunas, you name it, it has it. We didn't see much of all that, just the grill, but that was fine. The colours as I recall were mostly crimsons and scarlets, and shiny black, everything very shiny, candles on the table and orchids, you know the scene.

We went in a taxi, the Playboy is not downtown, but out along the Avenida Colón towards the airport, and when we went into the foyer and this Per Hedborg stood up to greet us I knew, the way a girl knows, that I had it right. Remember I'm tall, and thin but not skinny, and my skin is like the very best Swiss plain chocolate and feels like it when you touch . . . I'm quoting my admirers, of course, and that dress was made for me. I wish Ossie could see me in it.

So this Hedborg was all European charm, and I must say he is quite a dish. Blond, of course, a neat little moustache, and a tux that glowed the way only the very expensive ones do. So we went to the grill room, and sat at a table for four, and there was a scrap of dance floor which sight pleased me, as I like very much to dance. Of course all this elegance was made just a touch domestic by Zena's presence, carried hitherto in her Daddy's arms, until I put her in her Tamsit, a cloth affair that slips over the back of a grown-up chair, with a pouch in front and ribbons to tie, and what it does is convert an adult chair into a high chair. I must say we were tucked away in a corner a bit for which Per apologised. He had one of those pebbles-in-the-mouth really upper-class accents only Germans and Scandinavians achieve— the sort of thing that exposes the Kensington cockney in QEII.

We got well stuck into the sort of meal only a swish joint in a country like Costa Rica can put together. First a mountain of salad—mainly chopped avocado, but Lord knows what else in it—chunks of shellfish, lots of other fruits and veg, spices, too much tabasco, that sort of thing. Then the men had T-bone steaks with all the business of setting it on fire, and I had Lobster Newburg, but again to my taste too much cayenne. We drank wine which was quite something being as . . . since the grape doesn't grow between the Río Grande and the Columbian mountains, and the Ticos tax it, but we had a lot, all Californian including champagne, and that may explain my behaviour later.

All chatted away . . . amusingly, I suppose is the right word, cleverly, dare I say pretentiously? Kit is, was good at that sort of thing, always found the neat thing to set the table at a roar, as the Bard has it; Per Hedborg was suave and svelte and perhaps a little lacking in content, and I got away with being outrageous.

I found out long ago that's what one's betters expect from a beautiful, clever, black, working-class girl. And all went well with Zena eating Grissini bread-sticks and the odd bit of avocado or morsel of lobster, and drinking nicely out of her little beaker, which I could clearly see was a relief to Kit in spite of his recent conversion to the nipple.

In course of the clever jaw-jaw Per admitted that the reason why he was at the Playboy rather than the Gran Hotel was that AFI and the Playboy chain had an agreement whereby between them they picked up fifty per cent of the tab left by any UNAFO officer at assistant deputy director level or above. He also admitted that his stay in Ticoland was cut short on account of how very senior people in AFI were spending the Easter hols on the company island off Belize and they wanted him along to discuss various projects. This did not please Kit, but he hid his chagrin like a man.

Baked bananas followed, water ices, fresh fruits, coffee liqueurs including a home-brewed one the Ticos make a fuss of, made from bananas but no different from the stuff you turn out here on Tenerife.

All this time a black guy in a white tux tinkled away on a white baby grand, like he was in *Casablanca*, "Cuban Love Song" and crap like that.

At about this time another guy joined us who was to play, was already playing though none of us knew it, a considerable role in events. He was a humpty-dumptyish sort of man, sort of mousy gingerish hair in a halo, a round face over a round body. He was dressed about as crazy as you can imagine with a lacy sort of jerkin embroidered with flowers and quetzals and snakes over black trousers and black tie. He had round moony glasses that caught the light and sometimes hid his expression, and he was a touch pissed. I suppose we all were.

His name was, and I tell no lie, Charles Darwin Junior. Kit apparently knew him quite well, and though polite with him seemed not to be at ease. He was, it seemed, managing director of the Tico branch of Bullburger, the fast-food chain. Per was acquainted with him.

This Darwin then pulled up a chair and sat down at the end of our table, a cup and glass were brought for him, and straight off he started like trying to make some sort of a play at me. I mean he went to town. I was Cleopatra, the Queen of Sheba, why had Kit not been parading my beauty about the town, a treasure like me should be put on show, not locked away, Kit was a god-damn miser gloating over his ill-gotten gains, until Kit told him quite sharply to stuff it.

Darwin took the hint, took some sort of a grip on himself, ad-dressed himself entirely now to the two men so you could see what an MCP he was: the talk having shifted to "serious," we women is, are ignored. Naturally he asked Hedborg what he was going to look at in Ticoland and so they began to talk about Sant'Simon.

"They won't get tenure," said Darwin, after a time. "No chance."

"How do you know?" asked Kit. "You keep saying that."

"Because when something is put together the way this is, I mean a campaign like this, then something big and powerful is behind it, and big and powerful things A, don't give up, and B, always win."

"Okay," said my Kit. "Okay. That's all very well. Believe me, we know the facts of life. But what I ask is *why*. What big boys' toes are Sant'Simon stubbing? At least I'd like to know why."

"Actually I think I would too," said Per, his choice vowels purer than ever. "I think at least I shall spend a day trying to find out."

"Please yourselves, but you won't get anywhere. And if you do . . . well, take care." He beamed all round, glasses flashing. "Meanwhile—to change the subject. What I'd do if I had a day to spare right now and I knew a guy with a bit of clout, a guy like Chas. Darwin Junior, do you know what I'd do? Talk of Sant'Simon has put me in mind of it."

"What would you do?" asked Per, very steadily polite.

"I'd ask Chas. to arrange a trip further down the Río Remedios to the Milton University Canopy Research Station. You know about it? Knowing is not enough. It is absolutely the most mind-blowing experience you will ever have had, swooping and swing-ing about the last unexplored world of our planet, with all the freedom of one of its natural inhabitants, and I, lady and gentle-men, can put you in the way of enjoying precisely this experi-ence."

123

I was interested. "You can?"

"Sheba, I certainly can. They're winding the place up for the season right now. Tomorrow is the last day those aerial freeways are functioning. I'm coptering out there on the pretext of getting an on-the-spot end-of-term report. Really, I just can't resist the chance of one last swingabout."

"What," I asked, "have you to do with all that?"

Kit answered for him. "Bullburger financed it."

"AFI," said Hedborg. "After all Bullburger is part of AFI."

"Sure. AFI, Bullburger, what you will. But certainly any or all of you are welcome to come along for the ride. It'll be a better way of spending the day than shuntering around the San José bureaucracy, drinking coffee and listening to polite brushoffs. Hey. Look at this. A band."

He was right. The pianist had taken a bow and now a combo made up of electronic keyboard, acoustic guitar, a guy who could play anything from a stick and piece of corrugated wood to a tenor sax, a double bass, and a drummer were all up there, all black, and calling themselves Spadework. They blasted off into a Ska number from way back, "Yeah Yeah," by the Riots. I remember dancing to that on my Dad's sound system under Westway in '67 when I was seven. I wanted to dance now. Lots of other couples all round had gotten up and onto the floor. Why not me and Kit?

"What about Zena?" he mouthed at me, and pointed across the table at her. Certainly she was very wide-eyed, and bottom lip a-tremble with the racket, the deeper darkness and flashing lights. Still, I wanted a wriggle. I was aware this Darwin guy was now jogging about at the end of the table with both podgy hands stretched towards me. Maybe I acted impulsively. I plucked Zena out of the Tamsit and passed her across to Kit, and allowed Darwin to pull me onto the floor. In passing I saw Gentleman Per's eyebrows levitate a half inch or so before returning politely to base.

Darwin was a crazy but smooth mover, the sort of guy who you feel you can set yourself off against, make a show of yourself, let the music carry you on without you having to bother what he was up to. Ossie was a help too.

"What is that crazy garment," I screamed at him as we got close.

"Mexican wedding shirt," he bellowed back. "Say. Sheba?"

"Yeah?"

"Tomorrow? I'll have a car call. Ten o'clock. Right?"

"Ask the boss."

"Fuck the boss."

"Baby comes too."

"Ab-so-lute-ly."

The music crashed out, applause, then a tap on my shoulder. Gentleman Per.

"I'm afraid Zena is, as Kit says, kicking up."

Indeed in the comparative silence I could hear her. "Oh shit," I said and excused me to Darwin.

I went back to the table, took Zena who was indeed bawling up a storm, and did what came naturally, id est, pulled aside the skimpy folds of Ossie and let her have it.

All hell broke loose.

You know, they may or may not have topless shows in the grill at that joint, they certainly do elsewhere on the premises, yet they object to seeing boobs put to their proper usage. That's what I said in plain Spanish and plain English, to the head waiter, the restaurant manager, and the complex manager, one after the other in quick order, Darwin on one side mouthing, "Atta girl, Sheba, you tell them," Kit the Wimp, saying, "Come on Ezzie, it's not worth it, let's go home," on the other, and Gentleman Per doing the inscrutables in the middle. In the background Spadework belted out an old Maytal number called "Pressure Drop." The impasse was resolved dramatically by a fight.

Nothing to do with Zena and me. Music stopped. Glasses and crockery crashed. Screams. Some extra light came on, most people had scattered from the scene which was quite close to us, so all was plain to see. Three mother-naked characters, two men, Ladinos they looked like, black hair, neat 'staches, hairy bodies, fit, and a girl, *mestiza* with the most colossal misshappen tits you ever saw. She was crouching on the floor trying to cover them, but no chance. One of the men in front of her, like shielding her. He had a nasty cut, two inches long and gaping, across his shoulder. Blood just welling up and ready to tip out. The other, legs spread and bent, balls and prick dangling between, he was well-hung, in knife-fighter's stance, head thrust forward, knife searching to make another cut. Tableau, for the time being, vivant.

Then a swirl in the crowd and through it came the fourth character. No Ladino he. Tall, fair, short hair, dressed in a red silk dressing-gown, and as angry as Jesus on Judgement Day. He came straight up to the guy with the knife and chopped it out of his hand, then slapped him six times very quick and hard till the Ladino dropped to one knee, then he did a Bruce Lee kick to his ear. He turned to the other guy, and as he did, I saw the scar on the side of his face until then hidden from me, and I knew who the bastard was.

It was the would-be rapist from the Remedios valley Trevor Everton had saved us from.

I was already steamingly angry with the crass obtuseness, the piggish idiocy of the way those men around me had been patronising my body and its natural functions and now here was this degenerate Teutonic brute who had damn near carried those attitudes to their logical conclusion with the help of a Heckler and Koch, the bullying coward, and an SS knife, but now he had neither, so, still carrying Zena, though as usual she had come off the nipple to see what was going on, I surged across the gap between us. As I did, the big-titted *mestiza* whore, all right sister, tried to make her getaway by crawling round behind him.

There's a way of hitting a guy who's acting right out of order I learnt at a girls' self-defence group first year at Hume. Starting from behind the shoulder you jab, as hard as you can, with your fist open, aiming the ball of your hand at his top lip, but raking up into his nose with all your might. Thanks to big tits behind him, he went over like a felled tree, right into the middle of the dessert trolley, a big one, which, being jammed against a table did not roller-coaster away but collapsed satisfyingly around and over him. Jesus, did he look shocked! But I have to say the surprise shifted very quickly to extreme and wrathful hate which chilled me. He'd recognised me. Knew why I had done it. And he wouldn't forget.

I shrugged off the shiver, turned to Kit who was all ready to leap to my defence from somewhere behind me, no, that's cruel, I'd moved very quick, taken everyone by surprise, turned to him and said, "Kit. *Now* we'll go."

None of this take me home bit, you notice.

15

Steiner had lost face and the operation was compromised. Soldiers in real armies who no longer trust or respect their officers generally continue to function more or less as they should: they have been conditioned not subtly but well, like Pavlov's dogs, to do so. And if habit fails then fear of the penalties for disrespect, let alone mutiny, keep them in line. A small ad hoc group of mercenaries acknowledges no such sanctions. Steiner had boasted that he would survive alone in the jungle for twenty-four hours. He had said he was doing this to bolster the self-confidence of his men. In fact he had done it, and they knew he had done it, to demonstrate his toughness and independence. He had returned without his pack, without his SS dagger, and most criminal of all, without his Heckler and Koch. No. The loss of his gun was not the most serious failure: the lack of any explanation was worse.

So, at the Playboy, orders had been disobeyed. Two nights of debauchery, Sunday and Monday, had been encouraged and paid for. From Tuesday noon through to Wednesday 2 A.M. the men were to eat well and rest. But they had not. They had continued to carouse and Steiner's attempts to discipline them had failed, had finally failed when two Cuban exiles had chased each other all over the complex and finally into the Playboy Grill, determined to knife each other over a *mestiza* whore.

And there the second blow to Steiner's authority was struck. Both men returned, one albeit bloodied by the beating Steiner had given him, with the same story. Steiner had been smashed in the face by a nigger woman, and toppled into a trolley of trifles, gateaux and overripe tropical fruits.

The only thing that now gave cohesion to the group was the certainty that they would not be paid the second instalment of their hire if the mission failed. Since the first instalment had been handsome enough this was not as pressing a consideration as it might have been. Soldiers of fortune, all else being equal, are as likely to take the money and run as the rest of us.

A hired Ticabus coach collected them from the Playboy at two in the morning and took them to a private hangar in the freight area of San José's airfield. They changed into combat fatigues on the coach, and muddled the costumes. Inside the hangar they received their light weaponry, the twenty Armalites. The two M60 heavy machine-guns, the rocket launchers, mortars and grenades were already on the unmarked Boeing CH46 helicopter that stood on the bright moonlit tarmac.

Following standard drill they fitted magazines into their rifles, made sure nothing was up the spout, put on safety catches, and pulled the triggers. One gun went off, the report echoed in the cavernous space, and the bullet whined about, ringing off concrete and metal for perhaps three seconds during which eight of the twenty men flattened themselves on the ground. Steiner cursed them, and, with Coetzee his white South African "NCO," lashed out with malacca canes at three Hondurans, one of whom he thought might have been responsible, and all of whom he knew to be too cowardly to retaliate.

They then filed untidily onto the Chinook whose two large rotors in tandem were already slowly revolving to the low rev *chug-chug* of its engines. This particular one had a not untypical history. Used as a gunship it had made a forced landing in Kampuchea in 1972. Hill tribesmen beheaded the survivors and passed it on to a Pol Pot cadre. They, in turn fleeing their come-uppance, had got it across the Gulf of Thailand and into that country. They sold it to a small-time arms dealer for peanuts and he made a huge profit passing it on to a Philippine firm that specialised in leasing out military *matériel* on a no-questions-asked basis.

The pilot was ex-Royal Australian Air Force and knew what he was about. He would have liked a navigator but the one contracted for had lost his way at Heathrow and missed his connection. Since he had not been involved until now he was untainted by the collapse of Steiner's authority. Flight control gave clearance to a shipment of spares to a clear-felling site in Guánacaste—theirs not to reason why it should leave at half past two in the morning. The moon was bright and the pilot settled with some relief to following the ribbon of the Inter-American Highway north, keeping it always a couple of miles to his right and flying at a thousand feet. That way there was no possible chance of running into the *cordillera* and volcanoes that lay to the east.

In an hour the broad expanse of Lake Nicaragua, as glossily silver as Achilles' shield, its ripples that wonderful artefact's ornamentation, appeared in front of them and to the right. The next twenty minutes were a little more difficult. Having turned a corner through two hundred and eighty degrees he now had to fly south-east by south keeping the lake to his left, the *cordillera* and volcanoes to his right, and yet remain well within Costa Rican airspace. The jungle beneath was for a time almost unbroken.

Behind him the mercenaries were singing. Snatches of "Horst Wessel," "God Bless America," "Land of Hope and Glory" led by the Teuts in the group, the fourteen Ladinos smiling well, pretending to join in, and passing rum bottles between them. They did this in an entirely calculated way—just obviously enough for Steiner to see them do it, but not so obviously that he would have to take action to stop it. Thus his authority was yet further eroded.

Another forty minutes brought them over a second, very much smaller patch of water, Laguna Ceño Negro—Black Scowl Lake, the landmark for the last change of course. Steiner joined the pilot in the cockpit. The Chinook swung north again, lost height, and crossed the border into Nicaraguan airspace just west of Los Chilos, the largest border town, and sped on, the turbulence from its rotors now shaking the tallest of the almendro trees. Five minutes more took them across the Río San Juan. They were now over fields, and they left a small village to their left. Two minutes later the tiny moonlit complex of the agricultural field station which was their target floated into view through the Perspex blister at the front.

Two white single-storeyed buildings formed a right angle. Three smaller Controlled Environment Units placed in echelon stepped away from the end of one of the main buildings so the whole compound formed an irregular, squared-off U-shape. The Chinook swung over it all, only fifty feet off the ground. The pilot positioned it so it was pointing away from the buildings to present as small a target as possible, and then brought it gently to the ground, just about in the middle of the widest part of the U.

Led on one side by Steiner, on the other by ex-Sergeant Coetzee, the men tumbled out and quickly deployed into pre-arranged and rehearsed positions, blazing away as they did so. The last five remained on board but hefted out one mortar, one rocket launcher, rockets, grenades, and one of the M60s. The clattering motors crescendoed, dust and palm leaves swirled around them, the Chinook lifted, tilted, and roared away over the fields toward the river. There it dropped the five remaining mercenaries, commanded by Polack, ex-Marine Grabowski, who occupied an island in the middle linked by bridges to each bank. This they had to hold as otherwise the river would trap the main force inside Nicaragua. There was no question of the helicopter returning for them—there would be no surprise about a second visit and a ground-to-air missile could well be waiting for it.

Its mission now accomplished, the Chinook lifted off again, soared to a thousand feet, above the range of small-arms fire, and clattered briskly away to the safety of Costa Rica. There the pilot landed it on a private airstrip and swapped it for a Cessna Skylane crop-sprayer in readiness for the last stage of the operation.

At the research station things went at first according to plan. Although the rocket launcher did not work the mortars did. Within seconds the buildings were blown apart and burning well. The Controlled Environment Units—made of whitewashed glass with complicated systems which lifted and lowered each pane according to temperature and humidity—exploded in a particularly satisfying way. The only casualty was a Nicaraguan contra in the assault group, cut to pieces by their own M60 tracer. There was no opposition. There was no one there. One of the solid buildings was a laboratory, the other housed two offices, two storerooms and a lean-to shed. The six scientists and technologists who worked there lived in the village half a mile away, towards the river and the lake. The two small boys who had been on watch were already running towards it before the helicopter touched down.

Now things did begin to go wrong for the *Einsatzkommando* and not least because there had been no actual fighting at all. After a week of quite severe training, two and a half days of debauchery, and two hours of quite nasty suspense in the hold of the Chinook, this brisk and noisy firework display was an anticlimax. There wasn't even anything to loot or rape. Dazed by the noise they had made, bewildered by the lack of real action, the men wandered around aimlessly, shooting at shadows, passing the last of the rum from mouth to mouth, and ignoring Steiner's and Coetzee's attempts to get them to form up and march for the bridge.

With two miles to the river, six to the border, and less than two hours to daybreak, the situation was deteriorating. Steiner therefore shot one of the drunks squarely in the forehead with his Browning automatic. The 9-mm parabellum took the top off the man's head. The rest formed up more or less as ordered, but fearful, sullen.

Coetzee led the way, and Steiner came last having promised to shoot stragglers. He also feared reprisals. They followed farm tracks through maize and rice fields, the maize just sprouting and no more than a foot high, all laid out on a grid system. There was no way they could get lost, even though a thick blanket of mist was rising from the river, luminous and pearly in the moonlight. It was, however, possible to end up upstream of the bridge. Grabowski was expecting them to appear downstream of it. Meanwhile it was on the downstream side that a small group of villagers and agricultural technicians who had seen three years' work destroyed before their eyes were now establishing themselves. They were led by an ex-guerrilla and they had two Kalashnikov rifles that worked. They did not know that Grabowski with four men, the second M60 and a mortar, held the islet in the middle of the bridge.

They saw Coetzee and his men coming towards them, their heads and shoulders floating comically above the mist, and opened fire. Since the mercenaries were in line facing them only Coetzee was hurt, and not seriously. The rest, including Steiner in the rear, crashed to their bellies and disappeared.

Grabowski had seen the file of men approaching through the mist, heard the gunfire from the other side, and believed he had seen a section of Nicaraguan border guards, possibly professional soldiers, fired on by the returning mercenaries. He therefore promptly and accurately put down a carpet of tracer and grenades while his two spare men raked the area with their Armalites. Thus he and his four men killed or maimed all who had been at the research station except Steiner himself who, when the firing started, had contrived to get even further into the rear than he had been.

When half his ammunition had been used Grabowski ceased

firing, Steiner emerged and identified himself. He then came down the line of fallen men and shot any who were still alive. It was important that none should fall into Nicaraguan hands: apart from anything else they would testify to the monumental cock-up the whole operation had become and Steiner's credibility as an *Einsatzkommandoführer* would be destroyed.

The six survivors walked four miles down jungle tracks and back into Ticoland. The villagers, impressed by their firepower, ruthlessness and lunacy followed at a very safe distance. As dawn broke a Cessna Skylane flew north over their heads. Its pilot, the Aussie who had flown the Chinook, continued to enhance his reputation for competence. He sprayed, accurately and thoroughly, two hectares of specimen maize plants with a particularly nasty derivative of dioxin.

An hour or so after dawn Francisco Franco, as dapper as ever in a dove-grey suit but this time with a pink silk tie and pink silk lining to his jacket, sat on the verandah of a tiny clapboard hotel in Los Chilos drinking coffee and daintily managing a small plate of very oily *churros*. A small boy pushed dust off the boards with a broom inside the bar behind, and, as Paco checked his large gold wristwatch, Steiner appeared at the end of the narrow street. His face was grimy, he still wore his combat fatigues, and his pistol slapped against his thigh. Franco watched his progress with disapproval. To walk about so obviously armed might be all right in Guatemala or El Salvador. In Ticoland it could provoke arrest, or at any rate a polite query from the local police.

Steiner clearly had a lot on his mind. He stormed down the road, kicked a chicken that did not move quickly enough, and set chairs clattering out of his way to get to Franco's table. He slapped both hands down on it, hard. The coffee jumped, splashed. Franco's eyes flashed and he dabbed at the stain on his knee with a tissue taken from the dispenser on the table.

"We were betrayed," Steiner shouted. "Betrayed." He raised his hands to slap the table again. Franco pushed back his chair. "Ambushed. Oh yes. You can tell your boss the job is done. Perfectly. No problem. According to job specification. Operation a perfect success." The scar showed hectic beneath the dirt as Steiner strove to screw yet more sarcasm into his voice. Then he pulled a chair beneath him, slumped into it, and stared across

132

at Franco, eyes wide, filled with horror. "Fourteen men lost. Fourteen good men. Heroes. Christ!" he shook his head like a caged beast. "Jesus! The mother-fuckers were waiting for us. Waiting for us, I tell you. Shot us up almost as soon as we had landed. My men fought like heroes, like mad dogs. And we won. Drove the bastards off and then got on with the job. Fourteen men. Christ! I need a drink."

Franco snapped his fingers above his immaculate shoulder, without taking his eyes off Steiner. The small boy paid no attention. He tried again. Again no answer. Franco, aware he was losing face fast, got up, scraping his chair walked round it, caught the boy by the ear. He twisted it ferociously. *"Un cuarto de ron. Flor de Caña. Súbito."*

"The new laws against alcoholism. No drinks before twelve noon. . . ." His voice rose to a high squeal. Francisco glanced at Steiner, checked he was not looking, and shifted the boy's ear to his left hand and fingered out a hundred-*colones* note from his hip pocket. He hissed in the boy's free ear, "Get it, and this is for you." The boy got it, with ice and slices of lime too.

Steiner drank. Franco passed a thin hand across sleak black hair. "Are you sure? Are you sure they knew you were coming?"

Steiner wiped his mouth on the back of his hand. "That's better. Yes. Sure of it. We walked straight into it, into a trap."

Franco registered that this time they had walked into the trap that previously they had been dropped into but said nothing.

Steiner went on, "You tell your boss. He needs to check out his security. I'll do it for him. I can make dumb men, and women, talk. You tell him."

"I will. Right now. I will." Franco drank off the end of his coffee, dabbed at his lips with his bright handkerchief, and stood, shelling another hundred-*colones* note onto the table beside his cup. "But the job was done?"

"Yes. Perfectly."

"I'll tell him that too."

Part V

16

I thought I heard a lady's voice. In fact I did, but placed it in my dreams. It occurs to me now that if I had not made that unconscious repression and had instead insisted and got him to play the cassette, she would have lived.

Don Jesús, that's not quite right, not too honest. I said at the start I tell the truth. The truth is I heard Kit put on the answering machine and I heard the lady, his lady's voice, she sounded desperate and loving and he killed the tape. Now. I could have made a scene then and there and then he would have played the tape. But eight o'clock in the morning, with Zena asleep at last after a bad short night of snuffles and a bit of a cough, was no time to make a scene. Anyway, did I want to hear the voice of his lady, all loving and hot for him, and see how he went soft at the joints for her? No. It was a thing of the past, this was an echo from the past, let it go. Shit. I just did not want to hear her. I did not, even after he had gone, bother to find the cassette.

He came in later whispering some rubbish about a clean shirt and slacks and not wanting to wake up Zena. I went out into the living room. He said he couldn't open the chest of drawers without squeaking. *Men.* All you have to do is lift the drawer a little as you pull.

While I got them for him he poured some coffee for me and put out some magdalenas he'd got in specially. I can't stand Greenfinger Smalzers. So that was nice of him. Hell, he was nice, and I shouldn't knock him.

"That Charles Darwin Junior," I said, "is sending a car for me at ten to take me to the Río Remedios canopy research thing. Shall I go?"

He looked up with like horror. "With Zena? Hell, no."

"He says it's great, swinging like a mechanised Tarzan through the trees."

He grimaced deeper. "With Zena?"

"Okay. You don't want me to go."

He sighed. You could hear the word reverberating in his skull. *Women*. "I'd love you to go. I'd love to come too. But I think it's the sort of trip where you need two people so they can take turns looking after the baby. Maybe he'll be able to lay it on for us another day."

"As I understand it," I said, a little sarcastically using his favourite expressions in a discussion, "there won't be another day. They're closing it down this week for the rainy season." I could have added there'd be other people round to hold Zena if I thought it necessary, but I forebore. He didn't want me to go, and since there was still a bridge or two to be repaired between us, I gave in. "Never mind. I won't go. But it's going to be boring all day without you."

"I'm sorry. Let me see." Head up struggling in front of a mirror. Jesus, he's putting on a tie. These are important people he has to see. "Why don't you go to the Museo? It really is a very interesting place."

So I saw him off, straightened his tie at the door, and took a light kiss for my pains, all in the approved fashion, quite the little wifey, put on a housecoat and got on with what chores there were, which was very little we having ate out at the Playboy, and I did the washing and ironing the day before, and thought to myself if this life goes on like this I'll take up smoking again. I smoked at Milton Keynes as a protest against Benjamin and Nova, my foster-parents. They, being all wholefood, vegan, and similar shit—it's not that I don't like wholefood, it's the attitudes you're meant to take on board before you can touch the stuff—really hated me smoking. I packed it in at Hume. Couldn't afford it. I began to find I was rather looking forward to ten o'clock. Would Chas. Darwin send a Merc, a Caddy?

To help pass the time I put on one of my Reggae tapes.

Tears from your little sister
Crying because she doesn't have a dress without a patch
For the party to go
But you know
She'll get by
'Cos she's living in the heart of the common people

138

Smile from the heart of a family man
Daddy's going to buy you a dream to cling to
Mama's going to love you just as much as she can
And she can.

Of course Zena took off at about half nine so the trysting hour
went by in a flurry of a nappy to be changed, nipples, and a bowl
of Greenfinger 5 with some cream cheese stirred in. The poor
dear having to have her nose wiped, which she hates, and coughing every three minutes. Was she feverish? Should I get a doctor? All calm and back to order by half ten or a quarter to eleven
and no Merc or Caddy. Bastard. Stood me up. So what. I
wasn't going anyway, was I?

Still I didn't feel like heading for the wide open yonder or even
the Museo Nacional—give him an hour or so I thought, and then,
what the hell, I'll stay in, have lunch, and go out in the P.M. I
put on another tape, one of Kit's, *Flautas de Chile*, a composition
album, and was swinging around to that with Zena cooing and
laughing, a sort of dirty laugh she has at times, in my arms, snif-
fles for the time being better. Me, my baby and me, we dance
to anything, anywhere, anytime.

Then the door thing buzzed.

It was Chas. Darwin Junior in person with a small bunch of
gift-wrapped orchids he'd bought on the way. Not quite the big
deal they might be in London but still rating with say a half doz
of red long-stemmed. Nice one, Chas., I thought.

You know the bastard had the nerve to kiss me as he came in,
not heavily, on the cheek sort of thing, but giving my upper arm
a pat and a squeeze that seemed a touch over the top, you know?

And he talked. Would not stop.

"Sheba. I'm so sorry. I truly am very deeply sorry. Last
night you were so magnificent. The only word. And I felt a
deeper appeal too, I mean like we really have a lot in common.
So I was absolutely all set to give you the day of your life today,
sweep you off your feet. The copter ride over the jungle, a nice
lunch at the camp, a few daiquiris, up into the trees, all that
beauty so few humans have experienced, and the heavy pass.
You know?"

I had to laugh. "So. What went wrong?"

"Everything. Bad day at the office. I had to put our trip on the back burner, we'll do it another day, tomorrow, the day after. Say? Do you mind if I take out that crap? I can't stand those wimpish flutes. All moaning and whistling and mournful just because those Indians can't get off their butts and do a proper day's work." He didn't wait for my say-so, hit the stop button with a podgy finger. "Listen, I'll die if I don't have a coffee."

He followed me into the kitchenette, getting his fat feet caught in the cord that goes round Zena's babywalker and giving himself an excuse to get his fat hands on my rump. He smelled—of cologne and some deep sourness.

"Listen. Just now. You didn't react. When I said I was lining you up for the heavy pass, the works. Scarcely the in-drawn breath. Certainly not the smacked kisser. So tell me Sheba, does that mean it's on? Okay. So I don't look like Clark Kent or even Kit Carter, but I'm truly great in the sack, all the chicks say so. And. If we swing, then, as the words of the song have it, I'll make you a star. You've got such class, Sheba. You're wasted on a guy like Kit. Nice guy. Sure. But short on charisma, and short on get up and go—"

"But that's where you're wrong, Darwin."

"How's that?"

"He got up and went. For me. From a wife who was full of shit and a job ditto."

"Sure. Fine. The guy's a mensch. But is he the guy to put you in the showcase you deserve?"

"You in showbiz or beef?"

"Beef. But I have connections."

He was making the right play, and he knew it. Consider my background—showbiz was always the way out for girls like sport was for boys—my looks, my talent. I can sing Soul, Ska, Reggae in four languages. I can dance. Of course I know for ever I'll be wasted if I don't get my chance in the big time . . . but, hell, that's little-girl talk. I grew up out of that an aeon ago.

"Skip it, Darwin. Here's your coffee. So what went wrong at the office," said I, trying to change the subject.

"Everything. Foot and mouth on our biggest ranch in Guanacaste. Meat-packers on strike in Puntarenas—"

"Up the workers. So shouldn't you be in Guanacaste or Puntarenas?"

"No, no. The guys on the ground can handle it. But I have to be in the shop all day in case they call in. You know this Tico coffee you don't have to grind so fine. It's got body. It's got—"

"Don't you tell me how to make coffee. Why aren't you in the shop then?"

"A lull. It's wait and see time. So I thought I'd pay a call. I tried to phone you but all I got was hubby on the answering machine. So listen Sheba, do we make out together? Or don't we?"

"Jesus, Darwin, you've got a nerve."

"Listen, everyone loves me baby, what's the matter with you? I'm the second son of Mary Mild, a second cousin of Oscar Wilde. . . ."

"Twice removed from Oscar Wilde. I know that song. . . ."

"You know it all."

"Pack it in Darwin. Stuff it. GFY."

"If no one else will, I'll have to. Listen. If it's Kit Carter you're worried about, forget it. He had ass right here in San José right up to before you came out. Lovely ass. Not in your class, but class. Did you know that?"

"You're a bastard Darwin. Yes I knew that."

"Sure, I believe you. Okay. But sauce for the gander, sauce for . . ."

"Darwin. I think I'm going to throw you out. By the left leg and down the stairs."

I could have, too. Jane Fonda work-outs plus that self-defence course for ladies at Christbourne. He looked at me, his glasses winked like heliographs, he found a handkerchief and wiped his hands. He knew I could. I don't know why I didn't do then what I did later when I knew just how much of a shit he really was.

"Still. You must admit. That was nice ass."

My expression gave me away.

"Ahhh. You know he had ass but you don't know which ass. The name Rosa Portillo strike a chord? Chilean lady? Uhuh. That tape. Those mournful flutes. Not your style . . . but hers. Do you read me? Listen. How do you know it's not still going on? They were very close. I mean they were seen together. Often. Am I making you mad?"

"You might."

"Good. So how do you know it's not still going on?"

Again I must have given something away.

"Yes. You do thinks so. You've grounds for thinking so.

141

They're in touch and you know it."

Suddenly he relaxed, sat back in the chair and smiled like a Buddha, like a Buddha who's just pulled himself a nice one, it's all over but it was great. I should have guessed he'd worried out of me what he had come to find out.

"Okay. So where is Kit today? As of now. Laying Rosa in her apartment? No?"

"Shit Darwin. You know where he is."

"I do? Oh yes. Taking that cool Swede round San José. Save Sant'Simon campaign. Fat chance." He beamed some more, finished his coffee, then sat up as if he'd just thought of something. "Hey. Listen. You know that rape bit you told us about last night, on the way out, after you slugged that Kraut. Pow. What a beaut. That I shall never forget. And how this English guy Everton saved you?"

"Yes."

"Has he been in touch again?"

"No. Of course not. He won't be back until the rains raise the level of the river."

"No? But he's in San José today. Listen. Maybe when I take you out there, you'll take me to see him."

"I'm not going out there with you ever."

"We'll see. But could you do that? Could you find his bivouac?"

I remembered the way, the indications Trevor Everton had given us.

"Reckon I could. But, Darwin. I. Am. Not. Coming. Out. To. Remedios. With. You. Full-stop. Period. Finis."

"Okay, okay, Sheba. We'll see. Thanks for the coffee. Really it wasn't so bad. I was ribbing you. Never yet met a chick who didn't rise if I knocked her coffee." He leant forward, chucked Zena under the chin. Silly bitch smiled and gurgled at him. "Who's a good girl then? I'll let myself out."

And he did.

I looked down from the window to see what car. A big Plymouth convertible, metallic blue. Bastard knew I would. He waved up at me.

Later that day I met Trevor Everton. Coincidence. Except it wasn't. I should have had the sense to see that.

17

I felt restless after Darwin had gone. He'd given me the fidgets.
Excited me in a sort of way, but not a nice way. After twenty
minutes I got together the pushchair, shoved the Snugli in a large
soft basketwork shopping bag Kit had—did that Rosa give it to
him? It wasn't the sort of thing a guy buys. Never mind. And
off we went to the Museo. I have to admit I like museums.
And I liked them before Benjamin and Nova fostered me. I liked
them going from Brixton Junior School to the Natural Science
Museum and the Victoria and Albert. Never could I make up
my mind which I liked the better. Diplodocus or the Bernini,
the model of the blue whale or the Raphael cartoons, those tricksy
showcases with buttons to press that take you from sex to par-
turition or the Great Bed of Ware.

And the walk to get there, I mean to the Tico museum, was
great, though a full mile, and the grid pattern meaning I had to
cross sixteen or seventeen intersections. I wished I hadn't taken
the pushchair, just stuck to the Snugli, but you never can be sure
she'll put up with it for as long as you'd like, she has a scream
and there's not a lot you can do about it on your own. Just
how important this is will become apparent when my tale nears
its end.

Anyway, up Calle Central, eight blocks or so, and all the banks
and swish shops, and it still a nice clear morning, and not at all
too hot, and everything fresh and clean, and flower vendors, and
fruit stalls, and lots of colour and life as well as the banks, then
cut across the Central Park, a whole block to itself, with these
fantastic flowers, and palms and other trees, I mean it was like
the forest at Remedios laid out at Kew, the Palm House with the
lid off, and by now I felt like a little refreshment was needed. So
what did we do, my Zena and I, but pop up onto the terrace of
the Gran Hotel Costa Rica and order ourselves a coffee and bis-

cuits which turned out to be like sort of macaroon in cat's tongue shapes which Zena adores. I like doing that sort of thing, I mean like taking tea at the Ritz, and you know I carry it off. I carry it off. Probably they put me down for an oil-rich Nigerian in exile. I don't reckon the coffee was any better than mine. There we sat, under the arches, with another small park in front of us and watched the poor selling pineapple slices and bananas or touting to clean the gentlemen's shoes, and the Mercs, and Caddies, and Plymouths, and Toyotas and Datsuns, and a neat little car called the Caribe which is really a VW Golf assembled in Mex shunted up and down in time to the lights. The only Central American state where they obey the lights.

From where I was I could just see most of the façade of the Teatro Nacional which is quite something. Ticos don't have revolutions, they say, in case it gets damaged. Patti wouldn't sing in San José till they built it. The Paris Opera came to Ticoland and had, not pups, but a very pretty daughter.

Then off we went, continuing our perambulation, and, getting round the back of the Teatro, came upon a mess. The Cultural Centre it was to be. But the recession came in, coffee prices bottomed, and still it's a half-finished mess. And the boarded-up bits reveal through their graffiti what's really happening in San José, in Ticoland. "Work not handouts," "Free guns, why not free bread," "Yankee imperialism no—socialism yes," "The land belongs to the people," and most significant of all because the U.S. wants them to have an army again against Nicaragua and the growing dissent inside the state, "Guns for the people, not the police."

Four or five more blocks up the hill and there we were. The National Museum, Natural History Museum, et cetera, et cetera.

Well. It was not Kensington, but it was okay. Originally a big old house with thick walls set on a hill with views across the *meseta* to the volcanoes until they started building taller blocks. It was called Bellavista. In 1948 the last of the rightist regulars holed up here against the People's Army, and there are still bullet holes to prove it. Inside there's some pre-Columbian gold and jade, bits of pottery, and big round stones with spiral patterns on them, but really not much Indian stuff. There weren't too many in Ticoland anyway and the smallpox took them off by 1600. Some Spanish silver, some ceramics, you know the scene. Apparently most of the gold is in the Central Bank's Gold Museum. I never got to see that.

There were very few people about and almost no custodians. Zena and I wandered on, found a neat little courtyard in the sun where goldfish swam in a pond and a few orchids grew. Zena liked the fish, went *ooh, oooh, oooh* when she saw them. There was an old square tower. I found the staircase, dusty and circling, and climbed it, carrying Zena in my arms, and found now a really great view—green hills and Volcán Irazú, massive and clear after the rain, with a thin plume blown on the trades towards us.

Down we went. I put Zena back in the pushchair and we trundled on. I was in a bit of a daze: touch of a hangover still, the warmth, the quietness after the racket of the streets that was now a rumble in the background with the occasional squawk of a car horn. We drifted in to a largish room with a few showcases, and coloured prints, all of botanical specimens, but mainly boxes stacked like books in bookcases filling the walls. It smelt of spices and sandalwood. There was a long table down the middle and sitting at it with large sheets of thick paper all round him, taken from a couple of those boxes and with leaves, twigs, florets, seeds and so on mounted on them, was the neat, dapper figure of Trevor Everton.

At his elbow he had an electronic thing that looked a bit like a large remote-control unit, or one of those press button all-in-one telephones. But it had only six buttons, unnumbered, and as he read from a large volume bound in leather his fingers tapped away at them, and letters moved across a small display strip.

He didn't hear us until Zena gave her abrupt *Ah!* noise that means, "Why did we stop?"

"Good gracious!" He looked up over half-lensed gold-rimmed specs which immediately he took off. "Esther Somers. And the delectable Zena. What a nice surprise! What brings you here?"

I explained we were visiting the museum and had just followed our noses.

"To the National Herbarium. My home from home in Costa Rica. I spend a lot of time here. Theoretically, one day, it'll house dried specimens of leaves, flowers, seeds, bark and so on of every species in the country. Long way to go yet."

For want really of anything else to say, I asked, "You're here earlier than you expected, aren't you?"

He leant back.

"Interesting you should say that. Fact is, I came across something I felt I really ought to check out. I think it might interest you."

I tried to look interested. Truly I was, but it was a slightly artificial situation, you know the sort where you have to make signals rather than like actually respond.

"Sit down and I'll try to explain."

So I did, next to him, and straight off Zena put in a noisy protest. I hoisted her out of the chair, but she still wanted to fidget on my lap, reaching for the cards with the mounted specimens.

"Do you mind if I feed her?"

"Of course not."

I plugged myself in.

"You see, I think I've stumbled on why someone might want to see Sant'Simon closed down." Certainly, that did catch my full attention. He went on. "And I've just come up for the day to check it out. It hasn't taken me long, and I feel I could be right. Look. I'll show you."

He pulled two sheets of paper across so they were next to each other. One was old and yellowish and carried the rubber stamps of the Herbarium and had writing on it in brown or faded ink, done in a sort of copperplate script. The other was new, and the writing small, neat and clear.

"Would you say these are the same plants?"

Allowing that the older one was browner and more wrinkled and crumbly, I couldn't see any difference. I said so but hoisted a flag which said: I'm no expert.

"There's no expertise needed if you have a keen eye. I'm sure they are the same."

"What are they then?"

"A variant of *Zea diploperennis*. The collector who pressed the earlier specimen called it *Zea diploperennis talamanca*."

"Oh."

"*Zea* for maize. *Diplo* because it has dimorphic rhizomes. *Perennis* because it is perennial. As you know, ordinary maize is an annual. *Talamanca* because it is or was endemic in the Cordillera de Talamanca of which the Cerro de la Muerte is the most western eminence. Now, according to these records it was thought to be extinct in 1921. As you see, this specimen," he tapped the Herbarium one, "is dated 1916."

"I'm still not utterly with you." Not my usual way of speaking, still hoisting signals.

Actually I was by then guessing a bit, but I long ago discovered that men in the full flow of exposition do not like to be pre-empted by bright young females.

"Let me start by referring to this." He pulled towards him the large leatherbound volume he had been looking at when Zena and I emerged on the scene, and he slipped on his specs again. "This is *Science*, volume 203, for 12th January 1979. And it's an account of the rediscovery of *Zea diploperennis*, a new teosinte, in the Cerro de San Miguel, Jalisco, Mexico, made in 1978 by three botanists, an American, a Mexican, and an Israeli. First the habitat. It's very like that in the *páramo* above the coffee groves in Sant'Simon. Scattered oak, yuccas, tall grasses, that sort of thing, and small streams, growing at just over two thousand metres. At Sant'Simon it grows wild at twenty-five hundred to three thousand metres, but it's quite a bit further south. Then the description. Robust, erect, maize-like clumps of five to six culms growing from each rhizome to six feet or even higher, male inflorescences purple-tinged, female spikes bearing five to ten seed cases, a hundred mature cases weighing 7.12 grams. Okay. Have you placed it now?"

"Sure. As you say it grows all over the *páramo*, above the coffee. And the commune has fields of it growing down round the village, near where they have annual maize. When we were there the annual maize was being burnt off for the next season, but this stuff was flourishing, some in flower, some in cob."

"Right. I knew you'd catch on. I can always tell. You know, the way you listened and looked when we climbed back . . . anyway. This is the *Zea diploperennis* these people discovered in Mexico. And they're excited because diplo was thought to be extinct. Now. Look at the end of this article: "This new species should provide geneticists and maize breeders with a potentially valuable source of germ plasm, and may lead to the development of perennial maize." That was 1979. But still I haven't got to the heart of the matter. You see, this article is about *Zea diploperennis*, and what we have here is *Zea diploperennis talamanca*. . . ."

And at that point a shadow fell across the table. Actually of course I'd seen it coming but not poor Trev Ev, he'd been too carried away. A squat little man in a black silky suit, black knitted tie, had slid up on the other side of the table as if on soundless wheels. He had a sort of squashed white face, streaky black hair, bad teeth. I guessed at a glance that he was bad news, and guessed right. He spoke in Spanish.

"Señor Everton. This is most irregular."

"Ah. Señor Guzmán. Esther, this is Señor Guzmán, the deputy director of the Herbarium. Señor Guzmán, may I introduce—"

"Most irregular. This woman should not be here. Certainly this child should not be here. I must ask them to leave immediately."

Trev Ev seemed at a loss. I stood up, Zena popped off the nipple leaving it plum red and milky for Guzmán to goop at.

"I am sorry," I said also in Spanish. "Of course, we'll leave." Zena, not liking the look of Guzmán, plopped back on.

"You will do no such thing," said Trev Ev in English. Then back in Spanish, "I am very sorry, Señor Don Deputy Director Guzmán, if the lady's presence incommodes you or is at variance with the rules of the Herbarium. She will of course leave in five minutes or so. But first I know the renowned courtesy of Costa Rica, its reputation for civilised behaviour, will permit me to finish what I was saying to her. Five minutes will be quite sufficient."

"Five minutes, Señor Everton." He gave me a filthy look, and then the bastard looked at his watch. He slid away but not far.

"I say, I am sorry about that. Never liked Guzmán. And he's been hanging around me all morning. Almost as if spying on me. Never mind. Where was I?"

" 'What we have here is *Zea diploperennis talamanca*,' " I quoted.

"Yes. You really are on the ball. It's virtually the same plant as *Zea d.* in all respects except two. *Zea d.* has five to ten seed cases per spike, right?"

"Right. And . . . ?"

"And, as I'm sure you've noticed, the talamanca variety produces a cob much more like the cultivated varieties. In fact it can reach forty, and down by the village, sixty seed cases, and one hundred weigh in at nearly forty grams. For a teosinte, for a wild grass, that would be phenomenal. It suggests to me that what we have here is a survival from Indian cultivation four hundred years ago, a hybridised strain that has remained unchanged because of the lack of any other maizes in the area."

"On the ball I may be," I said, "but I don't see why this might mean someone wants to close down the Sant'Simon Co-op."

"Closing it down is probably incidental, the easiest way of achieving what they want."

"Which is?"

"Well, my guess is this. Properly developed it's possible Zdt could be used to develop a new perennial species of maize which would literally revolutionise corn production and the corn industry. Do you know, I reckon it could double the productivity of land under maize? I'm not qualified to guess what the industrial and social implications of an advance like that would be, but they would be enormous, take my word for it. And that's the sort of development powerful people like to have under control. I reckon someone, someone up there, has got wind of this and wants to take over the only known source of Zdt while they work out its potential. That's going to take some time, and meanwhile they really have to own it, and own where it grows, otherwise anyone else can walk in and get in on the act. In fact I think it's possible someone else already has."

"Yes?"

"I told you a friend of mine, Ignacio Morena, a Nicaraguan maize expert, was around at Sant'Simon a lot some time ago. Now I don't know much about politics and what I do know I find pretty sickening, but I would guess a lot of people would be very upset if Nicaraguan corn production miraculously doubled in the next year or so, just when it is U.S. policy to starve the Sandinistas into submission. Anyway. Look. It's marvellous you turned up. You can help me. Advise me. I think I should get a report on all this to someone very quickly, but who? Where will it have most effect?"

"The UNAFO area director is here right now. He's with Kit trying to persuade the officials to let Sant'Simon have tenure. But he's going this evening."

"I must get my skates on. I'm very nearly through here. I can get a preliminary report out by late afternoon. Where's this man staying?"

"The Playboy. And his name is Per Hedborg. But can you really get it done so quickly?"

"Oh yes." His smile came again, just a touch coy. "I'm rather into all the new systems. This little fellow," he tapped the press-button-box in front of him, "is a Microwriter. I've been taking notes on it. It has a memory, stores information. When I get back to my flat I plug it into my cassette recorder and it transfers its memory onto tape which I can then run into my word-processor, get it all on the screen. I jig around with that until I'm happy with it, press a button and I have a print-out. I'll have it at the Playboy by, let me see, four o'clock?"

Guzmán rematerialised. So we went. Me and Zena that is. Trev Ev turned back to his specimens and books and Microwriter, and that was the last I saw of him. As we left he was blessed by a shaft of dusty sunlight from a roof lantern above.

18

Miller watched and waited. Now that he had a commission to carry out he did not mind. With the prospect of a kill at the end of it he could remain still, quiet for twelve hours or more. The frustrating boredom that had so nearly driven him to chop down the black at the soccer match had quite gone. He sat at the café table, under the awning, watched the steady tipple of rain out of the leaden sky, the cars and buses swooshing brown sheets into the gutters, the hurrying umbrellas, the gleaming raincoats. He watched it all with steady, keyed-up equanimity. Occasionally he sipped a non-alcoholic cocktail of tropical fruit juices. Occasionally his fingers drummed on the day-old copy of the English-language *Tico Times*, and the current, evening edition of *La Prensa Libre* on the table in front of him. For the rest he was as still as a cat in a hedgerow, his drumming fingers taking the place of a twitching tail.

From the opposite side of the street, three floors up, Rosa Portillo paused in her packing to look down at him. She wondered who he was—for, like a black cat in a hedgerow, he was, after all, conspicuous. His clothes drew attention. Neither Ticos nor tourists dressed quite like that. She felt she had seen him around before, felt sure anyway that she had frequently been followed in the last two days. Still, neither the Costa Rican security services nor the CIA, nor even DINA, the murderous secret service of her own country, would employ for surveillance someone who stood out quite so obviously. She shuddered, drew the window to, returned to the packing.

It was a sad, a lonely business. It always was. This would be her third move since she had gone into exile. Always there were things to be left behind, stacked into cardboard boxes for the landlord to dispose of as he saw fit; always there were also things

151

which would have to stay because they were intolerably connected with relationships that would have to be forgotten: emotional lumber that had to be cut out, could not be allowed to burden her from the moment she stepped out of the aircraft at Charles de Gaulle or wherever to begin again a new life.

She folded up a man-size yellow wrap, held it briefly to her nostrils, shrugged almost with irritation and briskly folded it into a box. She hesitated over a book of love poems by Camilo Cela, inscribed by Kit, and that went too.

No point at all in taking the artificial flowers. The "folk-weave" curtains, of which she was very fond—they were not in fact the peasant artefacts Kit had taken them for but had been bought at Liberty's in London by her parents in 1950 when she had been conceived—she would take. It was always useful to have curtains, and these, being cut generously, fitted almost anywhere and instantly made anywhere home. Carefully she stood on a chair to unfasten the hooks. That man was still there. She folded them into a suitcase.

The peasant tapestry—villagers defending their school against tanks—could stay. In most capital cities in both the West and the East Chilean exiles sell similar artefacts. Individual and moving though it was, it was replaceable by another as good as soon as she re-established contact with her compatriots. *El pueblo unido jamás será vencido.*

A little later she cleared out the kitchenette. Most of that had to go—into the rubbish bags or the boxes. A three-week-old packet of Greenfinger Smalzers, hardly used. Perversely she tipped them out and thus extracted a small orange plastic figure: one of the "Masters of the Universe." She turned on her small Sanyo hoping for music. Padre Miguel d'Escoto, foreign minister of Nicaragua, had instructed his ambassador in San José to deliver a strongly worded protest at the incursion into Nicaragua from Costa Rica of a gang of contra desperadoes shortly before dawn. It was claimed they had all been wiped out by the local village militia with no loss of Nicaraguan life. However, totally wanton destruction had been carried out on an agricultural field research station whose work was entirely non-military and devoted to feeding the poor. Many years' research and labour had been undone.

The news flash went on: Comandante Zero, also known as Edén

Pastora, the ex-Sandinista guerrilla who operated from bases on the frontier further east, disclaimed all knowledge of the attack, and roundly condemned it. . . .

Rosa sat at her kitchen table, pushed her thin sparrow fingers up through her ebullient black hair and swore for a moment or two in Spanish. She felt sick, despairing. It all fitted in. Quite quickly over the last two days she had pieced together a scenario that explained what was happening in Sant'Simon, and this new outrage must be part of it. She was certain of it. She had tried to get in touch with Kit and explain. But obviously he had done nothing. Perhaps he did not want to. He had a new career to make something of. A wife. A child. A lot to lose, too much to lose.

She lifted her head, shook it. Even that Nicaraguan foreign minister had got it wrong or refused to spell it out. Feeding the poor by lifting the Central American peasant into self-sufficiency, unloading the burden of debt, interest, recycled debt, which puts more and more land under dollar-earning cash crops and drives the peasant off the land where they can feed themselves, anything that reverses these processes is political action, military action, for it aims a sword of justice at the heart of U.S. hegemony. But somehow, somewhere, often out of blind knee-kick reflex, the reaction always comes: savage, destructive, wasteful and often incompetent . . . but effective.

Coffee. Coffee and cigarettes. She wanted both. She snapped off the radio, looked round for her purse, glanced out of the curtainless window but at the sky, not the street. It had lightened a little. The rain had stopped. No need for the umbrella. She paused by the still unpacked mirror in the hallway, pushed back her hair and did up the top button of her frock, smoothed it over her waist and thighs.

Miller saw her come out of the street door. He had paid his bill some time before, always in such situations paid it when he was served. Briskly he picked up his papers, dropped them in a trash can, crossed the road, climbed the stair to her apartment. He had been here before without leaving a mark. He went inside and looked round, smiled grimly at the signs of packing—if she had gone before this moment had arrived he would have lost five thousand pounds.

A kitchenette, a bedroom, a living room. A tiny bathroom.

He settled on the bathroom which opened off the hall. She would have to come right past it and into the apartment before she could be aware of him. At the worst she would come straight in and stumble on him. He studied the way the door opened. If he sat on the edge of the bath he would be hidden until she closed the door. That would do.

He sat there then, hands on knees, and waited. It was very quiet. There was no window, only a vent onto the *patio de luces*, the well that was the core of the block. A dish clattered in a kitchen not far away. A baby cried and slept again. He could smell frying onions, tomatoes, pork. Time passed. Miller poked about in the few unpacked toiletries. Dental floss. A plastic compact with a Dutch cap. Eyebrow tweezers.

A key slid into the wards of the front-door lock. Adrenaline exploded into his blood and suddenly every muscle in his body was a coiled spring ready to be tripped by a hair. The cat in the hedgerow.

19

That same Wednesday, the morning after the dinner at the Playboy, the morning of Steiner's attack on the Nicaraguan research station where rhizomes of Zdt had been carefully nurtured for over a year, the morning of the day on which Miller killed Rosa, and Esther found Everton in the Museo Nacional, Kit had woken with a hangover. He padded nervously about his apartment trying to get together some sort of a breakfast, Greenfinger Smalzers and coffee, without waking Esther or Zena. They were both now in bed, curled up beneath the large cotton sheet that never any longer seemed to stay on his side, Zena cradled in Esther's arm and snoring steadily. She had developed a slight cough and a runny nose. Nothing to worry about: another tooth on the way. Neither had any clothes on—Zena just a disposable nappy which, Kit rather thought, was ripe to be disposed.

Actually he felt a bit pissed off with both of them. They had come in on a high of alcohol, good food, and excitement: Esther, in her Ossie Clark, had been glorious, magnificent, a goddess, and had made him feel like a god. After all he was a big man, they went well together, he gold and red like the day, she black and starlit like the night. Frankly he had been as randy as all get out, but she left him holding the baby while she had a shower; and then, when she was ready—still damp but perfumed, Zena refused to be put down. By the time she had been nursed into somnolence, fatigue and the first presentiments of hangover had crept up on both of them.

So now he pottered about, preparing himself for what would be a difficult day doing over the Costa Rican bureaucracy with Per Hedborg. He shaved round his beard, and cut himself over his Adam's apple. He took out his best slacks and hunted for a clean shirt. All his shirts were drip-dry. When he had washed them himself he had left them on a rack over the bath to do just that. Now Esther washed them, ironed them, and put them in the chest of drawers that squealed when you opened it.

Kit looked at his watch. He still had a clear twenty minutes before he needed to dress. Best not to disturb them. In truth he really felt the necessity of getting out before, or almost before they awoke. The business of coping with them and keeping together the papers he needed, and preserving his clothes from smears of Greenfinger 5, would all make his last minutes in the house a sort of battle, and leave him feeling harassed and nervous for perhaps much of the morning.

So what to do instead? He mooched idly round the living-room, settled in the corner he still managed to maintain as a sort of office at home. A tiny red light winked beneath the telephone. God, the answering machine. He had not touched it since the previous morning when he had reset it. And, he could see now, the tape was full. People must have been ringing all day. Who? Why?

The spools hummed, clicked off. He flicked a switch, turned up the volume. The buzz that indicated a caller then: "Kit, my sweet. This is the third time I've tried to call you. I have to speak to you, darling. I know you don't want—"

Hot with embarrassment, literally red-faced and in a sudden sweat, he killed the voice and sat dead still for all of two minutes. Zena snored on. Could he hear Esther's breath? Had he been able to hear it before? Had she been awake? Had she heard?

He tiptoed to the bedroom door. She had moved, yes certainly, was now half-way onto her back, her free arm flung out, pale palm dangling above the edge of the bed. But yes. She was, he thought, asleep.

He pulled the door to as far as he dared, moved quickly back to the machine, extracted the cassette, placed it in a plastic container with several others, loaded a clean one in its place. Then he breathed deeply, wiped his hands down his thighs, looked for a cloth.

The area in which most ministries and government agencies lie is small. Hedborg and Carter moved round on foot. Everywhere they were treated with sympathy and respect. UNAFO has patronage; Hedborg, especially if he got his promotion, could fund projects or refuse to, pay salaries within the Costa Rican bureaucracy, or find appointments for Costa Rican experts elsewhere. But no one offered much hope for Sant'Simon. For one official it was too small to be viable, for another too large for the available infrastructure. A third drew attention to the strain of coffee they were developing—a strain peculiarly vulnerable to *Hemileia vastatrix*, the fungoid disease that attacks the leaves. If that broke out the whole plantation would have to be destroyed. Carter argued that with the nearest plantations forty kilometres away and high *cordillera* between there was little chance of the wind-borne spores reaching Sant'Simon.

At the offices of the Sociedad para la Preservación de la Selva they were treated more frankly. The SPS is outside UNAFO's sphere of influence. Indeed the SPS looks on UNAFO as an enemy. Feeding people seems to entail cutting down trees.

This did not need to be the case, or not on the huge scale people imagined. Forest could be farmed and even support huge populations—the Mayan civilisation bore witness to that. No doubt Doña Pacífica Balboa de Castro had heard the arguments in favour of mixed cash and subsistence farming by peasants with tenure before. Certainly she was abruptly dismissive when Carter attempted to deploy them. Doña Pacífica was a tall, thin lady with grey hair beautifully shaped. She sat in a leather armchair in front of a magnificent colour photograph, poster size, showing a troupe of white-faced monkeys swinging through the crown of a giant Almendro.

She held to her position with an obstinacy unsupported by anything as boring as logic. It was the obstinacy of a mind introjected from birth with the certainty that people of her sort know best, even though they may not agree amongst themselves about what the best is.

"Of course we have been against Sant'Simon from the start. In the first place our concern was the forest they themselves cleared. . . ." She spoke a very pure English, a little archaic, much as Queen Mary used to speak it.

Carter tried. "Ninety per cent of it was clear-felled for lumber in 1952 when the highway became viable for large trucks."

"Thirty years is a considerable span in the life of tropical montane forest, Mr. Carter. A second growth of considerable interest was well established. Many species were spreading back into it. But of course it is not only what they have destroyed that we are

157

concerned with. These peasants hunt and bomb fish-pools."

"Both practises have been voluntarily stopped."

"And will be resumed as soon as the Rural Guards and Forest Rangers are committed elsewhere. But let me make my major point. The southern end of the Pacific side of our country is unique not only to our country, but to the Earth. There are many endemic species, many species flourish there that are endangered or extinct elsewhere. The most accessible part of this area, the Valle del General, has been almost totally ruined by the advent of the highway. The only unspoilt area is precisely that threatened by your land invaders. It still supports forest deer, coatimundis, tayras, tapirs, otters, peccaries. Ocelots, pumas and probably jaguars. The insect life and flora are unbelievably rich. The birds . . ." She spread her perfectly manicured hands in a gesture that suggested incalculable wealth. Gold and precious stones flashed as she did so. "All this is threatened by Sant'Simon. You see what you people will not accept is the fact that we have here, if we allow it to go forward, a precedent—"

"Señora, there is no question or indeed possibility of extending the cultivated area. The terrain will not—"

"So you say, Mr. Carter. But the same was said of parts of the Valle del General that have since been utterly ruined. No. It has long been an aim of the SPS to gain National Park status for the Remedios valley. What politicians call the economic climate is not on our side at the moment. However, I am happy to say that we have been promised a substantial donation from a private source, and once these squatters are removed we shall present a bill to the Legislative Assembly."

Hedborg intervened at last. "Doña Pacífica, may I ask who it is has promised this help?"

"You may ask, Mr. Hedborg. But I am not free to tell you."

Carter made one last attempt. "Doña Pacífica, I know at least one highly respected naturalist who disagrees with your perception of Sant'Simon as a threat to the ecosystems of the valley."

"Oh really? May I ask who?"

"You may. And I am free to answer. He is not secretive about his interest in and concern for the valley. I am speaking of Dr. Trevor Everton who is at present making a study of the riparian habitat in the upper reaches of the Remedios."

"Ah. Yes." Again the gold and stones flashed, this time dismissively. "We know Dr. Everton. Rather an eccentric young man, wouldn't you say?"

"Young?"

"Young in the ways of the world."

And with this cryptic remark the interview was closed.

After a working lunch with officials of the Consejo Nacional de Producción, which was no more productive than the rest, Hedborg and Carter moved on to their last call which was at the Union Club. There they met Don Diego de la Haya y Fernández, a part owner of one of the largest groups of coffee *haciendas* and the spokesperson appointed by Cafesa to speak to them.

The Union Club is opposite the magnificent and ornate General Post Office which must owe something in conception to the Post Office in Cibeles, Madrid. The Union was more elegant, more graceful then its brasher partner across the way, and inside, the atmosphere is one of refined extravagance, richness made comfortable by an indefinable shabbiness. It was the perfect habitat for Don Diego. He had silvery hair, a perfectly aquiline face, wore a turtleneck sweater made out of a wool as light as silk and as blue as the ultramarine of the deepest ocean, and perfectly tailored grey trousers. He was, of course, drinking coffee. The porcelain was Sèvres and not modern. The shabbiness was provided by flecks of cigar ash on his sweater, by the filaments of exploded capillaries on his cheekbones.

He waved Hedborg and Carter into chairs less sumptuously comfortable than the one he was sitting in, but grand enough, delicately placed his thin cigar on an ashtray and himself poured coffee for them. Carter looked round. There were a lot of paintings—mostly portraits, genre and conversation pieces done in the free, easy naturalism of Spanish painting at the turn of the century. One showed Minor Keith and his tiny Costa Rican wife, Cristina Castro Fernández, taking coffee on a terrace with a spectacular view of a volcano in the background. Along its flank ran the railway Keith had caused to be built and the smoke of the train echoed the plume from the volcano.

"I shall be frank with you, for I have no cause to be otherwise." Don Diego smiled. His English was as good as Doña Pacífica's, to whom he was almost certainly related. Perhaps the same lady, the daughter of an English bishop, had taught both.

The smile, however, revealed orthodontia that could only have been American.

"Our hands are clean. In its way Sant'Simon was a threat of a sort. Multiplied several times it would have become a problem. I'll tell you why." He embarked on a history of the Costa Rican coffee industry. "Until 1940 our coffee was renowned throughout Europe. Each *beneficio*, and there were hundreds, had its own mark, its own flavour. Especially was the taste of our coffee appreciated in England and Germany. The first coffee we exported went to Liverpool." This was not true: Costa Rica's first coffee exports went to Chile and Peru. "The war was a catastrophe. But Uncle Sam came to the rescue. We let him build his highway down to Panama so he could protect his canal. In return he guaranteed our coffee crop. An offer we could not refuse." Again the teeth. "The price was, of course, not good. And the crop went to the big American processors who blended it and converted it into soluble powder and liquid concentrates." He shuddered, sipped delicately from Sèvres.

"For the last fifteen years we have been trying to recover our reputation. Ever since the recession, and the formation of ICO which gives quotas for bulk, non-quality beans to each producing country. By re-establishing our reputation as luxury, carriage-trade producers we by-pass ICO and charge the prices connoisseurs expect to pay. We have had some success. Costa Rican coffee is now sold as such in European supermarkets for up to twenty per cent more than ordinary blends.

"This strategy depends on two factors. One, that our coffee is better. Which it is. Two, that we maintain its scarcity value. That is that we,"—a small but definite gesture included the whole of the Union Club—"do not overproduce our distinctively luxury blends. And that was where Sant'Simon suggested a danger. Its coffee is very good indeed, they operate outside our organisation, and are concerned naturally to produce and sell as much as they can. Of course Sant'Simon on its own was nothing, a drop in the ocean. But these things have a way of spreading. So. Yes. We were concerned."

Hedborg spoke: "And you filed a claim on the land they occupy."

"We did. And, frankly, not with much hope for success. As a delaying tactic merely. The land was clear-felled thirty years ago, under government licence, by a company which later became defunct. We bought it, its name, its by now useless shares. But the government licence to fell did not constitute any sort of ownership of the land. Previous use of it could be a basis, but since no one had touched it for thirty years. . . ." He shrugged. "No real chance of success. A delaying tactic. While we looked around for something better."

"Which was?" Carter asked, and now, at last, did not expect a frank answer, but he got one.

"Nothing. No need. Over the last two months it has become very apparent that a very powerful interest wants those peasants off that land. Someone is doing it for us."

"Who?"

"Why?"

Don Diego shrugged again. "Some say so and so, others say otherwise. I don't know. Listen. By the standards of this part of the world we are not a corrupt society." He leant forward, looked to left and right, and dropped his voice. "But we are a very small country. It needs pressure only on one or two senior civil servants, or a minister, for a *feeling*, shall I say? to percolate down. You see what I am saying? Given enough, what do you say? clout, a powerful organisation can get things like this done quite easily. There . . ." He tipped the coffee pot to show it was empty. "No more coffee and nothing more really to be said." He stood, brushed the ash from his sweater. "I should add, no one *here* has that sort of clout anymore. On Wednesday afternoons I play billiards with three friends. I can see they are waiting for me."

On the steps of the Union Club Hedborg and Carter paused, watched the traffic streaming across the intersection of Calle 2 and Avenida 1.

"I have to say," said Carter, "I did not expect to hear a coffee baron admit there is something more powerful in Costa Rica than the oligarchy."

"Really?" Hedborg's pale eyes searched for a taxi.

"No army. No political party with enough support to form a government on its own. Even the police, in spite of U.S. attempts to modernise them, are still a joke to most Ticos. Who else?"

20

Hedborg had not enjoyed his brief stopover in Costa Rica. Dinner at the Playboy had been a disaster, tramping round the ministries had been hopeless and tedious. And Carter was a disappointment. A year ago he had looked like a promising candidate: a mature man, fluent Spanish, excellent qualifications, committed. That, perhaps, was the problem. Carter was overcommitted. Clearly he was obsessed with Sant'Simon, which was, after all, a relatively small business, and one which UNAFO was not directly concerned with. And Carter's understanding of the parameters within which UNAFO can operate was at fault: both Darwin the night before and now Don Diego were right—if someone that big and powerful was interested in closing Sant'Simon then resistance was futile and a waste of time. During that awful evening before he left, Hedborg had mentioned the CIA. For Hedborg that was good enough.

And Carter's wife! Really. She was over the top. Hedborg blushed and inwardly squirmed at the memory of how she had behaved at the Playboy. It had not been possible to call her for the interview when Carter had been appointed. A mistake. Always you should see the wife when you are filling an important post. Clearly she was a most unstable person, and clearly a man who could choose to marry her at the best lacked judgement, at the worst was probably unstable himself.

Back at the Playboy he called for his account, went to his room, showered, packed his soft leather grip and the red plastic document case that said no animal died for me. At reception he settled up using his UNAFO American Express card and was handed a large manila envelope that had been left only ten minutes before. By whom? A small neat man, that's all the girl at the desk could say.

A taxi took him to the airport and a jet airbus to Belize, stopping at Toncontín airport for Tegucigalpa, and Ramón Villeda Morales for San Pedró Sula, both in Honduras.

Once in the air Hedborg tore open the envelope and pulled out six sheets of word-processor print-out. Attached was a brief note. "Dear Mr. Hedborg, Forgive the impertinence but I feel I must take advantage of your presence in San José to acquaint you with a really rather startling discovery I have made in the *páramo* where the springs of the Río Remedios rise, not far above the Co-operative of Sant'Simon. . . ." That was enough to demolish Hedborg's interest at a stroke. Clearly the obsessed Carter had put Everton up to this. Nevertheless he was a conscientious man and he read on. He soon began to wish that he had not. When he had finished it he put the document on one side, let the back of his seat drop, closed his eyes and thought.

Beneath the plane, forest slipped away to the east and the Pacific took its place. For a brief spell they were avoiding Nicaraguan airspace: not because there was any danger, but because the U.S. authorities who controlled the airlanes liked civil aircraft to do so. As they turned west and began the slow descent to Toncontín Hedborg zipped out a Sharp pocket calculator. It confirmed what he already suspected: that *Zea diploperennis talamanca* could pose a very serious threat indeed to the operation of any corporation heavily involved in the production and processing of corn derived from conventional maize.

He thought it all through some more and found a lot of niggling questions had been answered. He discovered, and fear blossomed in his mouth and stomach, that a large new question had appeared. What the hell was he going to do about it? In a couple of hours only, just about at nightfall, he would be setting foot on Greenfinger Cay, the guest of AFI. This he realised was scarcely coincidence. Possibly it was not coincidence either that Roberto González did not have to worry unduly about the staggering fees at the clinic that proposed to cure him of smoking and emphysema. And certainly it was relevant that he, Hedborg, was a strong candidate for González's post.

The plane climbed briefly, making the short hop on to Ramón Villeda Morales. What to do? The answer was clear. Nothing. Nobody could be sure he had Everton's document. Certainly the people he was to talk to at Greenfinger Cay would know nothing about it. Officially he was going there to discuss the AFI pro-

163

posal to finance crops of cane and citrus on the marijuana fields of Belize. It was a good scheme. Quickly he leafed through the relevant documents, refreshed his memory. Within twenty minutes he had decided he would do whatever AFI wanted with regard to Belize. Hopefully that, and silence, would be all they would require of him.

Only four passengers went on from Honduras, which was not surprising. If Central America is the United States's backyard then Belize is the outside loo, though while everywhere else it is an American presence that is perceived, here the British linger on. The anti-aircraft missiles strung with camouflage netting along the runway of the small fly-blown airport are manned by pink, large, and generally overweight recruits, with tattooed arms and thighs exposed below short sleeves and khaki shorts.

Hedborg expected to be met. With sinking heart he realised something had gone wrong. On his last visit to Belize a smart, clean black had driven him in a new Toyota Corolla to the harbour, and then on a smart motor launch straight out to Greenfinger Cay, an islet just inside the Barrier Reef which AFI maintained for private conferences and the use of its directors and senior executives. It was everything that advertisements for Caribbean rum, smart caper films and James Bond fantasies might lead one to hope for. Hedborg had been looking forward to a second visit. Not to be met was worse than a disaster, it was a catastrophe, for the only alternative to this dream world was Belize City and the Fort George Hotel.

It is a settlement more than a city, intersected by a series of inlets from the sea, and everything is brown. The water is tea-brown, the square clapboard houses are set on timber stilts and are coffee-brown admittedly streaked with flaking pale-blue paint. Their square, squat, pyramidal roofs are the rust-brown of old corrugated iron. In the film *The Dogs of War* Belize City was asked to simulate a corrupt West African capital. It failed—it was too seedy.

At the Fort George the desk clerk took seventy-five dollars from Hedborg, the minimum charge, and showed him to a room in which the air conditioning did not work, the door would not lock, and the sheets were dirty. He used the lavatory and dirty water rose in the bowl. The smell was a concentration of all the smells outside. Hedborg found telephone numbers that should have put him in contact with Greenfinger Cay, but none of them produced an answer.

Twilight and swift tropical nightfall were less than an hour away. The fastidious Swede, driven by despair, decided to have one last look round the harbour in the hope that he might yet be plucked from a limbo that bordered on hell. Not trusting either the lock on his room nor the desk clerk, he took his money, plastic, and passport in a small black leather purse fastened by a thong loop to his wrist, but left the rest of his baggage in his room.

He walked along a quay pock-marked with wide puddles of brown rainwater. A notice proclaimed that no persons under the influence of marijuana would be employed by the harbour board. The reason perhaps why almost nothing was going on at all. Mud crabs scurried. A flight of laden pelicans passed by. Shearwaters were busy. Otherwise the only activity was carried on by a section of British soldiers loading a landing craft with large tins of English baked beans in a country where the same beans are staple and possibly where they came from in the first place, and Heineken lager: for once refreshing parts no other European beers can reach. Nearby a smart motor launch nudged the tatty jute fenders as the tide listlessly rose. Hedborg quickened his pace as much as the puddles and refuse would allow. Yes. It was the same as the one he had been ferried out on before, immaculately white, with polished brass fittings and a large Yamaha outboard. The wind, which only ever drops in Belize towards dusk, was still strong enough to stir the pennant at the stern to show the AFI logo, the "I" a green and gold finger of corn.

Back at the Fort George, Hedborg found the black who had met him before waiting in the tiny bar, drinking Pelican beer. Profuse apologies poured through white teeth set in a dark face. A minor failure in the Yamaha, a valve. Yes, of course he was expected at Greenfinger Cay, they would be worried because he had not yet arrived.

Hedborg stormed up the wooden, rackety stairs and faced the worst shock of all. His room had been broken into, his red plastic document case rifled, and the only thing that had gone was Everton's report. The fear flooded back. There was only one place it could be, only one place it could be on its way to—like him, it was going to Greenfinger Cay. And he now had precious

165

little time to work out what he was going to do about it. Could he still plead ignorance, that he had not had time to read it properly? Or a different sort of ignorance, that he had not appreciated its significance? He imagined himself saying, Of course UNAFO officials at my level are plagued with this sort of thing, crackpot schemes for feeding the world with plankton or seaweed. Would it wash? Perhaps. If it did not there was only one thing for it—to persuade the men of AFI that he was on their side, that they had nothing to fear from him. And convincing he would have to be. Cursing Everton and Carter and his own folly in not destroying the document as soon as he had read it, he realised that he knew too much.

It was a very frightened Hedborg who packed up his rubbished belongings and rejoined the man in the bar, the black who almost certainly had the document safe in an inside pocket. Five minutes later they were on the motor launch. Its engine roared, its bowwave settled into a marble sculpture carved out of the choppy sea, and it whisked them away to the tropical paradise of Greenfinger Cay.

21

We, me and Zena, spent the rest of the early afternoon very nicely. I wasn't at all sure at that point that Everton was not a crank, and not that convinced that Zdt was such a big deal. So my main thought was: I've done all I can by directing him to Hedborg. Of course I'll tell Kit all about it when he comes home, but there's no point in trying to contact him while he is trundling Hedborg round all the agencies and ministries, and I'll never make contact even if I try.

So, using a deli I got myself together a neat picnic—tortillas with a spicy pork mince filling and *tamal asado*, a sort of baked custard which Zena took to be the food of the gods, a couple of papayas and a can of Coke. And these we took to the National Park, right on the topmost bit of San José. It is a swell place. Like from the tower in the Museo nearby you could see for miles, or at any rate the hills and volcanoes miles away, and the air fresh and clean up here away from the traffic, and of course as usual these marvellous trees, flowers, ferns and bromeliads, humming-birds and tiny parrots.

And right in the centre a huge bronze monument by Auguste Rodin, no less, depicting, in allegorical form, the defeat of William Walker, the notorious filibuster, who tried to annexe most of Central America in the 1850s aiming to make them slave-owning states in the U.S. of A. Modern Yankee imperialism is no less overt or more subtle—it is more ruthless and efficacious.

Anyway it was a good time, a happy time, and we chatted to all and sundry who passed through and took a shine to Zena, the way all who see her do, and the rain held off till later. I mention all this because it was the last happy time I had in Ticoland, maybe ever.

Pleased with the day I had and longing to tell Kit all about Everton and what might turn out to be good news for Sant'-

Simon, I pushed Zena all the way back, and got to the apartment at about half four.

I'd hardly got in when the door buzzer went again. Maybe the guy had been waiting outside. He was tall, pale, dark hair, looked like any Tico official or clerk or whatever, except he had a fringe of beard round the edge of his jaw and chin. He said his name was Miguel Saavedra, and he had urgent news for Kit to be delivered personally, and could he wait. Of course I said yes. He sat on a chair but fidgeted a lot, refused coffee, then accepted it, was clearly under stress.

"Is this news bad?" I asked.

He stopped his fidgets and fixed me with a long hang-dog stare. "Very," he said.

I hate dramatics, got on with what I had to do Zena-wise and put together the makings of a light supper.

About five Kit let himself in. He did not look pleased to see this Saavedra character, asked him what he wanted, and got the bad news bit.

"What bad news?" Kit asked.

"I think you should hear it first on your own."

"Christ, Miguel, Esther is my wife."

"Yes. Indeed. Just so."

"Come on. Tell me. Here and now."

Saavedra shrugged. "All right. This is it. Rosa. Rosa Portillo is dead. She committed suicide some time early this afternoon in her flat."

Kit went pale. Dead white. He sat down. I didn't know what to do. How does the dutiful wife behave when her husband learns his beautiful mistress has snuffed herself?

Kit whispered, "How? How did she do it?"

Saavedra flinched away. "Do you really want to know?"

"Of course I bloody want to know."

"She hanged herself from the light fitting in her living-room. She tried first in the bedroom, but the fitting broke."

Kit now moved fast, to the bathroom. I followed. He hates vomiting. On the two or three occasions he has, I've held his forehead while he retched. I did then. Something to do. But I was having reactions too. He was very, very upset. I knew I should master my resentment at this, but I wanted to grab a fist full of his hair and bang his head against the bowl.

He wiped himself up and went back to the living-room. I offered him a drink, he said no, he'd have coffee. I went to the kitchenette to see to that but could hear all.

"She did not kill herself."

No verbal reaction from Saavedra. Kit paced about.

"I am certain she did not kill herself. She loved life. She loved people."

"Perhaps. But she was seriously depressed at times."

"She was a lover, not a hater. You know that. That's why Pinochet's torturers could do nothing with her. Sad she could be. A sort of melancholy at times. Despair, never!"

"Torture marks people. They're never the same again. There's never the same . . . balance."

"She was all set up to go. To Paris, to a new job. A new life. People don't suicide at times like that.'

"So. She changed her mind."

This sounded callous, pulled Kit up. He turned and faced Miguel, stared at him for a long time.

"You think she did it because of me?"

Miguel shrugged. "People will say so. That's why I came. To warn you."

Now that is charming, I thought. People, Josefinos and Josefinas, will see tall, black Esther and whisper, her husband's mistress suicided when she turned up. Charming.

"Well. They're wrong. She was killed. Must have been."

At this Miguel, who really was not too likeable, gave a sardonic snort. "Why?"

"I don't know exactly why. But it could be to do with Sant'Simon. There's been pressure. Something going on I've not got to the bottom of. You were pressured, someone leant on you to write that lying report about educational attainment. And someone leant on Rosa and leant very hard, because she would not lie easily or well. There's something there. Something to be found out about. And I'm going to clear it up."

"This is stupid. You're distressed."

"Yes. I am distressed. But I'm right."

He paced about a bit more. I thought of bringing through the coffee which was now ready, but thought, no, this is not the moment.

"And what better way of starting than by having you tell me

why you put in your lying report."

"It was not a lying report."

"But it was, Miguel. And you have to tell me why you did it. Really you do."

"I do not."

"Oh yes you do."

"Why?"

"Because I am going to thump you until you do."

I knew he would. Kit did not anger easy, but he angered well. Once on an anti-racism march in London, a skin shouted out something about how carrot-tops shouldn't fuck black minges and Kit just went and thumped him very hard on the nose, and got back in the march as if nothing had happened. All were so surprised, including the nearest filth, that no one did anything, and that was that.

Miguel sneered, which was silly. "Well-known liberal humanist resorts to torture, eh?"

Kit reached down and got hold of his shirt front up under his neck, and hauled him up and bopped him on the nose, hard, like he did to the National Front skinhead. Then he dropped him, and Miguel blubbered and held his hanky to his bleeding face and went on about how Kit had better not do that again. Kit said, nevertheless, he was about to do that again unless Miguel talked, so surprise, surprise, Miguel talked.

It was not worth the effort of clearing up the blood on the floor. Miguel's boss had come to him and indicated without saying as much that a report condemning Sant'Simon would be appreciated, and that while Miguel's post was not of course in question, his chances of early promotion might be. No, of course he had no idea of what or who was behind it, no, he knew nothing else at all, and now please could he go?

He went.

The next twenty minutes or so was not nice. Kit was mourning, no other word for it, but guilty-feeling too about me, so not ready to let go. I tried to tell him it was okay but he wasn't listening. I tried to tell him about Trev Ev and Zdt but he thought I was trying to be tactful and change the subject. So we blundered about and got in each other's way, Zena woke up, had a bawl while chewing on her fist, poor little mite, the nasty toothy-peg,

170

nearly through, didn't your mummy give you some nice Calpol then . . . ?

At last it dawned on me. The poor man wanted to play the answering-machine tape, and didn't dare say so. So I said, "Listen Kit. I heard that machine play back a second or two this morning. I know you want to play it all now. So go ahead. I'll take Zena out walkies, if you like."

At which he gave me a long, big, sad hug and said I was a great girl, which I am, and after a moment's thought said no, he'd rather I stayed, unless I preferred to go out. You know, Don Jesús, it was a hard moment that. I'd heard the beginning remember, all loving it sounded, and I think we were both frightened Miguel had it right, and the gossips, and that Rosa did kill herself for love, and this last message coming up could be pretty devastating. I was tempted to run for it. Let him tell me his own way when I came back. But I could see he wanted me to stay.

So, he found the tape, slotted it in and let it run. She had a lot to say and only half a minute each go, so had to keep redialling. And once someone else got in the middle, nothing significant, but it was extra hassle. But I'll give it to you straight. I've had time since to take a transcript.

Kit, this is the third time I've tried to call you. I have to speak to you, darling. I know you don't want me intruding on you, and I don't want to either, but there's something you've got to know, and I'm going to go on recording on your machine until the tape runs out.

It's to do with Sant'Simon. First of all, I was coerced to write that report. But not by jealousy of your wife or any silly nonsense like that, and it really was very silly of you to suggest that was the case. Never mind. I wrote the first factual part as it stands. My comments and comparisons with other studies showed there was nothing to fear from in-breeding more than at hundreds of other tiny settlements all over the country. I attacked the Chilean and Puerto Rican reports for being unscientific.

It all came back with a polite request I should reconsider my interpretation. I ignored it. It came back again with the last two-thirds rewritten with a request I should put my signature to it. And within an hour I had a telephone call from my cousin

171

in Santiago saying that my mother had been arrested and no one knew where she was. She's seventy years old, in poor health, a bourgeois widow interested in spiritualism and quite unpolitical. She has always had a comfortable life. . . . Kit. I won't defend myself on this, but she simply is not a person one can allow to . . . Kit. I know Sant'Simon is more important than my mother. But.

I did not make the connection until a nasty little man in a sharp grey suit interrupted my lunch at the "soda" where you used to meet me sometimes, and told me my mother would be brought home just as soon as I signed that report.

Kit. Santiago is thousands of kilometres away. Whoever wants to close Sant'Simon is very powerful.

I signed. I'm sorry. And I fretted and worried about it for days, even after I had spoken to my mother on the phone and she had said she was quite all right, the people from DINA had made a silly mistake, and she was only very slightly bruised.

I decided I should leave here. I had betrayed . . . myself. I should go somewhere I was less vulnerable. This Paris connection is a good one, there are many Chileans there.

Then I realised I had not done enough. After you had called on me. I did not know what to do. But I decided I should at least spend some time making an effort to find out just why Sant'Simon was being so singled out for persecution.

I found out very quickly and easily that Sant'Simon has a Comité Campesino affiliated to FUNTAC—Federación Unitaria Nacional de Trabajadores Agrícolos y Campesinos. Manuel, who you have told me about, is chairperson. I have friends in San José who are CP, and I went to them. They directed me to the right person in FUNTAC, and he knew all about Sant'Simon and its troubles. He told me something he has kept very quiet about because if ITCO got to hear of it it would be bad for Sant'Simon. It could be too easily made to look as if Sant'Simon was being set up as a foco, you know, part of a Communist network of focal points across the countryside. He told me only after I had convinced him that ITCO was about to withdraw support anyway.

January before last, a Nicaraguan Sandinista botanist was shot to pieces on the steps of Branch Twelve of the CP. His name was Ignacio Morena. Officially he was in San José to do some research at the Herbarium. Unofficially he had been invited to look at some plants Manuel had found. That was all my contact could tell me. Typical of a CP cadre he had registered all that was irrelevant and nothing of importance. He could not tell me what the plan was.

I did some more homework but it involved going to the Nicaraguan Embassy here and making a fuss. Fortunately one of the people there knows me. I found out that Ignacio Morena was a specialist in cereals and that he was running a field research station in Nicaragua not far from the border, where they specialise in improving strains of rice and maize. They also knew that he had been carrying some roots of a plant when he was killed, that these had been snatched from him as he fell, and that he had already taken many specimens across the border.

That's it Kit. Find out what that plant is and you may save Sant'Simon. And maybe do more than that. Anything the other side is so eager to destroy must be something good for the people. Adiós, Kit. *Besos*.

Don Jesús, I wept when I first heard that, and I weep now to read it out again. Rosa was a lovely woman. Kit was lucky to have known her. She killed herself. Not by hanging, but by going to FUNTAC, to the CP, to the Nicaraguan Embassy, by drawing attention to herself.

I dried my eyes and told Kit I knew what the plant was, told him about my meeting with Trevor Everton in the Herbarium. He knew the address of Everton's flat in San José. If Rosa had been murdered then Everton was in danger. He tried to phone him but no answer. So he decided to go round. I wanted to come too, but he would not let me because of Zena. We kissed, love perfect again between us, and he went. I saw him again only once, for perhaps half a minute before that man killed him.

22

Everton's apartment was near the markets, some twenty minutes away on foot, and that was the way Kit Carter went. The rain had started again, most Josefinos were on their way home from work, and all the taxis were spoken for. Tall, red-skinned, bearded, he was made doubly incongruous and conspicuous by the large, green, stoutly made Greenpeace umbrella held high like a standard above all the other umbrellas round—Stop Acid Rain.

Everton had an *ático* at the top of a narrow block of flats: it was cheap, had only a small hallway and no *conserje* or *portero*. The lift was not working. With umbrella unfurled, but lowered and dripping, Kit climbed the six flights of stairs to the top. On the third floor a small girl kicked and banged at the lift doors. She smiled at him as he went by, said in Spanish, "Someone has not shut the doors properly—fix them if you pass them." He paused to answer her and was aware that footsteps half a flight, one turn of the stairs below him, had paused too.

On the lower floors there were three apartments on each, but at the top just two *áticos* set on either side of the lift shaft, each with a large balcony. Everton's door was open, had very clearly been forced. It was all very quiet now—only distant traffic sounds, a radio playing tangos, the steady sussuration of the rain on the roof above his head and on the balconies. Thunder rumbled distantly.

Fear fell on Kit like a python dropping from a tree, cold coils immobilising his limbs. Then he shook his head and said audibly, "This will not do." He grasped the wood handle of his umbrella more tightly.

He pushed wide the door and waited. Nothing happened. He moved into the tiny hall. A large poster, a photograph of an Amerindian fertility goddess, lavishly hung about with gold corncobs, had been ripped across. Three doors—a kitchen, bathroom, living-room—and an almost overpowering reek of alcohol and formalin. The living-room door was also ajar. Kit called, "Everton. Trevor. Are you there?" A gust of wind rattled the slats of a blind, and the fear seized him again. He pushed this second door with the ferrule of the green umbrella.

The room was longer and narrower than he had expected, and, apart from a narrow bed, very much a workroom. There were bookcases, deep sets of shelves on which dried specimens were stacked, and shelves for jars containing pickled ones. In the middle was a small word-processor, tape player, printer, and the Micro-writer Everton had been using in the museum. But the place had been wrecked, the books pulled to the floor, the screen of the word-processor smashed, most of the specimen jars broken and emptied.

At the far end of the room a glass door was set between two ordinary windows. It was open and the blind, a quarter-dropped, rattled again as the wind gusted. The door swung. Kit moved towards it, ducked under the blind. The balcony was large, L-shaped, but protected under the walls by the deep eaves of the sloping roof, designed to provide some protection from the rain and sun. Beneath them, on the corner of the L, stood a tall, fair-haired man with a thin moustache, and a long jagged scar down one cheek giving one side of his face a permanent rictus. The large automatic he was holding was already pointing at the very centre of Kit's stomach.

The danger had materialised and the fear went. The berserk rage, passed on from family to family since Viking times, gripped him. This man had threatened Esther, Zena and him with hor-rors, had, for all Kit knew, killed Rosa and Everton too. Fuck his gun, I'm going to kill him. He swept the heavy umbrella in a short, two-handed hook that caught Steiner on the wrist, smashing it against the projecting windowsill. Steiner did not fire—perhaps because he knew they could be seen from neigh-bouring blocks, perhaps because he did not believe that Kit would attack him with an umbrella.

Kit followed the first blow with a hard, vicious jab to the solar plexus. Greenpeace umbrellas have three-inch metal spikes. This brought the German's head down in a reflex spasm so Kit could catch his face with a rising knee. Steiner jerked back and col-lapsed, gasping and moaning, blood pouring from crushed lips.

He huddled himself against the wall, trying to protect his head with an upflung arm.

Kit wiped the rain out of his eyes, stooped without taking his eyes off Steiner, felt for the gun with his free hand. As he straightened lights exploded behind his eyes and an electric current generated at a point just below his fourth vertebra shot down every feeling nerve of his body.

Miller delicately squatted beside, careful not to let his trouser hems touch the wet terrazo, checked he was still alive. He straightened, pleased that the blow had been perfectly judged, then stooped again to hook his large strong hands in Carter's armpits. He hauled him, face down banging against Miller's knees, into the living-room and let him drop. Then he sat on the bed, knees spread, chin on heavy clenched fist, and thought. Throughout he had ignored Steiner, and he continued to do so.

Miller was not happy. It was a principle of his that he was a killer, nothing less. That's what he was hired for, that's what he did. But because he smuggled tiny amounts of cocaine into Tenerife whenever he could because they bought for him the services of the German girl surfer who had most buzz, he had been conned and blackmailed into behaving like a common hoodlum. He had been told to kill Everton and make it look like accident. Okay. Everton had answered the door. Miller had said he was police and shown him an American Express card. As Everton's head dropped to look at it Miller had placed his left forearm behind Everton's neck and forced his head back with his right hand placed flatly over the forehead. Back, then sideways over the fulcrum, disconnecting its vertebrae and killing him instantly. He then banged on the lift door. Steiner, on the ground floor, called it down. Miller, using the same techniques that had opened Rosa's door, opened up the lift shaft and dropped Everton's body down it. So far so good.

But now he had been told to do things other than kill. Steiner walked up to search the apartment, while Miller went below and kept watch. At their preliminary briefing he had objected but Franco had reminded him that cocaine trading on Spanish soil was a very serious offence which could well lead to deportation back to England where far more serious charges might be brought.

The situation had continued to deteriorate. Steiner's search of the apartment was clearly rubbish, not a search but a pointless trashing job. Who was going to believe Everton had accidented or even suicided when his flat had been trashed? Not even the Tico police would believe that. And how long would it be before an engineer came and fixed the lift? How long before the body was found on its roof? Miller had experience and he knew it could be hours, even through to the next morning, but that was not the sort of guess he liked to gamble on.

And here was Carter, breathing noisily and already occasionally moaning. Miller knew who he was—he was on Paco's list of possible targets, though he had not yet been specified. What was to be done with him? Miller stood up, moved into the tiny hall where, miraculously in view of the destruction Steiner had wrought, the telephone was still intact. He dialled the number Paco had given him. Steiner staggered by, heading for the bathroom.

Paco arrived ten minutes later. By then Carter, still not properly conscious, had been tied up with light flex and gagged. Steiner, holding a cloth to his smashed mouth, sat on the bed above him and rhythmically, savagely kicked him. Miller, sickened by the alcohol and formalin fumes, stood in the open glass door. Rain still clattered onto the balcony from a black sky, lit by distant forks of lightning as the storm crashed around the volcanoes.

Paco took in the scene, lifted Carter's head, let it drop, wiped his hands on his large turquoise-blue silk handkerchief.

"This is the guy whose wife you were going to rape."

Steiner looked up, wary.

"But Everton scared you off."

Steiner twisted away and spat bloodily.

"Sure it is," Paco went on. He had not asked questions, he had made statements. "So he'll know how to find Everton's place in the forest."

He went back to the hall, dialled a number. While he waited for the connection to be made he shredded down a strip more off the poster of the goddess, carefully curling the tear round her left breast. He spoke briefly, came back into the living-room.

"Right. We have a safe house on a private estate off the Heredia road. We'll take him there. Can you make him talk?"

Steiner's face slowly lit up, a small boy promised a heavenly treat. Paco nodded slowly, his question answered.

23

"You asked for my assessment. I have to give it."

Outside a rising wind off the sea clattered the palm fronds. Distantly the thud of the surf on the Great Barrier Reef increased. On a glassed-in balcony three men and one woman leaned towards each other over a smoked-glass table mounted on heavy chrome tubes. Glasses frosted with cold chimed when moved and the scent of classic martinis sharpened the warm air. Greenfinger Cay was perfect, whatever the weather.

"All right then, Jethro. Speaking for myself I'm man enough to take it. And Ike too, I daresay. And we all know what an unflappable toughie old Maureen is."

Jethro, a dark man with deeply pock-marked skin and crinkly hair greying in front of his ears, drew a small sheaf of folded foolscap from the inside pocket of his white tuxedo.

"This," he said, "is dynamite."

He shifted two glasses, inverted cones on spiralled stems, and spread Everton's report.

"Just," he went on, and his voice had an untidy rasping quality, "as we thought we had wrapped up Weedkiller, this comes along. This guy knows—"

"Knew." Matt dropped the word as if releasing a pebble into a well. He was tall, had thin gingery hair, mottled skin. He hated sun. He hated Greenfinger Cay. His accent was Connecticut through Harvard Business School, and he was the only one of them whose evening wear was entirely conventional. He was also in charge.

Jethro said, "Knew. Fine. Knew a lot. He has it right. His analysis of Zdt, done in the field, is as good as our labs came up with. Furthermore he has made the appropriate connection to the destructuring of Sant'Simon."

Maureen, dressed in a minuscule network of jet beads, and

178

very little else, with brown eyes and dark hair streaked with white, recrossed her bare legs. The dimples on the backs of her thighs, and the sagginess below her upper arm betrayed a not unsexy middle age. They did not indicate her achievement quotient.

"And Hedborg has read this?"

"The envelope has been opened."

"And he is still here. He has not turned round and gone back to Costa Rica? He is not blowing whistles. What's into this guy?"

Jethro shrugged. Matt looked from each to each, picked on Ike, squat and hairy with glasses heavily framed in black. He wore a purple cummerbund shot with gold threads, and he had taken off his jacket.

"Ike?"

"He has an accident. Tomorrow. Scuba diving on the reef."

Maureen shifted, and the leather beneath her squeaked. "You miss the point."

"I do?"

"Listen. Hedborg has read that and dismissed it, no sweat. Or he has read it and comprehended it, and still comes on. Why? Because he knows we're behind this thing, knows there's no way we're going to back off now. Above all he knows we have very decisive influence on who gets the Middle American Desk at UNAFO."

"So?"

"So. We leave him be. Keep him here a day or two longer than he expected. Under total surveillance, of course. Meanwhile make sure the Costa Rican end is properly sanitised, and then reconsider his position."

"Okay." Matt was decisive. "That's for Hedborg. Now Jethro, how, as you perceive it, does this . . ."—he tapped Everton's report—"call for restructuring of our overall strategy in Costa Rica?"

"Basically not at all. The way I see it, this is an isolated, one-off thing, a gremlin. We offed Everton. Now we have to take out everything to do with him. We can do this. He was a loner, no family, no base, no backing. If we delete everything he did and was, we're okay."

"So what's left?"

Maureen recrossed her legs. "Do we get a refill?"

"Of course. Unless you'd rather blow coke?"

But already behind them ice was rattling. Black hands protruding from white cuffs were briefly perceived as liquor trickled into fresh glasses, which frosted instantly. Jethro went on. "Everton had a hideaway. A place about two miles downstream of Sant'Simon, two miles upstream of the Milton University camp. That has to be found. He may have left notes there. First drafts. If everything Everton ever did or had has to be deleted then that has to be very much included."

"So it's found and taken out."

"Not easy."

"Why not?"

"It's tucked away in the jungle. Need not occupy more than five square yards. You could look for it for ever and never find it."

"So no one ever finds it."

"Tomorrow someone, anyone might just walk into it. By accident."

Matt leant back, peered out into the thrashing night.

"Who else knows where it is?"

Ike spoke but first tipped his spectacles onto the end of his tumescent nose.

"We gather Carter and his wife Somers have been there. Probably."

"Then both of them, both, must lead us back there. How do we make them do that?"

"Carter is already in-house and we're working on his orientation. I do think Hedborg could assist here."

"How?"

"Carter needs security and promotion. Probably too he needs to stop being hurt. If Hedborg puts security and promotion on the line, tells him he's blown both if he doesn't take us to Everton's hideaway, that might tip the balance. Also have the Eichmann effect, let a man know he can do something that might be wrong because his boss said so."

"Yeah," Maureen drawled. "And if Hedborg agrees to do that, we'll know whose side he's on."

"Right." Matt straightened his back, turned to them all with a cold smile. Jethro, can you talk Hedborg into giving that sort of message to Carter? If we can patch in a connection to him, that is."

Ike chipped in: "I know where he is."

"And Somers? The woman?"

Maureen too was confident. "We'll get to her."

"So. One way and another this Everton gremlin is open and shut."

All assented.

"We can go down to dinner then. I suppose Hedborg is waiting for us. Are you sure you don't want to blow some coke first?"

Part VI

24

Don Jesús, I'm mad again. You know why? That Nova and Benjamin, my *ex-*, please note that, very ex-foster-parents have turned up. They want to take Zena. Mother Superior here wants them to take Zena. Mother Superior says Zena is an unsettling influence on the Casa de Corrección. So they have her on their side. But listen. They have absolutely no legal rights to do this, no right at all. There's talk they can get a magistrate's order if Mother Superior says Zena would be better cared for with them, but that really is bullshit. Zena is just fine with me. She's had another tooth since we've been here, she understands when I say things to her like "give-a-mumma-a-bikkie," and then she offers it, she's put on weight and is all laughs and smiles to everyone.

No wonder they want her. Trouble is Nova, who is a great big fat arse of a person, wears ethnic kaftans to hide the size of her bun, eats beans and bugger all else, is a course tutor for the Open University in, you've guessed it, infant management. And Benjie Wenjie is a child psychologist under contract to the Ministry of Defence to do research into the effects of a nuclear war on the surviving under-fives. They've no children of their own, of course. Anyway they want to take her back to Milton Keynes and fill her full of shit until what Benjie calls my spot of bother has blown over.

Yeah, I said, and suppose I get twenty years for murder? And he just looked sad like yes, I probably will and what will become of Zena then? Do I want her in an orphanage on Tenerife brought up to be a chambermaid in the hotels and the time-sharing? Or a nice decent upbringing in middle-class Milton Keynes? You know, Don Jesús, given the choice, I'd go for the orphanage, in spite of the fact it would be churchy. Better the fucking Roman Catholic Church than the British brand of middle-class liberal humanism.

But it's not going to happen, is it? I mean justifiable homicide, two years in the pen, and Spaniards who understand mothers will let me keep her, or better still sentence suspended, that's the score, the way you told me, isn't it? Isn't it, Don Jesús? I'll tear you to bits if it's not. I'll tear her to bits rather than let her go. No. That's not true. But. Don Jesús. They can do anything in the world with me, but they don't take Zena from me, my baby, Kit's baby.

Two hours after Kit had gone I commenced to be very worried. Or like my anxiety reached a point where I had to do something. So I rang Everton's number. A strange voice answered, in Spanish, and would not say who he was, unless I said who I was, but then he blew it, said I'd better tell him because he was a police officer investigating a serious crime, and he wanted to know anyone who knew Everton. I hung up on him sharp.

Why? Because, Don Jesús, my life has taught me not to like, or trust, or want to have anything to do with the filth, the pigs, Mr. Plod, Old Bill. I had a nice Daddy. He was easy-going and fun, and apart from knocking us about when things got on top of him, he was really okay. He went in for the Rastafarian bit, dreadlocks, sound systems, *ganja*, the lot, all a matter of style, not because he believed it. The filth knicked him on sus and put him away for two years for possession and trading, and that criminalised him. Two years in a British jail does that to you, you know? So now he's doing ten years for robbery with violence.

And that was only the start of it. I got nicked in the 1983 general election when peacefully picketing for troops out of Ireland, and again in 1984 when pregnant with Zena, for collecting outside a supermarket for the Welsh coal mine the university had adopted, and both times strip-searched, holes and all. Why? To intimidate me, or because the WPCs were dikes. Okay. I'm not at all against lady gays, not at all, no way, but those WPCs really enjoyed themselves, believe me.

Pigs are pigs the world over. Ticos make a joke of their pigs, but they've had a lot American advice and training over the last few years. Believe me, I saw them in their true colours forty-eight hours later.

Nevertheless, another hour went by and by then, about nine o'clock I reckon and the thunder circling back over the city and

Zena whimpering and refusing to settle like she knew something was wrong, I was pretty near frantic and just about to see if the pigs were still there and knew anything about Kit, when the phone went.

"Sheba?"

Oh Christ I thought—Darwin.

"Sheba?"

"Darwin."

"Chas. Sheba, is Kit there?"

"No."

"I thought not. Now listen, Sheba. You've got to trust me in this."

"Trust *you*?"

But you know, Don Jesús, at that moment I did. I had been in Ticoland less than a week. My husband had disappeared. The only other nice guy in town likewise. A girl, a nice girl had been murdered. The only other people I could trust were fifty miles away on Sant'Simon.

Chas. Darwin Junior was on line to be trusted. Who else?

"You must. Listen Sheba. I think I know what's happened to Kit. I can't explain now. Not over the phone. But . . . you've got to believe this. You do what I say and I'll find him. Safe and sound. Because I reckon you hold the key. I'll tell you tomorrow. Listen Sheba. You do this and you do this right and Kit'll be okay. You sit tight. You don't open the door or answer the phone. And tomorrow morning a guy will come for you. Francisco Franco. He'll put a card under the door, with his name on, printed, and then you let him in, and go with him, no questions. That way we get Kit out of the mess he's in."

"He's in a mess?" My heart sank.

"Nothing irreversible. If you just do as I say. Okay?"

"Zena comes too."

"Shit. I'd forgotten about her."

"Forgotten!"

"Hell, Sheba. All I can think of is you. Okay, Zena comes too. But bring what you need for her for a day or two. Right?"

And the bastard rang off.

What could I do? What could I have done?

Half an hour later the phone rang again. Darwin had told me not to answer it. It rang again and again. I couldn't go on not answering it. But I was frightened too. So I sussed out what to do, and fixed in the answering-machine. It rang. The tape turned. Stopped. I played it back. It was Kit. He sounded wretched and strained.

"Sweetheart Ezzie. If that's you. If you hear this. Please do whatever Darwin says. It will be for the best. Love. Kisses. I love you."

Next morning, buzz on the door buzzer and a card slipped under the door. I looked out of the window and there's that big Plymouth again. I picked up the card. Francisco Franco. Bullburger's Costaricense, SA. I opened the door. He was a sharp character, short, dark, touch of the Indian with those cheekbones, slightly Chink eyes. And dressed like a dude in a sharp suit. I gathered up Zena wearing her on my front this time because she likes a dodo, a sleep in the morning, and I like to be able to see and hold her when she's asleep, and the Mothercare drawstring bag that holds her life-support systems—disposables, babywipes, biscuits, a beaker of orange juice, a packet of Greenfinger 5, and a small vacuum flask of warm water. I checked I had a key and the door was properly locked and off we went, me following Paco into the lift and out into the street.

The ride in the Plymouth convertible was okay, you know? Roof off, those big soft seats, the sun and warmth and freshness of the morning, the avenues and parks. Then out onto the Heredia road—a lot of *tugurios* filling most of the roadside, but coffee *haciendas* too with the white blossom here just fresh. We took a side road, a track, and the Plymouth rocked in the potholes like a boat in an ocean swell. We reached a barrier with an armed guard, and Paco had to hand him plastic which was slotted before the barrier went up. Now we were on tarmac again, but smooth like purple velvet. Above flowering hedges I saw nubile girls scissoring off diving boards into pools I could not see. A line of white board fencing kept a couple of playful Arabs (the equine kind) at bay. Finally we reached a neat *finca* on the top of a conical hill. Andalusian it looked, red tiles, white paint, geraniums and gladioli-like lilies, deep scarlet.

A white arch led into a courtyard with a well and standing right in the middle a Messerschmitt-Bolkow-Blohm, the dinkiest of midget 'copters, the sort that is just one round blister, and blazoned on the boom AFI, the "I" the green and gold corncob.

This Franco was not about to hang about. He opened the Plymouth's fat door, let it clunk behind me, marched over to the 'copter, vents in his sharp jacket swinging, handed us up into the passenger seat, gave me a pair of ear muffs. What about Zena? He shrugged. So I pressed one of her dainty ears to my bosom and covered the other with my hand, and then bang, bang, bang, clatter, clatter, clatter the rotor swung and in a moment we had lift-off.

Where the hell are we going, I shouted but if he heard he wasn't bothered to answer.

He swung us round and we headed off almost due west following the road and railway towards Puntarenas, but long before we got to the coast turned south. Bananas and cane below, then pasture of a sort, stumps of charred forest trees sticking up out of yellow and brown with herds of thin black cattle drifting across it, desolate it looked after the greenness of the *meseta*. Some hills and fields returned, with newly sprouting maize and some rice, then flat again and groves and groves of citrus laid out in grids. Not many villages. Not much work. But a lot of money.

The coastal plain narrowed and the giant *cordillera* on our left came nearer and there were patches of uncleared forest below us slowly coalescing into quite big areas, and the ocean, white, sandy, chalky-looking shallows, green then deepest blue to our right, it was becoming a great ride. The *cordillera* closed towards us, those heavy forests gashed with rivers and waterfalls and it dawned on silly me where we were going. The valley of Río Remedios for sure, but which part of it?

I looked down at Zena. She sort of half smiled up at me, awake now, and a bit bothered, perhaps especially because I'm holding her like I was so she's not deafened. Not long now, my chick. Nor was it. Paco swung the M-B-B inland, low hills to the right, cutting off sight of the coast, then to the left and in front el Cerro de la Muerte, blue uplands shrouded in mist, and I was pretty sure this long zigzagging valley ahead was Remedios and so it was, for quite suddenly a square of cleared forest appeared below us and the M-B-B dropped, slowly turning this way and that, and the debris below began to stir with the blast from the blades. I felt the skids touch, we dropped another foot, and Paco gesticulated. He wanted me out. But he had not turned off the engine. Fuck that, I said. I'm not going to be dropped just like that. He pulled back his jacket and I saw he'd got a small gun in his waistband. He flashed his teeth in what I expect he thought was a grin, so I did as he said. Just five steps down and I'm hardly on terra firma than the blades crescendoed again and the blast whirled up my dress and scattered leaves and muck all round me and Zena, and up he went. In a minute the 'copter was making less noise than the three large bees that had homed in on us.

I looked about. We were in a shabby square of cleared forest. It's a funny thing how great the forest looks untouched and how tatty when it's been got at. Now we were down on the ground the hills looked a long way off and the mountain not visible, just a patch of cloud seen between the crowns of two of the taller trees. Coming in closer it was just trees, and you couldn't see much of them. Like a wall of silvery trunks with lianas on the edge of the clearing, and dense growth up to twenty feet or so because the light had been let in. As the silence settled, or rather as the bombardment of the 'copter was rinsed out of our ears, there were bird calls intermittent and distant, the buzz of insects, and the rustle of . . . what? Ants, spiders, scorpions, rodents, snakes!!! at my feet. I was commencing to be very miserable, then pulled myself together. Come on, Ezzie, I said. The river's not too far off. Find that and at the most you've got six miles of hard grind to get to Sant'Simon and then you're okay. . . .

25

AaAaAaAAAAAAaaaaaah!

What the fuck's that?

The fat idiot jumped through a screen of liana and landed five yards off. He'd taken off his shirt and tied it round his waist so it looked like a loincloth. Mercifully he had kept his trousers on.

"Me Tarzan, you Jane."

"Shit, Darwin, you gave me a fright."

"Sure I did, Sheba. All part of the service. Welcome to the Charles Darwin Tropical Jungle Theme Park."

The fat bastard made as if he was going to kiss me, even with Zena between us, and this time I was so angry at the fright he gave me I did slap him, and knocked his specs crooked. For a moment his eyes, which were an unusual gingery colour, blazed, and his mouth narrowed to a slit like a shark's, and I thought oh dear, what next. Especially as I'd smelled the rum on him.

Then he laughed, straightened his specs, swatted a large insect that landed on his shoulder, and pulled his shirt back on. The view was a lot better now I couldn't see his hairy tits.

"Come on," he said. "There's a lot to look at."

"Hang on Darwin. Where's Kit?"

"He's okay. Never mind about him. We rendezvous with him later. About three-thirty I reckon."

"Where?"

"Everton's bivouac. You know where that is?"

"I could find it."

"Great. Sure as hell, I can't."

"Listen, Darwin."

"Chas."

"*Darwin*. Either Darwin or Fat-Ass."

"Darwin."

"Darwin. I don't like any of this at all. What's happened to them? What's going on? Kit went to Everton's last night, both have disappeared, and the filth are there instead. How do you know they'll be at Everton's bivouac? Everton was in San José yesterday lunchtime. I met him at the Herbarium."

"You did? Why? Do you know what he was doing there? Christ Sheba, what were you doing there?"

He was all shark-like again. I stood back and a stick or something snapped beneath my foot.

"Shit! Listen. You could have told me we were coming here. I'm not dressed for this, you know."

"What were you doing with Everton at the Herbarium?" Said nastily, with threat.

I bravoed him out. "Just visiting the Museo. He happened to be there. And another thing. Kit won't be anywhere near here. At three o'clock he'll be at the ITCO meeting on Sant-'Simon."

"No chance. That's fixed. Tied up. And he knows it. He'll be humiliated if he attends." Suddenly he relaxed though it like took an effort. "Come on Sheba. I know a bit of what's going on. You'll have to trust me. It's now half eleven. Kit will be at Everton's bivouac at half three. How long will it take to get there?"

"Two hours. Maybe three. If there's a cleared or marked track up to Sant'Simon, two will do."

"As I understand it the way up is marked. What's not known is where you turn off."

"I can find that."

"So we have two hours to kill. I aim to do what I said I would and show you the canopy. In comfort and style. Come on."

He pulled back the lianas and pushed into the vegetation, very thick at first, but after a nasty moment or so, when things seemed to grab and catch and pull, buzz round you and drop on you, we were through. It was even grander, more awesome than it had been up at Everton's. Here the ground was almost flat, we were maybe five hundred metres lower, and both those factors make a difference. Here the trees were taller, the canopy thicker, the debris on the floor wetter, more rotted and deeper, the hot smells of fungi and compost richer. It was darker too, eerily dark with only sprinklings here and there of sunflakes so bright they burned your eyes and sent little puffs of vapour up into the air above where they settled. It was quiet too, coming into the quiet time of day, a few distant bird calls, screeches and cries, no song, and echoing down from more than a hundred feet above us.

It was very hot, very humid. Darwin's shirt in front of me was black with sweat, Zena in the Snugli was like a ball of wet cloth clinging to my chest below my tits, and the straps on the shoulders began to chafe. And all I was wearing was a dress, a cardigan I'd looped into the drawstrings on Zena's bag, knickers, and, would you believe it a pair of soft leather coasters. No one had told me we were going jungle trekking. It was impossible. After a hundred yards I took a decision, not an easy one with only a billion creepy-crawlies all over the ground and in it, and stepped out of them. Their value had been purely psychological—they were no practical use whatever.

Anyway I go barefoot whenever I possibly can, always have. I hold the one hundred metres' ladies' record at Hume, and won a silver in the Inter-Universities 4-by-100 metres relay, and all done on cinders, barefoot, before Zola Budd got to secondary school. All the same it wasn't easy, really quite creepy—if I stood still more than five seconds I could feel the life in the compost wriggling between my toes. The worst thing though was when I stubbed my toe really hard and sharp. After that I watched where my feet went. Darwin was following a blazed trail from the clearing to the camp and most of the large obstacles like fallen limbs or trunks had been cleared.

In ten minutes we were there. You could see it before that because they had had to take out some trees and trim limbs up in the canopy. The result was the area was lit like with floods and spots, like the stage in a theatre in the round like at Hume Arts Centre. And of course they'd kept down the vegetation that would have sprung up in the light, and had only been gone a day so it was still clear. Two large oblongs marked where tents had been, and some smaller shapes showed stores or whatever, but all left neat and tidy, like these were really very ecologically minded scientists for once.

What did stand out was two sets of lines of very bright yellowy orange that dropped like plumb lines against all the sinewy elegance of the vegetation. The nearest seemed to drop out of one

of those trees with great buttress roots, thin triangular plates supporting the lower structure of the tree, and one of these provided
anchorage maybe ten feet or more out from the trunk. Darwin
went up to this and fiddled about with clamps and things for a
moment or two and held up like a webbing sling or harness with
two lower stirrups.

"All aboard, Sheba."

"I'm not getting in that."

"Sure you are, Sheba."

"No way."

"You afraid of heights?"

"No."

"Okay, come on then. Maybe it'll be easier with the picka-
ninny on your back. Can you do that?"

He moved towards us, podgy hands reaching.

"You keep your hands off of me. I can manage."

It's a bit of a struggle getting her off the front because that way
the straps should be crossed on your back, but easy then to get
her onto your back just like a backpack. She gave a whimper or
two, but not much, far too interested in all that was going on.
This harness thing though was another matter, and Darwin had
to show me where to put my rump, and my feet, and how the
buckles went, and of course took the opportunity for a grope.

"Why are you such a randy bastard, Darwin?"

"Come on Sheba. With a figure like yours and a pelt to match,
you must be used to the odd feely in public places. And this is
private. Fine and private."

I knew what he was getting at and shuddered. The grave's a
fine and private place. He knew I knew because he was certainly no fool, and he was prodding my mind in the direction of
my predicament, the chief factor of which was, I didn't know
what the predicament itself was, just that it was there. In short
he was putting in a little touch of the frighteners as well as a
feely.

"Right. This can operate manually. These clamps are jumars,
used in rock climbing. When you pull on them they clamp the
rope, when you release the tension they release too. You lock
this top clamp by hanging on it, lift your feet so the bottom clamp
releases, raise them as high as you can, then straighten your legs.
That pressures the bottom clamp and locks it higher than it was.

Release the tension on the top clamp by raising your arms, raise them as high as you can lifting the top clamp. Then lock it by pulling. And so on. Up you'll go. It's hard work, the platform is over a hundred feet up. Luckily though we don't have to use steam except if things go wrong, because we have this."

He patted a small Honda generator, checked the fuel gauge and topped it up from a can. He then made a few more adjustments and connections.

"If the harness is fixed right you will be comfortable and safe, even letting go. If you feel you do want to hold on, that's okay. When you get to the platform step out of the stirrups on to it, then bang the release catches. Ready? Let's go."

He yanked the lanyard on the engine, it coughed, roared, settled back into a quiet hum.

"Neat machine. Three hours at two hundred and twenty volts. More than we need."

He threw a gear, the rope above my head tautened, the harness gripped my bum, then we were off, up, and away.

It was a glorious ascent and blissfully not quick. The harness twisted slowly, but would stop if I swung against it, or gripped the cable—yellow flecked with a scarlet thread.

The first thirty feet or so were relatively clear dark space, filled with subaquaeous greenness, little colour, the tree trunks like pewter, ranging from elegantly thin saplings to the larger though never really massive pillars of those who had made it to the top. It all changed as we passed through the tops of the saplings which mostly had thin, transparent leaves, groping to make effective use of the wheeling sunflakes that lit on them, made them glow gold with inner-veined fire, pale-green gold.

Now it was lighter, the hum of the generator receded, and a few moths and other insects circulated lazily in the wider beams of sunlight. This was the area of the epiphytic gardens, and suddenly I wished for Trev Ev, and knew with a stab of sureness he was dead, longed for him to tell me what was what, which was epiphyte and which was host until I recollected these indeed were gardens hanging densely down from higher limbs and the trunks themselves cascades of plants, each growing on each, bromeliads providing pools chaliced in succulent leaves for tree frogs to nurture their tadpoles within, and indeed mosquitoes and other nasties too—but we'd had all the injections, Kit had made sure of that, I had nothing to fear from the forest, only the fat bastard below.

Flowers now too—orchids mostly I suppose, and I remembered the dying ones the fat bastard had brought and I'd put them in the trashcan before leaving since they'd wilted fast and gave off a nasty smell. These were fine: mostly in that spot small, with pale colours, yellows and browns streaked with crimson and some bell-like in shape.

Here too I saw two large birds, crows flashed with brightness, yellow, white and red with huge beaks streaked a rich red brown, toucans I suppose. Our approach had disturbed their siesta and they cawed and jabbered and slapped and drifted through the sunbeams. And then best of all, Don Jesús, a three-toed sloth, a lady because like me she had her own little Zena, but carrying hers in front, clinging to her fur and licking from mother's lips the fragments of leaves mum had been chewing. She looked out at us from the trunk she was clinging to, over her shoulder, her wide-spaced eyes blind-looking caught in a sunflake, her face caped in fur and her whole coat shaggy and green with the algae that lived there. Jesus, Don Jesús, I loved her as we went by.

At last clusters of dripping yellow flowers, cascades of them, dropping walls of gold showed we were almost there and there were scents so heavenly you cannot describe or comprehend them, with a great multifarious concourse of pollinators sharing in am-icality the richness of nectars.

This miraculous ascent concluded as we broke slowly into clearer and blissfully cooler air, at least it moved, and through all the flowers and leaves I caught glimpses of the slopes and crags of the valley climbing above us, and so reached, some surprise this was, a platform constructed and roofed too, in what could only be pre-cast aluminum, a treehouse of aluminum suspended from the strongest limbs of a forest giant beneath its crown but above those nearby.

Are you afraid of heights?

No, I had said. But I am, somewhat. No need to be here, for the crowns of the trees below closed beneath our feet save for the round hole into blackness through which we had climbed to this wonderful platform. For a moment or so I looked out over the glory of it all, undulating up into the mountains, and here and there across the sea of trees, crowns were in full and glorious blossom, yellow and gold, some lilac, some creamy white and thus on and up through declivities and slopes where I saw white water streaked to the fan-shaped quarter bowl of Sant'Simon, and beyond it shadowed into mauve and blue beneath the gathering cumulus that would be our P.M. rainstorm, the long lump of el Cerro de la Muerte.

I snapped off the harness, stepped out of it. It clattered to the metal floor which was ridged for footholds, and then it snaked off as the cable started again and took if off down into the subarboreal shades through which it had taken me. Five minutes or so before fatty would be up here too. I turned the other way, hoping to see the ocean but a range of low hills lay between us and it, yet there was a distant sort of whitish haze that hung above and beyond, the haze you get above fine-sanded beaches pounded by ceaseless surf.

So now I took in in more detail the canny treehouse we had arrived at. As said, I think it was made of riveted or bolted aluminum specially cast, the floor about sixteen feet square with the trunk of the tree coming up through the middle at that point with a diameter of perhaps six feet. A sloping roof came down to open sides, railed with benches. Below the benches the sides were solid so nothing could roll accidentally off, not even where a gap took the place of the bench, the point where the cradle had landed me.

There was a trap in the floor. I lifted it and a short ladder dropped six feet to another smaller platform from which two more sets of lines looped horizontally away just above the crowns of the lower trees. And all around us these great swathes of yellow blossom filling the air with almondy sweetness, not unlike the mimosa scent that drifts across your island, Don Jesús. And always too there was a gently rocking motion, not really like a boat on a swell because it was, I realised, circular. It made me a touch dizzy at first but was soon, in that calm, late-morning air, forgotten.

The line whirred on and I swear I smelled him before he arrived, the thinning gingery hair round a balding patch rising greenly cadaverous through the shades till the sunlight hit it. He hooked his legs over the low wall, straightened and carefully placed on the floor a square plastic red and white coolsack.

"Din-dins," he said and grinned, his round glasses flashing in the splashy sun. Then he broke the harness, clipped it to the rail, and threw a switch. Down below the hum of the generator died.

At this point Zena suddenly bellowed—got his number at last I thought. I wriggled the straps down, sat down, slung her and the Snugli across my knees, unzipped her, extracted her, pulled back my dress and plugged in. She shut up.

"Excuse me," I said.

He grinned again. More a leer. "Be my guest. Can you drink or eat at the same time?"

"Drink, certainly."

He unzipped the coolsack, firked about in it, came up with a long, tall plastic beaker with a cap which he unscrewed. He handed it to me. Beaded bubbles winking on the brim and even a cube of ice. It was deliciously cold, sort of crushed strawberry in colour, and was about half rum, good rum. The rest tropical fruits, but mostly passion fruit.

He stayed kneeling a couple of yards away, still leering.

"Okay?"

"Fine."

"Will she sleep after that?"

"If I mix up her dinner, she eats it, and I change her, then make her comfortable or carry her."

He nodded, the grin fixed still.

"While you do all that we'll have a couple more drinks, some food, and then when she's gone off, we'll fuck."

"We will?"

"Sure Sheba. That's what we're up here for."

"Darwin, suppose I say no."

Out of that sack he had lifted four or five plastic containers and taken the lids off. Chicken pieces. *Palmitos* salad. Crispbread, and yes, caviar. Now he took out a short-barrelled Smith and Wesson .38, and put it on the bench beside him.

"Sheba! How could you?"

This man, I thought, is mad. He spooned caviar onto crisp-bread, handed it to me.

"Virgin sturgeon needs no urgin'!"

Zena came off, looked round. I put her on the floor, sitting up. The nipple had just been to quiet her, not a proper drink. The tree rocked a little and she swayed with it, looked as if she might keel over, so I caught her.

"Look. You'll have to hold her while I mix up her dinner."

I'm sure he looked more put out by this suggestion than I had at his of rape. Zena began to cry again. Now any mother knows that a baby under one crying is the most unbearable noise in the world. She knows because she finds it so herself, but she knows it too because of the way other people react. In a crowded shop you want attention, stick a pin in your baby and management itself will give you prompt attention to get you and the screaming baby away before the shop empties.

"If I don't hold her, you can't mix up her feed, and she goes on crying?" he shouted.

"That's right."

He took off his specs, wiped them on his shirt-tail, put them back on, reached for her, then drew back. She's not dirty, I thought. But what was bothering him was his gun. Which I might grab for while he held the baby. He put it back in the coolsack in the far corner of the platform on the other side of the trunk, as far from me as possible.

"You try to get it, and I'll chuck her over," he said.

I gave him one of my looks. He took her as if she was a thin glass bubble filled with vitriol, but she stopped crying and made a grab for his specs.

Moving slowly, believe me I was in no hurry, considering a fate worse than a badly stubbed toe awaited me, I dug out the Greenfinger 5, the flask, and Zena's red eating bowl, and began to mix up.

"Nothing but the best for baby," said Darwin, and signed his death warrant.

Greenfinger with the "I" a corncob set over a clenched fist. "Who makes two ears of corn, two blades of grass grow where one grew before deserves the lasting gratitude of all mankind," on the packet. Wrong, I thought. What Swift actually said was ". . . does more essential service to his country than the whole race of politicians put together." AFI emblazoned on the 'copter, and the "I" a corncob. I scanned the small print. Greenfinger Inc. is a member of Associated Foods International. Darwin was boss of Bullburger Costaricense, SA. And Bullburger, the fastest fast-food in the West, is also part of AFI.

The whole scenario fell into place. Maybe I have the odd detail a touch wrong. Sure as hell I have the gist of it. Adding up all I knew—from Trev Ev, from Rosa, from what I'd seen and heard in Sant'Simon, this was it: *Zea diploperennis talamanca* is a plant AFI wants to obliterate or own. Why? Because in ways I'm not expert to analyse it threatens their whole maize operation. Look at it this way. Supposing a strain of perennial maize is developed that increases the productivity per hectare of small-holdings and co-operatives from China to Peru by ten to fifty per cent, Trev's figure, the world corn market will be blown apart.

Maybe that's not all. Manuel at Sant'Simon—and I glanced out of our eyrie across the rolling forest to that fan-shaped space in the *cordillera*—saw more to it than that. Chop that percentage off the price of staple corn and fodder and the knock-on effect he spoke of could take place. When the poor of the world are allowed to feed themselves they will be able to jack up the price of their cash crops, reduce production and put the rich over a barrel—just like the OPEC countries did.

So no wonder Ignacio Morena got shot to pieces, no wonder now Sant'Simon has to go and the *páramo* where Zdt grows will go too. And all of us who know. Rosa. Trev Ev. And now poor Kit and me too, but not until we have led them to Trev's bivouac where his rough notes, diaries and so on might still be a threat. Kit will take them there because he knows they've got me. I'll take them there because I know they've got Kit.

And Darwin? He must be the mastermind of the Ticoland end of the operation. So what was he playing at now? Was he really such a monster that he would get me to give him a fuck, then lead him to Trev's bivouac, then murder me? And Zena? Or did he have something else in mind?

Such were my thoughts, clearer as I lay them out here but basically the same, as I stirred the shit together and began to push it into Zena's mouth. Silly bitch. She loves it. Why not? Good quality product, Greenfinger 5. Darwin still held her on his knee as if she were a stick of sweating gelignite.

"Those lines out from this tree," I said, more to keep the tempo calm and slow than out of much interest at that point, "what's with them?"

"Our skilled ensemble of acrobatic researchers from Milton University, Iowa, get into harnesses like the one you and I just used and swing themselves out. When they reach the point they want they drop into the canopy below. The thing is, you see, it's a triangle. From this tree at the right angle to that Monkey Pot and that Almendro, and the line between the Almendro and the Monkey Pot, makes the hypotenuse. The line the researcher hangs from is attached to that hypotenuse, so by having a crank turned on the Monkey Pot tree its end can be shifted towards the Almendro or back again. That way every inch within the triangle can be covered."

"Why have they left it all up?"

"Cheaper to come back next season and repair any storm damage than ship the whole thing out and back in. Next year, if we give them the dough, they'll set up three more triangles and cover a complete circle. That's the second time you've dropped that shit on my trousers."

"Darwin. I reckon I've rumbled you."

"You do?"

"I reckon, when Kit and I have shown you Everton's hideaway you'll rub us all out. Off us."

He looked pained. "Rub you out? Off you? We're not gangsters, you know. We're a very big organisation."

"Like the Mafia. Come on. You're fucking gangsters."

He continued to looked pained. "Listen Sheba. I don't want to kill you. I don't even want to rape you. That gun's a joke."

"It's only a joke if it's made of plastic. And then it's a bad joke."

"It's real. It's a joke if you think I'll rape you with it."

"You're joking if you think you can."

"Shit, Sheba. Shut up and listen. Has she finished?" He handed her to me. I began to make with the wet wipes, the dry wipes, the disposables. Disposables? Where in an aluminum tree house one hundred and odd feet above the ground do you dispose of disposables and Zena's nicely shaped ball of biodegradable? Do you know, I screwed it all up in a plastic bag, twisted a tag on it, took it back to San José, put it in the trashcan, so the garbage men could truck it out into the forest and dump it. Ironic! I digress. Sorry.

Meanwhile, hands on fat knees he did his owlish bit. Solomon the Wise.

"Look out over that jungle, Sheba. What do you see?"

I felt embarrassed, but I said it. "Paradise."

"Sheba, you're wrong. It's warfare. Total warfare."

"You're crazy."

"Everything out there is fighting everything else. Trees pushing and shoving for the sun, the ones that don't make it dropping back onto the floor where they rot and their nutrients feed the ones that do. The lianas and the epiphytes fight each other to destroy the trees they live off. I've seen a pillar of lianas and epiphytes, and the tree they'd been on had died in the middle, dropped to wet sawdust, and the winners still stood, already tagging into neighbouring trees they were getting their suckers into. It's the same the whole way through. Insect against insect, birds against insects, snakes against the little birds, the big birds against the snakes, the rodents eat the mushrooms, the monkeys strip their favourite trees of leaves, the eagles get the baby monkeys, and the puma goes for the big ones. And the sex is the same. The males fight each other and the females offer their asses to the winners, whether they're quetzals or jaguars. Losers lose, winners take all, and what I'm getting round to is this. Carter, ITCO, UNAFO, Sant'Simon, they're losers. At best they get the leavings, what we don't want, but let them make a play for something we do want and it's the boot, the knife, the gun, the banks, the army, the police, the politicos, the churches, we own them all. We don't lose. Ever. It's a law of nature. Like what goes on out there."

He reached for his tall plastic beaker and drank. From the larger container in the coolsack he topped it up again. That, I thought, should make him more than half-way pissed. I was a touch tipsy on half a beaker. He picked up a chicken breast and ate half, then a hard-boiled egg.

"The mother and child reunion is only a moment away." He ate them together. I toyed with caviar on crispbread. It was not doing a lot for me. Maybe that arch-snob Shakespeare was right. Or maybe I just wasn't in the mood to eat unborn children. A small flight of orange-chinned parakeets flashed by below, broke into a short glide and settled chattering in a tree with long woody pods just below us.

"Now Sheba, you're no loser. You're a winner. As of now we have to get you onto the right side. You walk tall. You walk in beauty like the night. I can make you a star. . . ."

"You said that before."

"You name it, I can give it you. Money—no problem. Can

you guess what AFI pay me to run the Tico end of their operation? What I pick up in kickbacks, perks, share-options? Come live with me and Ossie Clark will take your measurements himself. I can set you up, you can be your own boss. You'd be great. You could handle a bank. I could get you into real estate, right here. It's booming. The real fat cats don't want Miami any more. They're building properties right here that make the best Miami condominiums look like tenements. Travel. On your own if you like. In style. Just come back to Daddy when Daddy feels lonely.

"You sing. You dance. You speak languages. I could get you into movies. They're looking for a big black star right now. Someone with your grace, height, style. . . . Shit, Sheba. You know I can do this. What can Carter do? Sure, he can fuck. I'll bet he can't fuck like I can fuck. And there's only one way you can find out. What else can he do? He's even fucked up his job here stirring us all up over Sant'Simon. He's a loser. A born loser. Be a winner. Join the club. Life membership here on offer now."

Don Jesús, do I have to say I was tempted? When you start life ten to a room the world of glitz looks good. I got out through middle-class foster-parents and playing the education system. Big deal. But not matching up to childhood visions of glamour. And Darwin could deliver. Sure he could. Not for nothing did he run the Tico beef industry. I stood up, rocking my baby very gently and cooing at her and I looked out over forest towards the silver haze above where the ocean lay. A breeze was coming off of it now, and six miles away as it was I felt I could smell the sea amongst all the fragrances coming up off the hot wet forest.

A large hawk came by riding on the breeze so his wings had only to give the laziest of flaps every now and then to see him home. He flew very close, and just below us, dark brown back, long black and white barred tail. He had in his talons a thin snake, almost a yard long. Its body was almost evenly divided between black and coral pink hoops. No head. Hawk had left the poisonous head behind.

I smelt rum and garlic, felt the heat of his stomach pressing into the small of my back, his fat hands sliding down my skirt into the hollows between my tummy and pelvic bones. He was firm, but not rough.

"Guaco. *Herpetotheres cachinnas*. Laughing snake-eater. The snake is a Coralillo, *Micrurus nigrocinctus*. Very poisonous."

"No longer. Guaco has bitten his head off and left it behind."

"They always do. Now watch."

Guaco soared a little, you could see how only a slight curling of his primaries achieved this, and called, "How, how, how, how, how, how," and brought himself round in a lazy semicircle towards a tree that lay between us and the Almendro. It stood just inside the lines and I guessed had been pollarded to allow them to move across it. The guacos, should I not say guacas, had built their next in a large hole left by a fallen limb, just a few feet above the nearest crown. We could see it all quite well. It was less than eighty feet away.

Guaco landed on the stub of a branch just below the hole, taking the snake in his beak as he landed, and now Guaca appeared, and she took the snake from him with her beak, clamped it under her right talon and snapped at the head end.

"Checking out Daddy's done a good job on the poisonous bit." His splayed finger ends began to ravel up my dress, simultaneously scrabbling in the pelvic grooves on either side of my fanny. He knew what he was doing.

Guaca, satisfied that Coralillo was not about to up and fang her, held it on her perch, lifted her head and began to call, "How, how, how, how, how, wac, wac, wac, wac," and Guaco joined in in the bass with, "Wah-co, wah-co, wah-co, wah-co." It was really quite a racket, and went on for two or three minutes, maybe more.

Darwin's fingers remained an inch or so away, just on the edge of my swatch, very gently kneading, and still outside my bikini-style knickers. I looked down and of course copped full-beam headlights from Zena's dark blue eyes, touched with violet. With her coffee skin and those eyes all she has to do is keep her figure. Meanwhile Darwin's prick was getting spongy, I could feel it between my bum-cheeks.

Guaca now did something that looked almost as obscene. She held the headless neck in her bill, kept the tail anchored under her left talons, and began to knead what lay between with those on the right. The headless body began to writhe, and only when it was really going again did she suddenly dodge into the hole, her nest, and filled herself and her chick with good meat. Proper the chick should feel the dead snake writhe. How else would it know what to swoop on when it reached puberty?

"Nature red in tooth and claw."

"Can't you manage to say anything without plundering the obvious?"

His fingers tightened a little, then began to move the half inch down to get under the hem of the crotch of my knickers. The warmth and pressure behind me got heavier. Fine. He was rushing himself.

"Anyway, she's just feeding her baby. That's all. And so is he. He could have eaten that snake and buggered off. And all that snake was to him and to her was something wriggly and very edible. They didn't . . ."

Poor Darwin began to breathe rather heavily. Maybe he'll come, I thought, and we can all relax. I looked at Zena. She was relaxing already. Missed most of her morning nap. Headlamps dipping, long black lashes drooping. The treehouse suddenly swung down a little and then rose, and up over Sant'Simon and into the fastnesses of el Cerro de la Muerte thunder distantly crackled. It was very black up there now, though still pristine blue above us. Suddenly I was rather frightened, wanted to get it over, get down. Fatty lurched away from me as the newly gusty wind gave another push. Cables and pulleys squealed. Rope hissed. But still really it was nothing, nothing to what was to come.

He stood back from me, round, red face flushed, brown shirt plastered over his boobs. He pushed his specs back.

"Okay, Sheba. Do you join the club, or don't you?"

"Fine, I join the club," I said. The tree rocked again. "What do I have to do?"

He stood back feet splayed.

"Put the baby down. She's asleep isn't she?"

"Quiet, anyway."

"Put her down."

I spread out the Snugli, laid her on it. She rubbed her eyes, grinned, stuck her fist in her mouth.

"Now what?"

He lurched towards me. Already I was kneeling above Zena. He began to pull down the zip of his jeans.

A Catholic would say he now achieved an act of grace. If that's right, and I don't for one second believe it, then maybe he's gotten himself to Purgatory after all. The tree rocked again, throwing him off balance forward. To regain balance his left foot searched for the floor and *refused to tread on Zena*. Maybe bonding occurred while he held her. As it came down, shod in a cleated Pro-Ked, it hesitated just above her face. I caught it, and pushed, gave him the bunk-up he needed to go over the low parapet, and drop. Caught him by the left leg and threw him down the stairs.

26

It was a long way down. He didn't scream *a-a-a-a-a-ah* like they do in films, but I could hear branches smashing for several seconds. Then the squawk of the toucans, their siesta disturbed again. I had better, I thought, get down and see how he is. But it took more than a minute or two to get Zena into the Snugli, and the Snugli onto my back. My hands shook. All of me really, all shook. And then I didn't know how to work the goddamn lift. He'd turned the generator off from up here. Perhaps it would restart too. There was a junction box and three large buttons, but I was frightened of it. Supposing I got it wrong and somehow lost the harness, or couldn't control the speed so it dropped us down too quick?

I went down by steam, by my own weight and manipulation of the jumars, and it took a bit of time to get the hang of it, so even going down it was ten minutes before I reached terra firma. On the way I saw mother sloth was twenty feet lower now, just dropping into the top layer of the lower canopy. They go all the way down, once every four days or so for a piss and a shit, and then go back up again.

Darwin wasn't going back up again. Whatever damage he'd suffered on the way down was nothing to the crack he took as he hit the hard edge of one of the blade buttresses six feet above the ground. The awful thing was he had stuck on it, his belt or something, legs and torso hanging straight down, upper back, arms, head, at right angles, cantilevered out over the floor. He was broken. And dead. Head flung back, glasses gone, eyes open, insects already skirmishing round them. I was sick. First time I had real caviar, and I was sick.

I tried to pull myself together. My watch, a neat flat gold Seiko Kit gave me, showed right on one o'clock. I had Zena's life-support system, her Mothercare bag, but I'd forgotten Darwin's gun.   Should I go back up?   I hadn't that sort of time or strength to spare.   I had to be at Everton's bivouac before half-past three, well before, if I was going to do anything for Kit.   Which way was the river?   Three trails led out into the forest—one of them back to the landing square for the 'copters, so not that one.   Eeny, meeny, miney, mo, catch a nigger girl by the toe.   I picked the right one.   After five minutes I could hear water.   Darwin had said there was a trail, and there was.

The river was much wider here than up by where Trev Ev's bivouac was, wider, deeper, slower, and the edge less rocky.   But the screen on the bank was very thick and dense indeed, and the trail actually stayed inside the screen where there was less ground vegetation, so the way was, to begin with, quite easy, and marked by machete blazes on the trees.   Everton himself maybe did them or maybe the Sant'Simon men in the days when they came down to stun-bomb for fish or hunt the forest deer.   Anyway it was quite easy, and mostly squashy under foot so not too difficult— it's amazing how quickly feet readapt to going bare so long as you don't put a thorn through them, or stub your toes again.   It was hot of course and humid, but not too many insects of the winged sort—as said, these mostly live in the canopy itself.   Mercifully Zena slept, I could feel her go limp as she dropped into a neat little ball inside her double pouch.

We went on for a hour much like that, and my mind had time to cope with what had gone before.   Perhaps it was trying not to be over-anxious about what was to come.

I have to say I felt sort of angry with Darwin.   Have you noticed how we all do that?   Work up an anger with anyone who has made us feel guilty.   Reason told me I had no need to feel guilty about Darwin.   He was a crazy shit.   A murderous fat bastard.   But I didn't want to have had to do that to anyone.

He was wrong too, I told myself, as I stumbled and loped through the shady, eerie, creaking forest.   For a time I could hear wind rushing through the highest crowns above, a sound like a hundred distant trains, then the rain came, but down here it fell in a fine, warm, hazy shower, which, with my plunging feet, released new odours of fungi and decay.

Wrong.   Nature in the Middle Ages was a hierarchy, a chain of being, a pyramid from the many at the base to the One at the top.   A description that mirrored the society that described it.

For the first industrialists and the Age of Reason it was a machine, an engine, a thing of many distinct parts held together by checks and balances like the American Constitution, and expected to work like a clock or a factory. For Charles Darwin Junior, for AFI Nature is a state of War, of endless ruthless competition between the strong, and repression and exploitation of the weak by the strong. But what is she really? An endlessly, incomprehensibly complex web of interactions, of dependencies in which the whole is infinitely greater than the sum of the parts, and where no parts are intrinsically more important than any of the others. Is that really what she is? Or is that Nature the way a socialist society might want to see her?

Deep thoughts, and, of course, because of them, I lost the way. The trail touched the edge of a pool which looked a bit like the one where Scarface was getting his act together to rape me, just before Trev Ev took charge, and I scouted about to find the indications he'd told us—a big palm, find a gully, go round the top and so on. But I'd forgotten he'd said there were big waterfalls below there that took you down through a gorge. So, I found a big palm and messed about for half an hour, then gave up. Tearfully I considered the possibilities.

"They"—whoever they were—were bringing Kit to Trev's hideaway. They had to be coming from the top, from the Inter-American Highway, el Cerro de la Muerte, Sant'Simon. So even if I couldn't find Trev's hideaway my chance of running into Kit and doing something to save him depended on going on and up, which I now continued to do.

Quite soon we came to said waterfalls and gorge, and a very tricky bit of a climb up its side I had of it. Still, it's always better going up that sort of terrain than down. Little did I know. Huge rocks piled on top of each other, horrendously steep scree in places, and in others vegetation crowding in while the waterfall crashed from step to step and pool to pool, through a hundred metres or more. Birds swept past the columns of water, dragonflies scouted over the pools, sweat poured off of me, and of course Zena began to stir. But we made it. At 3:10 precisely we really did stand on the rock where we had been when Scarface intervened. And now of course I recognised it entirely. How could I ever have mistaken that pool lower down for the same one? Recognised it, yet it was different. With the rain the river had risen, the rock from which I had dived was almost completely submerged. The edge where Scarface had crossed was now knee-deep in rushing, boiling water. But I was on the right side of the river, no problem. I would have liked to rest. I was bushed. The last climb had taken it out of me. But my watch said 3:11 and still we had to find the bivouac. Zena was fed up of this and her whimpers became more serious. I found the palm, the top of the gulley, the fallen Sotacaballo, and there we were. 3:23 P.M.

It was unchanged. Why should it be otherwise? He'd only been gone a couple of nights and he'd set it up neatly, pegged down the thatch of his low roof, tied down the mosquito net all round—but for its whiteness you could have walked past it ten yards away and not seen it. Under the net it was all there—the hammock, the cooking utensils, kettle, tins. I could of done with a cup of his fancy tea. His Walkman and Beethoven tapes. His notes. The notes and the plant presses would be what they were after.

All there, including the guns. I crouched down at the head end of the hammock feeling in the gloom for the large oilcloth-wrapped bundle. It was really almost dark in there, for the sky was now deeply overcast and no sunflakes or sunbeams arrived to spread that diffused, subaqueous light. The snake was even more frightened than I. It shot over my arm, dry and silky, me of course stumbling back and thrashing so it shot off to land on the ground a yard or so away. It was small, prettily patterned, with a bright red underbelly and it moved off out of sight between the roots of a tree like curly lightning. This of course set Zena off, she broke into a very serious loud howl. Only one way to stop that. But first I grabbed the bundle—it was heavier than I expected, and backed off, but as I did it unwrapped itself and the shotgun thudded out.

You can't think straight when a baby is screaming like that. I held on to the Heckler and Koch, and scrambled away twenty yards or so to a spot where branches had fallen, let in light, and there was a fair patch of undergrowth, ferns and saplings. And Lord knew what further snakes and other creepy-crawlies. Actually three large rat-like creatures, as big as small dogs or piglets, but with white blotches down their backs, went scuttling and loping away, almost as quickly as the snake had done. Right in the middle of this thicket I found their nest, a hollow of pressed leaves with some hairs and fur just big enough for me to crouch in. I unslung Zena and got her to the nipple. This time I didn't take her out of the Snugli—she wasn't smelly, and anyway I was short of time. I just got the lot off my back.

She shut up of course, straightaway, and with my free hand I finished unwrapping the Heckler and Koch. It was a dinky evil little thing, smaller than I remembered, not much more than eighteen inches long, with a pistol grip, and another roughened section just behind the muzzle. I could see your right hand would grip the pistol butt, and your left the other bit. I turned it over and found a catch. Three settings—*S*, *E*, and *F*. I guessed *sicher* for safe; *ein* for one or single shot; and *fährt* perhaps for go, for automatic fire. I switched it to *F*, then switched it back. Just testing.

I hefted it about for a minute or so, getting the feel of it—it weighed maybe five pounds, perhaps six. Heavy for its size—a solid, no nonsense affair. I hate to say it, but I felt better having it.

Then I heard them. In the stillness of the forest, only the drip of rain from leaves, the distant chortle of the river, I heard them from quite a distance, maybe almost as far as the river itself. Three pairs of boots in the deep wet litter, branches and twigs snapping. Voices. I put down the gun, eased Zena off the nipple and she looked at me as if I'd farted in church but mercifully did not start a new yell. But I knew she would if I wasn't careful, if I didn't do the right thing. The right thing was to carry her on my front so I could whisper to her and tell her lovings, give her a finger to suck, or a twig to play with. That meant doing the crossover with the straps and getting my head through, and all without setting her off. I managed, forcing myself to go slow and nice and easy and baby-talking *sotto voce* all the time.

They were in sight by the time I had finished, walking round the rim of the gully, a hundred yards away, in single file, three of them. In the middle, Kit. I longed to cry out. He looked bad, ashen under his freckles. Three fingers of his left hand were roughly bandaged together; there was blood on his shirt and trousers, dry, not fresh. My poor, poor Kit. What had they done to him?

The man in front I knew, knew too well by now, it was Scarface himself. The man behind I did not know yet. In the next

211

few hours I got to know him well. Oh yes. He wasn't tall, but he was stocky, very well built. Like Scarface he was in paramilitary fatigues, jungle boots, but wore a woolen hat, dark green, instead of the Aussie-type bushwhacker thing Scarface had. Both had small haversacks on their backs. Neither seemed to be armed.

I could hear Kit.

"Not far now. Bear left a little. Follow the line of that fallen tree." He sounded weary, soul-weary.

They headed where the Sotacaballo pointed, passed ten yards from our thicket, and came thus to the bivouac. Have I said it was in a slight hollow? They were all now just a little below me: Kit and the stocky man—who, I may as well now admit, was Sergeant James "Dusty" Miller, ex-SAS, though of course I knew none of that then—with their backs to me, and Scarface beyond firking about in Trev's bivouac.

He said, "This is it all right. Funny thing."

Miller said, "What"

Scarface raised the short-barrelled shotgun.

"This was just lying here. As if it had been dropped."

"Not by Everton."

"No. Not by Everton." Short laugh. "Nothing else disturbed."

"There are footprints," said Miller.

"Where?"

"All round you."

Shit a fucking brick, I thought, and moved from *S* to *F*.

Miller crouched. "Bare feet. Very fresh. Only one person. Indian?"

"There aren't any Indians. A few in the south on the Panama border. None round here."

Scarface firked around a bit more. I knew what he was looking for. I held it in my hands. The, *his* Heckler and Koch should have been with the shotgun, but it had gone. The footprints were fresh. It might, right now, be pointing at him from the forest. It was. But he couldn't say so, couldn't tell the whole story of how he had lost it.

Zena began to cry. Just a whimper. A starter. I made tiny noises, and gave her a finger to suck. She twisted her head away in pained disgust—a very irritating little gesture she's developed. If she wants to communicate so perfectly she should learn to speak.

212

Then she lifted her head and said very loudly and clearly, "Di, dah, di, dah, dah, dah, dah."

"What the hell's that?" said Miller. Scarface said something in Kraut. They were all facing our way now. Scarface had the shotgun. There was nothing else for it. I let her go on doing it.

"Di, dah, di, dah, dah, dah, dah, dah. Aaah!"

It worked. It had to.

Kit, looking like a saint to whom God has just spoken personally, said, "A bird?"

For ten seconds they remained like that, then the muzzle of the shotgun dropped, and Scarface turned back to the bivouac. Miller, though, remained very alert, very poised.

"Where's the other man then?" he asked, speaking to Scarface. He had a slight accent I now realised was Dorset or West Hampshire. I know because like Hume University, Christbourne, is on that border. "The man you said would meet us here."

Kit spoke now. Quite loud and clear. Louder and clearer than he needed. "Why should he come? The only reason for him to come was so my wife could lead him here. You know, and he knows my boss has told me to bring you here. There's no need for him to be here. Or *her*." The last word said with a lot of emphasis. He knew I was there. He'd recognised Zena's voice. He was trying to tell me to lie low. "Why don't you take what you came for and go?"

No one answered. Somewhere a bird called, "Trrr, trrr, trrah."

"Di, dah, aah," said Zena. They paid no attention.

Scarface came up beside them. "I've got everything we were told to get." They turned again, had their backs to us. He was carrying the notes, the diary. The shotgun swung from a webbing strap against his thigh. He turned, went back, came up with an armful of pressed specimens.

"We're to burn these," he said.

"Then what?" asked Miller.

"Kill Carter."

Miller took a couple of paces, one way, then the other. A sentry. I could see him clearly now. Older than I had thought, grey eyes close together, small nose, big nostrils, thin lips, very thin grey moustache. Skin a touch blotched, otherwise he looked very fit.

"Kill him first," he said. "Now."

"Why?"

"You've told him. What do you think he's going to do? Stand around and wait for it?"

Scarface dropped the pressed specimens, swung the shotgun round. Miller backed off sharpish.

I stood up where I was, Zena swinging in front of me, pointed the Heckler and Koch as if it was, were an extra finger straight at Scarface's diaphragm, and squeezed. No. I did not shut my eyes. Something warned me not to do that.

Boom, boom, boom, boom, boom, boom, boom, boom.

I wanted it to go on for ever. The slugs tore him apart, sent him thrashing backwards, then spinning away to crash into the bivouac. But it stopped, would not go on.

I turned. Miller had made a grab for Kit, held my husband now in front of him, with one forearm tucked up under his chin. Zena was screaming. The fucking gun was empty, useless.

Miller looked at me, over Kit's shoulder. We were thirty feet away from each other. That's all. I saw the fingers of his other hand come up over the crown of Kit's head. Kit smiled at me. I think. Then Miller did it. He pushed Kit's head forward and screwed it at the same time.

Don Jesús. He was dead. And I was running. I had a ten-yard start and a baby to save as well as myself. There was really no point in staying. Really not. Maybe your *juez*, your judge is going to say I should of, is going to say this is indeed evidence that she did not love her husband. But he was dead. Like Rosa. Like Everton. Who risks all for the dead? I ran. Jesus, did I run!

27

As already said you know I am athletic and fit and a sprinter.
So I sprinted. As well as I could over that ground and cradling
Zena in the Snugli with my left arm while my right protected my
face against whatever the jung . . . ooops! forest threw at me. I
headed back down the way I knew till I came to the river, about
three hundred yards, which is about my limit full out. I sat on
a rock, hauled in breath, began to slap my calves, kept peering
into the dark I'd come through, mercifully speckled darkness, the
sun had come through again, the first storm now banging away
over the coast I reckon, mercifully because I caught a glimpse of
him when he was still sixty yards off.

You know, I'd run like hell, most of the time out of his sight,
and so he was *tracking* me, and yet was only maybe half a minute
behind me. Less. He was jogging briskly, looked up, saw me,
and of course accelerated.

I took off. Had to. Didn't stop to think consciously, but I was
right, I headed downhill. Right because I could sprint longer
downhill, get the distance between us greater. Right because I
knew the track and he did not, whereas uphill we would have
been covering the ground he'd just come down. Right because
if I kept going and kept going at the bottom of the hill a short-
nosed Smith and Wesson .38 waited for me in Darwin's coolsack
on the top of a forest giant.

But in bare feet it was murder. At least to begin with, down
those waterfalls, patches of scree, through the gorge. Coming up
my toes had been a help, searching out footholds, getting a grip
in the trickier places. Going down in a big hurry they got in the
way, for I reckoned often I could leap and jump, and then I stubbed
them on some projection or other, and couldn't even stop to see
if I was bleeding or not. Trouble was this stretch, though I think
it gave me some advantage, gave me no time to think. And

thought was needed if I was going to come out on top.

I thought well enough to get into a thicket at the bottom of the last waterfall that exited the river out of the gorge. I needed the rest. I needed to know how Miller was doing. We had a long way to go yet and I needed to know how he rated. I needed to reassure Zena that though the world had turned into a roller-coaster, it was still a world with nipples. I picked my spot well. From it I could see two hundred yards of the trail I had come down, and then the waterfall which was especially beautiful. I could see nothing above its edge but sky. Those weeds Trev studied, like naiad's hair, streamed in the water that cascaded over it. The sun had now gotten behind us so there was a rain-bow in the spray. Dragonflies, butterflies and birds dodged each other through it.

Miller was committed to my tracks until he could see me, and I made sure he couldn't. We kept very still and very quiet. One of those Riverside Wrens Trev had shown us perched within six feet and never saw us. Zena, worn out by it all, took a nap.

But not for long. Again far sooner than I would have thought possible there the mother-fucker was—compact, solid, dark against the sky. He paused for a moment silhouetted against clouds black and nasty that were thickening up again. His round head with the woolly hat still on was dropped over his chest as if contem-plating the mysteries of the universe. Or the splashes, drops of blood, occasional footprints, and torn vegetation we'd left behind us. Then he was off again, leaping down the boulders in his jungle boots.

You know Don Jesús, the newspapers here in Tenerife have filled in what Miller was: SAS jungle-trained who got to Indo-nesia pickets in Borneo no one else could get within shooting distance of. Of course I did not know that then, but I could see he was good. I find it difficult not to respect skill used to what-ever evil ends. Right then, respect was what the situation de-manded.

Okay, so I could sprint and rest, but he could go on for ever. Okay, so I could no way be sure that whatever I did in the way of concealment or deception would throw him off or even delay him. Okay, so . . . And then thanks to a sudden patch of sun another factor was revealed to me. He was coming at me with his bare hands. No shotgun. Why not? Perhaps because Trev's shotgun had revealed itself to Miller's professional eye as useless. Perhaps because its range was short anyway and if he was going to get that close to me, he'd use his hands. He could use his hands. Poor Kit, Poor, poor Kit.

I let him get to thirty yards and then I was off again, happy now I was on the flat, more or less, running through the forest litter which was much like running through well-composted horse shit, rather than dropping down boulders and scree, and happy that I knew where I was going and he did not. Of course this meant breaking cover, but I didn't mind. I wanted him to know I knew he was there, wanted him to know I was in charge. In fact to prove it I turned on him and jerked my clenched fist at him. As rudely as I could.

Nearly served me right. About ten minutes later I passed under a Kapok tree that had self-pruned a limb and ran a fucking great thorn into the ball of my foot behind my right big toe. How do I know it was a Kapok? Because Trev told us it's the only big one in those parts with both buttresses and thorns. It hurt like hell and I bled like a pig when I yanked it out. I nearly fainted at the sight, and worse still suffered a spasm of despair. How the fuck was I going to get away with this? I was already pretty well bushed and hungry too, that very nasty deep hunger that says feed me, or I stop. I fed. Off of the last soggy biscuits in Zena's life-support system.

Hardly had I swallowed the last crumbs than here comes Miller. And this time I was lucky to see him some way off, since I didn't plan it, maybe two hundred yards again, and not moving too fast. Two hundred yards is a long distance to see someone over in rain forest, but we were in the lowland now where the trees are more widely spaced, the cut-off of sunlight more complete, so not much undergrowth. And, with the exhaustion, weakness, bleeding, and pain I made a grave error.

I reckoned he'd not seen me. I reckoned I could keep him in sight while he couldn't see me, and so move at his speed, slower than mine, and that would be a heavenly relief. Then, when I felt better, I'd make a sprint and get right away.

The bastard sussed me out. I think he must of. After five minutes when I turned to check for maybe the fifth time I found him closer than before but the clever sod was facing obliquely the wrong way. He's spotted my turn before I got him in vision.

Grandmother's footsteps was the name of the game.

I turned again, and Jesus Christ, I couldn't see him anywhere. I really twigged then. Didn't bother to check him out, I just ran, and do you know he'd got so fucking near I heard him.

"Shit."

He said. And I heard his feet, his breath, thankfully heard them recede as I pounded on, on and away. Believe me Don Jesús at that moment I flew, and Zena was no burden. She it was and her precious life so nearly smashed, gave me wings.

But, of course, I didn't look too closely where I was going, didn't pick up the blazes on the trees like I had before, forgot for half a mile or more that the river should be heard if not seen on my left. I dropped Miller behind all right but got lost. I forced my breath to quieten, clamped Zena on to a nipple, and tried to work it out. It was hopeless. No sound of the river at all. Bird calls way up top, more of them now, then suddenly so it frightened me rigid, it really came without warning, a wailing screaming cacophony from almost directly above, and fragments of leaves drifting down through the gloom. Howler monkeys. A troupe of them, the males sounding off maybe because they'd spotted me, or Miller, or another troupe, or just heard the thunder rolling round el Cerro.

In fact the whole forest had been waking up for the last hour or so with the rain and the wind and the heat of the day lessening a little, but I had been too busy, and too newly widowed, to notice.

None of this was helping. Which way was the river was problem number one and how far behind was Miller was problem number two. Anxiety, exhaustion, despair hovered like evil angels at my shoulder, but something better—nothing mystical you understand, just my life-loving instincts—directed my attention to the forest floor.

There I discovered that I was not the only creature that left footprints but that I was on a narrow path, maybe only a foot across, that snaked away from me round trees and fallen limbs, in two directions. Deer. Small ones like British roe, so they'd be brockets I suppose. I knew as much because Hume University is like near the New Forest and the boyfriend before Kit used to take me there on nature walks which actually did take in the wild life as well as the Wild Life.

This deer path then connected two places of interest to them. Uphill verdure to their liking, in reach for browsing, downhill to the river for water. Trouble was—which was which. Just there it all undulated.

A butterfly flapped by, and I mean flapped not fluttered it was so big. It was iridescent blue, darker on the outer edges and on the underside it had a row of peacock eyes. You could see all this on account of its lazy gliding flight. Then three, four more. All heading one way and keeping over the deer path. Okay, Morpho, I said, I'll take your word for it, and I loped off after them, soon passed beneath them, but the deer tracks held up and led me on.

In no time I saw the glow of greens and yellows, smelt the flowers, saw the glow widen into the screen of dense thicket by the river and heard again its merry clatter above the rush of blood in my ears. A moment later we picked up a blazed tree.

We jogged smartly on a hundred yards, long enough to realise we had looped back and were now covering ground already covered, and I was just wondering where the fuck's Miller, went round a tree and there he was, two yards from me, not lying in wait, but having a pee. I suppose the sound of the river had masked my approach. The look he gave me was evil, deadly evil.

"Shit."

I said. And off we went again, with a bit more of a start than really I deserved, he having to shake his peg and zip up.

I realised now that if I was to get harnessed up and working those jumars out of his reach and up into the canopy I needed to get a better distance between us than I'd so far managed. How to do it? I worked out a strategy: he was a long-distance man, even a marathon man. That sort goes on for ever at a mean ten miles an hour. But make them sprint, like at the end of a race with a close competitive finish and that does for them. One big effort, so long as they think it'll be worth it, is what they're capable of, then they're cracked, broken.

So I gradually slowed, like it was me that was blown, and truth to say I nearly was, really blown, thresholds of pain I'd never dreamt of already crossed, especially after that thorn got me, and others now flashing like livid streaks of sheet lightning on the horizons of my mind. I let him come closer and closer so I could hear the splosh, splosh, splosh of his boots, the steady well-spaced pumping of his breath, and then I sensed him turning on the juice, splish-splosh-splish-splosh, and gasp-blow, gasp-blow, so I lengthened my stride and quickened too, and he stayed with me, and I turned it up a bit more, and then he fell back.

He'd rumbled me again, sensed what I was up to, dropped back to his steady jog, knowing I'd never get right away, knowing he'd wear me down in the end.

So we pounded or sloshed on. The forest grew darker, the warm haze of droplets began to drift down again, the wind rushed through the canopy, and suddenly thunder cracked, right above us. If Zena howled I couldn't hear her. Nor could I hear Miller, if he was near of not. All I could do was pick up the blazes on the trees as I passed. Whoever did them did them right. On both sides of the tree, big white splashes and more easily seen in the gloom than they had been when the sun shone.

I reckoned not far now so really pushed myself into a final sprint that must leave Death behind a bit, and sure as anything they took me right back to the camping place of the Milton University Canopy Research Team. And I didn't mess about when we got there. Yellow and red cables and the harness of the floor, ready to step into. I stepped in. Realised it wasn't on with Zena on my front, so switched her round to my back as quick as I could and fuck the fact she screamed up a storm to rival the one above. Did up the buckles, hoisted the top clamps as high above my head as they would go, put on pressure, they held, hoisted my feet, the bottom clamps gave, pressed down with my feet, the lower clamps gripped, and there we were, two feet off the ground. Two feet!

And where was Miller? Shaking the rain from my eyes I took a look around. He was a hundred paces off and moving well. Just time for two more yanks, and now my feet were six feet off the ground. I looked down. Wet streamed from his face, plastered his short hair, his woolly hat had gone. His barrel chest was heaving, in spite of the storm I could hear him gasping. Christ, I thought, he's as bushed as I am. Yet his hands reached for my ankles and caught them.

As they did I heaved again, breaking his grasp and getting clear beyond his reach. He tried to follow, rope-climbing, but even for a jungle-trained, ex-SAS killer the circs were too much. The cable was a running stream of water, a conduit for all the rain that fell on it and on the leaves and branches around it. Yet, thank not God but the dialectical historical materialist process, the jumars, made for wet mountain conditions, continued to work a treat.

After two sliding pulls he dropped off, and I went on and up. Slowly, laboriously. It was, after all else, a killing climb. The last, I thought, straw. But not the last. As we got into the under-storey between the lower and upper canopies, amongst the epiphytes, bromeliads and orchids, and the line began to sway more as draughts and buffets of warm wet wind banged by, I got the sense something was wrong. It just was not the same as that first ascent made, it seemed, an aeon ago, and of course I'd not seen Darwin's smashed body on the ridge of the buttress, in fact, I realised with a sudden shock, we were not going up the same tree at all. And one thing was for sure, whatever awaited us at the top, it was not going to include a short-nosed Smith and Wesson .38.

Of course it had to be one of the two other trees linked by looping but basically horizontal lines to the big tree, it had be the one on the corner of the actual camp, the Monkey Pot, in fact.

I climbed on. Nothing else for it. Sure as hell I was not going down. Presently we were pushing up through the canopy, and then, there we quite suddenly were: this was a lower emergent than the other, the platform actually set in the lower branches of the crown rather than suspended from them, and much smaller, made of wood, much more like a kid's treehouse.

The scene and the storm now were scarcely to be described. Huge purple clouds swept down the valley and hit new air currents streaming in over the low ridge of hills on the ocean side to create all round us, it seemed, and certainly not much higher, a terrible warring turbulence of thunder and lightning out of which cascaded torrents of driving rain. The crowns of the trees thrashed, leaves, blossoms, branches, limbs were whirled away or sometimes spiralled upwards as small cyclones formed and vanished and formed again. The Monkey Pot we were in heaved and swung and bowed and sprang back.

The lines that linked it to the other two giants in a roughly right-angled triangle, with the big tree with the tree station set at the right angle, all still held as far as I could see, four lines in each case. Here they came in at standing height above the plat-form which was well railed, and ran through small pulleys that in turn were anchored very firmly to the central limbs of the tree. From them harnesses hung, like the one I had come up in but clipped onto the rails so they didn't thrash about. There was also a small winch whose purpose then I wasn't too concerned to fathom out. My main aim was to keep more or less upright, ungarrotted by flailing ropes. I also wanted to bring some sort of comfort to Zena whose terrible screams penetrated the roar of the storm, but that meant getting out of the harness and moving her to my front again.

It could not be done. We would both be plucked from our perch and hurled into the crowns whose crests billowed and broke about our feet—yet it had to be. I spent time on it. Worked out ways of clipping myself into other fastenings in the treehouse before undoing the ones that held us safe, yet even so there were moments of dread and horror as when I actually dropped one loop of the Snugli, then the other, thought for a moment that I was in a dreadful tangle, then all came looser than I had thought possible or even intended, and my tiny mite still balled up in her sodden double pouches was held only by my fumbling arms while I struggled to get the crossed straps over my head and re-anchor her to me.

Oh the poor sweet—she had a scratch on one cheek that was taken up again on her plump little shoulder, and she was dirty and the dirt and blood streamed in the rain over her face, but it wasn't bad really, probably she was not as frightened as I, and certainly not as tired. Yet again I lengthened the straps on my shoulders and let her droop to where my poor sore boobs could yet give her some comfort and sustenance, though for how much longer if I did not get food and rest, who could say?

This all took time like I said. Imagine my horror then when I looked through the wrack at the tree that supported the main station and saw Miller there, large hands spread and braced on the metal rail, clothes sodden, hair plastered down, peering out at us from under the tortured swags of yellow blossom across the tossing chaos between. He turned away, crouched or knelt, then his legs dropped through the trap in the floor, onto the lower platform from which four lines looped to us. And there he put himself into one of those harnesses.

222

Oh Christ, I cried, the fucking bastard's *still* coming after us?

What could I do? Having just shed the harness to get Zena round to my front there was no way I was going to get it on again and drop down. Could I fight him off? He was coming now, already, swinging from a main pulley above his crotch with two stirrups supporting his feet, his cleated jungle boots led the way. A third attachment gave stability above his head and all he had to do was go hand over hand beneath the cable till he got here, feet first, and maybe now with the S and W .38 for all I knew.

There were big nuts hanging all over this tree we were in, not unlike coconuts, I could lob them at him. That was not good enough. I knew it. I had to do better than that.

Undo his cable and drop him. Fine. But it was anchored to a pulley attached to one of the lines that ran to the Almendro and that in turn was bound and anchored to our tree in what at first sight looked like an impenetrable tangle of tackle. Certainly no chance I'd get that lot undone in the two or three minutes I had before he'd be knocking at the door. He was swinging down the line to the manner born. Of course SAS-trained for Borneo all this was second nature. I didn't know that. Just amazed the bugger was fit enough to keep up with me, and steeped in enough jungle lore to track me, and now swing about the canopy like a fucking ape. . . . What was this guy? He like had me unnerved, I can tell you.

But I kept my head. What was all this *for*, all these ropes and machinery? Darwin had said so they could cover every inch of the canopy they liked within the triangle. How? I remembered the winch. It took me a moment to unlock the red handle which clipped back into the wheel itself. He was near the outer twigs of our tree, but going slower. On account of the slack he was going uphill. I saw no sign of the gun. He knew what he could do with his hands. I knew. Poor, poor Kit. I'll kill you you fucking bastard, I will, I know I will somehow, I cried.

I got that winch turning and miraculously it did what I hoped it would. Lots of slackish line had to be taken up, but then came the pressure, the strain, just as he was getting into the outer branches, maybe only twenty feet to go, then came the strain and I had to use all that was left in me to get the thing going, every last ounce.

I think his fat ass was snagging on a branch.

223

It gave, it shifted, the winch which was neat, geared, power-efficient, pulled on a line that went right across the hypotenuse of the triangle, from us to the Almendro, round a pulley and back to the end of the line he was hung from and it pulled that line from my tree towards the Almendro, and Sergeant James "Dusty" Miller with it.

His face was a picture.

But looks can't kill.

Still he was on to what was happening quick enough and was soon backpedalling or rather overarming above his head as fast as he could, towards the main tree. And then, just when he was about half-way, and I had the end of his line about half-way down the hypotenuse so he was over the very middle of the triangle, it all fell apart. Almost.

It must of been the storm blowing out of el Cerro de la Muerte, smashing into that coming off up out of the Pacific, coupled with the fact, I suppose, that well-engineered and tested though it all was, it was never presumed canopy research from aerial rope-ways was anything other than a fair-weather sport. Anyhow, something snapped and dropped him in it.

28

Don Jesús. The papers here say Miller had done parachute jungle drops. I didn't know that. But I knew plenty. He killed with his bare hands: Rosa, Trev, and Kit. He could outrun me though maybe twice my age. So, he could drop into the crown of a tropical rain forest tree with a long rope in his hand and get down. One thing he could not do was get back up again. He couldn't get to me from the main tree because the harness was at the top. He couldn't get to me from the Almendro because the lines were down. And he couldn't shin up forty metres of wet rope. Not unless he had been born on Krypton, which I was not quite ready to believe. For the time being he was down there and I was up here, and that was that. But I never forgot he might still be alive, if not too well.

In the morning I'll think of something. Meanwhile there was my cherub needed attention, poor soul that she was.

One thing: the storm seemed to have climaxed with the turbulence that took out Miller. It was leaking away like water from a bucket with a hole. Within twenty minutes the wind had almost dropped, the rain came only in occasional gusts, the thunder had moved on—a giant black anvil cloud above cumulus way out over the Pacific. The sun, also on the downward path now, got through in short jabs of light which for all they were short were hot, drew up instant mist around us and below, spreading magical shreds and puffballs through the tree crowns and again sucking heavenly fragrances from the blossoms.

Birds began to sing—not just cry or squawk. A couple of macaws, bright green, red and blue flapped across below us trailing banners the colour of lapis lazuli, the Laughing Snake-eater stuck his head out of his hole, looked this way and that, clambered onto its ledge, launched out on lazy pinions. As the motion of the tree settled I got Zena out of the Snugli. Oh dear, what a mess! But she didn't seem to mind, was soon gurgling and *di-di-dah*-ing as I sponged her down and dried her. Through all our vicissitudes I had managed to keep her Mothercare bag tied by its drawstring to one of the Snugli straps. So I had cotton wool, four disposable nappies, Savlon, a tiny tin of talc. Soon she was clean and fresh as a daisy. But hungry too. Me likewise ravenous and of course still sore all over and very very tired. I used some of the Savlon on my legs and feet. But what to eat? The one thing missing from the bag was the Greenfinger 5—I must have left it in the big tree.

The answer was soon provided. A busyness manifested itself over seven or eight of the larger trees on one side of us, that tree by tree came nearer and was now clearly seen to be a troupe of white-faced monkeys, capuchins, foraging through the crowns for leaves, flowers, fruit and nuts. We kept very still, Zena and I, and watched as four of them swung up into the lower branches of our tree from the top of its neighbour.

The largest scampered closer, saw us, stared with big black eyes framed in the white fur of his cowl, ran nearer a few steps, his long bushy tail erect but for a crook in the tip, jabbered at us, then spread-eagled and using his tail as well, hoisted himself into the leaves only a few feet above us. There he plucked one of the woody cases like the coconut part of a coconut fruit but not hairy, it looked too big for him but he managed, pulled at the end and like removed a lid. He rummaged inside and came out with a nut. He chewed off its brown outer covering, spitting it out, then ate with great relish the hard waxy flesh. He found four more nuts like that inside the pot before throwing it away and reaching for another.

By now he had been joined by his friends and relations, maybe wife, sons and daughter, for one had her little baby on her back, peaking over her shoulder as bright and intelligent-looking as Zena who went *ah! ah! ah!* and *pss, pss, pss* at them and tried to clap her hands. This amused them and Daddy swung in nearer. Looking up I saw a bunch of these cases just above my head. On three of them the cap, which was on the bottom as they hung down, had come away on its own and I could see the thumb-shaped nuts inside.

"Oh no, you don't," I said, and holding Zena on my hip, reached them down for myself.

With a bit of leaning and stretching but not too far you can be sure, I managed to collect eight pots which yielded thirty sound nuts. They were sweet to taste, very much like Brazils. I chewed them well, then, following the example of my newfound gossip with the baby, who perched in the angle of a branch twelve feet away, gave the chewing to my Zena, who relished this mash as much as her furrier cousin did. So after all we dined, and none too badly.

Shortly our friends moved on but were replaced by three more of the tribe, just as the sun was setting, who made their roost in the thickest branches above us, and for this company I was quite grateful for in the very last of the light three large bats came swooping and crying by and one perched upside down over the open end of a nut pot and contrived to shell out the nuts. It looked like a large black rag wrapped over it and I could see not so tiny fangs, piggy face and foxy ears. It could of been a vampire! It really could. Save it was eating nuts so was probably a Jamaican fruit bat. Nevertheless!

Before that though the sun set in a glory of reds and yellows and molten golds fanning up out of the Pacific over almost all of the sky, except for cloud palaces lit by its last rays above the distant Cerro.

Before the dark could sweep right in and shut out all, and while those bats flickered and squeaked around, I zipped Zena up again and crouched with her in the centre of our tiny platform with my back against a solid branch and rocked her gently thus and crooned a lullaby until I knew she slept.

Rinde, rinde, rinde	Let go, give in
tan chiquitita la negrita	such a tiny black babe
que no quiera dormir	to not want to sleep
cabeza de coco, grano de café	nut-head, coffee-bean
con lindas notitas	with sweet little notes
con ojos grandotes	with your great big eyes
como las ventanas	like windows
que miran al mar.	which look out at the sea.
Cierra los ojitos	Close your eyes
negrita asustada	little frightened black babe
el mandinga blanco	the white bogeyman
te puede comer.	might eat you.
Ya no eres esclava	Now you are not a slave

y si duermes mucho	and if you sleep a lot
el señor de casa	the man of the house
promete comprar	promises to buy
traje con botones	a suit with buttons
para hacer un rumbo.	fit for a party.
Rinde, rinde, rinde	Let go, give in
duerme mi negrita	go to sleep little black babe
mmm, mmmm, mmmm,	mmm, mmmm, mmmm,
cabeza de coco	nut-head
grano de café.	coffee-bean.

But sleep, I could not. For now the horrors and exertions of the day being finished and hunger too, and for the time being all mortal danger, I found space to grieve. I mourned Kit Carter. I grieved for the whole man—his straight body, his freckles, his incipient baldness, his prickly beard, his comic prick (really they all are, aren't they?), his balls, his hole, and his toes. His pale blue eyes, the spots on his shoulders, his tummy that had spread at Christbourne with the Ringwood bitter he liked to drink but had since gone slack, the varicose vein on his left leg.

I grieved the hang-ups he had had about his mother who was not too likeable in old age, and his father who may have been a saint but I knew only what Kit told me of him. Kit searched for him after his death, perhaps saw him in the prof at Hume, perhaps even in Hedborg. So. He had his hang-ups and who of us does not?

And his virtue was, when all was said and done, he was decent. Is there a better? Several. Activist, freedom fighter, revolutionary. These he was not, but those who are could learn from him decency if nothing else.

He threw up, and throw up is the right word, he sicked up his bonny career as senior lecturer with tenure to help grow two ears of corn . . . that's how I knew Greenfinger had got that quote wrong. So, he was a man. A decent man. I grieved and mourned and remembered him.

And out of my grief there rose with the moon from behind el Cerro de la Muerte, a day past full but huge and bright, an anger that heats me still but then when it first swelled in my breast I felt would consume me and my baby, burn us up like the phoenix herself, perched in her nest above the forest. And out of the anger came resolution. If Miller was not dead already I would kill him.   And I would find out all that lay behind the murder of my Kit, and his Rosa too, and what had happened to Trev Ev, find out all about *Zea diploperennis talamanca,* and why the men of AFI and Greenfinger had done so much evil and I would do what I could do to undo that evil.

This resolution brought with it a sort of calm and as the moon slipped past its zenith above our heads and those of our neighbours above us who whimpered and chattered and were restless with it, on down its silver track to the ocean, I felt a sort of languid warmth spread through my aching muscles, and I slept too.

29

Came the morning I was brisk. With that resolution now like a steel spring in my soul I got a move on. Because of the Cerro, light came before the sun and its heat so all was shrouded in thick mist, which may be was just as well, for the first thing I had to do was perhaps the scariest of all, and not to be able to see what I was doing was an advantage.

I didn't know what damage the storm had done. I didn't know for sure we would not be dropped into the misty abyss below. But using one of the lines that still linked our tree with the main one, and with Zena on my front, and using the harness we had come up in, I hauled us across the gulf. Two capuchins came down to the extremest end of the Monkey Pot that had fed and sheltered us so well to see us off. I was mad still, and didn't care, but it was a crazy thing to do.

Nevertheless I did it and ten minutes later clambered up through the trap into the aluminium tree station. Nothing was as we had left it. Scavengers had torn up the remains of the chicken, drunk the rum punch, and consumed the caviar and crispbread. Which was a shame because I needed breakfast. But there was a container Darwin had never got round to opening and in it a genuine Camembert made in Monte Verde, now a touch over the top, in fact runny, but full of nourishment. Best of all what I had come for, the S and W .38.

It's the simplest of guns which is why all over the world they give it to Mr. Plod. Not even Old Bill can get a short-nosed Smith and Wesson wrong. It's so simple even a simple black girl like me can make it work. The trigger has a long pull which takes back the hammer and winds the cylinder so it turns the next chamber, the next round into place for the hammer to drop on it at the end of the pull. Easy.

I hated the fucker. I hated the heavy but easy way it sat in

my hand.   The Heckler and Koch I had not time to get to know.
I just fired the shitter and tore its owner apart, and that was that.
I carried the S and W for almost a week and I got to know it—
its handiness, the six neat slugs in its heart, its infallibility.

Anyway I took it.   And I took it to be sure that if I found
Miller alive I'd be able to kill him.

But I have to say this.   I was so fucked up with exhaustion
and grief that I was taking chances all the time.   I'd have been
happy then to die, even, forgive me, take Zena with me, just so
long as I went in the cause of killing Miller if he was still alive,
then of getting even with Greenfinger.   My steel was not as true
than as it is now.   My attitude then was, Okay, if the bastards
have done for us at least we go down fighting.   Now I want to
win.   Still, at that time the attitude was the right one because
risks had to be taken and you don't take risks if you want to live,
you hang on and hope a better chance turns up.   But then I
mourned Kit, I still do but in a different way, then I mourned
him in such a way I could die with him—now I want to stay
alive, and help get the world to rights.

I checked out the harness with the jumars, left up there by
Miller, switched Zena onto my back, clipped up, swung over, and
dropped through the mist to the clear air below.   I quite had the
hang of the thing now, and we were soon down safe and sound,
but much bothered by an enormous cloud of flies we disturbed
off the cadaver of Darwin which revealed they were by no means
the only carrion feeders who had shown an interest.   This was
nasty but a timely warning too of what to expect when we reached
Everton's bivouac.

Then, with equaliser in my hand and ready to fire, I scouted
out into the forest and found the end of the snapped cable that
had dropped Miller, and no sign of him at all.   Lacking his jungle-trained skills I had to guess where he was.   Not difficult.
Either he was lurking, seeking an opportunity to jump me without getting his head shot off, or he was hurt and wanted out.   In
which case he'd gone back the way he came.   Since that was the
way I wanted to go too, indeed the only way out I knew, that
was fine.

Near the river I found a wild papaya which had handily dropped
three of its pale orange fruits in the storm, and while one was
already half eaten by wasps, the other two were sound.   They

were not as sweet as cultivated ones and the flesh was cream-colored instead of rose, but they kept me going.

With the last one in my hand I turned to set off again and as I did got the fright of my life—a sleek, black shadow dropped out of the papaya tree I had stooped beneath, a black cat. I stood as still as a statue. It looked at me from great yellowish-green eyes and I saw that it wasn't exactly black but that in the blackness like floating below its surface there were the mariposas, the butterfly markings of a jaguar, especially visible when she moved and sunflakes drifted down her back.

She? Oh yes. My sister. She rolled onto her back and wriggled and squirmed for a moment before righting herself. Then she gave herself a shake, yawned, licked her shoulder, and stretched up the papaya on her back legs only and had a good scratch at the bark before dropping back down. On all fours her shoulder was not as high as my knee but still I reckoned she must of weighed in not many kilos behind me. Don Jesús, she was lovely.

She began now seriously to wash, so I saluted her and moved gently off. She stopped washing for a moment, then went back to it. A hundred paces on I stopped and turned. She stopped washing again and came after me at a gentle trot like she knew I might be company, but stopped ten paces short of me and waited so I went on again. Zena saw her and said *psst, psst, aaht; psst, psst, psst, aaht*, which is what she usually says when she sees furry animals. We went on thus for perhaps a quarter of a mile, then when I stopped and turned for the fourth time she had gone and I never saw her again. But whenever I make a list of friends in my head I put her in with the sloth and the capuchin monkeys, but especially her.

The mist had cleared from all but the higher crags by the time I reached the bivouac. I paid as little attention as possible to the bodies. Kit's was less preyed upon than Scarface's, I suppose because less damaged. Scarface's certainly was a mess, and I had to cope with bits of it to get into Everton's bivouac, the blast of bullets having thrown him into the side of it. Fortunately the storm had toppled a tree quite close by and so there was much more light than hitherto.

I found a diary of rough notes, written in a neat, clear hand. Out of habit or training, he wrote on the spot wherever he collected a specimen, and made a fair copy each evening. This was the rough on-the-spot version. No doubt he'd taken the fair-copy text to San José. There was, is, for of course I still have it, an account of *Zea diploperennis talamanca* on the last pages used. Also he had a dried specimen, all its parts, mounted on paper. Once I had identified this from the bundle Fritz dropped when I blasted him I stuffed it with the diary down between the inner and outer pouches of the Snugli, and so kept my hands free.

I was about to leave after less than five minutes on the site when I discovered something that gave me another fright. The small camping gas stove on which Trevor had boiled up water for a nice cuppa for us was standing about fifteen yards away, and on it a saucepan of water.

The water was steaming.

I went over to it, but with the S and W leading the way. There was only half a cupful but it was still quite warm. On the floor beside it the mug Kit and I had shared, a strainer, and Trevor's caddy. The mug had a quarter of an inch of undrunk tea at the bottom. Miller. Who else?

I was ready to press on after him as fast as I could, but first I had to say some sort of goodbye. Kit looked peaceful, but his face was in the ground. I stroked his hair for a second, but did not move him. How could I? What for? Don Jesús, it was the living man I loved and want to remember, not a corpse. Tell the judge that, will you? Then I strode off as quickly as I could, and as quickly as the tears would let me, first to the river, even more swollen now, pounding and crashing through the riparian screen, and then on and upwards towards Sant'Simon, determined to catch that man up and execute him for what he did.

30

A pall of smoke, black and grey, hung above the settlement and a cloud of big black birds, King and Turkey Vultures, soared above it. As I got nearer, I could hear, through the roar of the waterfalls, shooting. Once on top I could see that the grey smoke came from burning crops, the black smoke from the flame throwers the police were using on the cabins. I put the S and W in the Mothercare bag. Even the leafy roof of the unfinished church was going well: flames flickered along the horizontal bar of the plain wooden cross that stood on the altar which was dressed in black. I remembered it was Good Friday.

The shooting was of the animals. Most were left where they fell and those found in the fields, notably two lovely mushroom-coloured, dusky-faced milch cows, were already a feast for the big flapping, hopping, tearing birds. But I saw the bodies of four piglets in the back of one of the Daihatsu jeeps, like Kit's but painted dark green, with bleeper lights on their roofs. One of the policemen also carried four live hens trussed by their legs and he tossed these in with the pigs. There wasn't anything else worth looting.

So, I thought, the jokes about the Costaricense police are . . . just jokes. This lot, Rural Guards, Rangers or whatever, acted like pigs the world over. Not pigs, filth. They were trashing Sant'Simon and humiliating the rightful owners as I quickly found out for they took me for one of them. Why not? There were Guatemalan Indians, a Honduran *mestiza*, why not a *negrita* from Puerto Limón. Anyway, next thing I knew as I walked past the jeeps I was pushed and then pinched hard in the ass and told to get a move on. I checked out no sign of Miller and did as I was told.

I walked as quickly as I could up the narrow road the commune had so cunningly built over five years so they could get their coffee beans up it. The coffee blossom now looked a mess—the brown rot streaking out from the centres of the flowers which hung like dirty cloths and gave off a sweeter smell tinged with decay. A lot of it, and a big harvest to come in five, six months, enough to make one man rich for a year instead of a hundred people tolerably comfortable. Was that what it was all about? Sure. One way and another.

The road wound on and up into the trees. Shortly the last stragglers came in view. The very old and the very young, Miguelito, Minerva's grandchild, amongst them. He recognised me. Us. And ran on up the line, but not far because Minerva was finding the climb heavy.

"Nana, nana," he cried in Spanish, "here is Ezzie, the English gentleman's woman. So he must be near and will make all well, and we'll be able to go back home after all."

She stopped, turned, five feet tall and five feet round, with her straw hat on to hide her clerical tonsure. Her face and dress were blackened, her eyes red with weeping and smoke. I stopped at such grief a yard in front of her and she turned back, climbed on, stumpy veined legs in flip-flops smacking the greasy road. I fell in beside her.

Presently she said, "They murdered Manuel."

I too began to cry.

"Yesterday. A band of men came with petrol and flame-throwers, and tried to fire the *páramo* above us. You know. Where the wild maize grows."

I knew.

"It wouldn't burn. Too wet. But Manuel and two others went up to stop them and they shot him. His friends brought him down. He died this morning, not long after sunrise."

We walked on, came to the point where the road crosses the shoulder of the spur and you can see much of the valley and all of Sant'Simon. She did not pause, walked on.

"He said, before he died, that we were defeated because we did not unite. Amongst ourselves, of course, yes. But not with the millions like us. *El pueblo unido jamás será vencido.* He said that this morning and died."

A few more turns and we came to the *recibidores*, the barns with shoots where trucks can turn and load up with coffee cherries. Parked in the bay beneath giant yuccas was a huge Mercedes

Ticabus—all yellows, reds and flashing chrome. Most of the commune stood round it, their bundles on the floor beside them, not getting in until made to.

Carmen came and stood by us.

"Has she told you about Manuel?"

I said she had.

She went on. "Three bad men brought Cristóbal"—she meant my Kit—"down to Sant'Simon in a big American car. Just after Manuel and Ipolito and Umberto had left for the *páramo*. Two of them took Cristóbal, who was hurt, down into the forest. The other waited for them until dusk, but they did not come back. He went away but came back this morning in the same big car, just after the police arrived with their eviction order. Do you know about this?"

"Yes. They killed Cristóbal in the forest. I killed one of them. I will kill the other when I find him."

"He came out of the forest not long before you. You nearly caught him. He was hurt quite badly in the arm. I think it was broken. He went off in the big car, they passed here only half an hour ago. I am sorry about Cristóbal. Very sorry. He did his best for us. I am sorry if it was because of us. . . ."

They wept but this time I did not. The anger was with me again now I knew for sure Miller was alive. My anger spread to include the commune—not because Kit had died for them, but because they were doing nothing. They stood round in their sloppy clothes, their worn, tired, dirty faces beneath their broken straw hats as expressionless as sheep. Waiting for the butcher. Why the fuck didn't they fight?

Rebecca joined us and Conchita. Rebecca, the Honduran with black and Chinese blood, had been beaten and abused by the filth precisely because she had these qualities. Now she had bad uterine pains. Conchita, the forest Indian from Guatemala feared she would abort and she had had no time to find the herbs and prepare the infusions she felt might save the baby.

The jeeps came roaring up the hill. Police with riot sticks pushed them, us, into the coach. It was a big coach but there was only just enough room even squashed three or four to a double seat and ten or so of the younger adults had to stand. Four police with guns like mine got in too. The bundles were loaded into the luggage holds. The big diesel engine coughed and roared, the doors hissed shut.   Come on, I thought, jump the pigs, get the guns, shoot them, do something.   But the gears ground and the engine roared as we began to swing up the bends and on to the *páramo*.

Beneath the oaks and yuccas, in bright sunlight, the wind caressed the russet and green sending a swell across it.   An alien shadow came in low, so low we could hear the roar of its engine; a Cessna Skyplane with the AFI logo on its side swooped over us.   And as it passed it began to shed a thin, sick orange mist that streamed from its asshole just in front of the tail-unit.   It spread out and left a swathe across the corn.   The Cessna climbed, banked, the sun on its wings, then back it came, evacuating its poison.   It could only be dioxin.   It will be rain-washed into the becks that rise in the *páramo*, it will drain into the Remedios, and it will destroy the valley.   The animals will suffer the diseases that afflict the women of Vietnam and Seveso, they will abort their foetuses or produce monsters.   The *páramo* will be destroyed in days.   The valley will die more slowly but just as surely.

The coach reached the highway, turned left, put the summit of el Cerro de la Muerte behind us, and suddenly we were back. Oh yes there were still great views from the watershed, out to the Pacific, across the rolling expanse of the Caribbean lowlands, and near to the great oaks of Costa Rica hung with mosses and lichens, and then, as we began the drop towards Cartago, the Swiss-like meadows with their huge pale cows, the lushlands where even the fenceposts sprout, and the volcanoes superb in the distance.   But the highway was giant trucks, buses like ours, monstrous logging machines on the move, diesel fumes, police on motorbikes, boardings advertising Coca-Cola and Greenfinger 5. We were back.

Zena was awake now.   I dandled her on my lap, then played pass the parcel with her.   She didn't care.   She was all right. She chortled and "di, di, di, dah," she said, and blew raspberries through her lips.   Oh yes, she raised a smile or two as the bus swung and roared on.   Minerva unwrapped a cloth and gave her a tortilla.   The last batch from Sant'Simon.   Maybe the last from *Zea diploperennis talamanca*.

Minerva said, "Babies like yours do us good.   Happy babies. They see the world as new and grand and great, they re-create for us all its possibilities and we believe again.   Even if we can do nothing else we should go on making babies. It keeps the hope alive." She took my hand in hers and patted it.

Behind us a guitar began to strum. Someone snapped fingers. The bus roared on.

Hacemos esta muralla	We must make this wall
Juntando todas las manos	By joining all our hands
Los negras sus manos	The Blacks their black hands
Los blancos sus blancas manos.	The Whites their white hands.
Al ruiseñor en la flor	To the nightingale in the flower,
Abre la muralla!	Open the wall!

31

Sun shone from a cloudless sky. Atlantic rollers showed what surfers call glass, carried long combs of spray, and a steady but not bothersome wind blew off the ocean, enough to keep the palm fronds alive, the flag moving, the air cool.

The vice-president stood at his desk high above it all, sipped scotch and watched through binoculars a girl thirty years his junior, who swam like a dolphin, surfed better than he had thirty years ago, and did it topless. She had sun-white hair cut very short, set off by very dark skin, which, because of the colour of her hair, he took to be the tan of those few sun and surf worshippers who never, ever leave the beach. Her breasts were small and firm and she had a small tight ass. Tight ass, tight pussy. Probably she knew, of course she knew, that senior execs, even directors, could see her through the bronze-tinted glass of their office suites. So. She had come to market. The question was, how much? For all he got horny whenever he saw her, he did not intend to get into an auction situation.

Here she comes. Here I goddamn near come too. She's on a real curler this time, should hold it all the way. The vice-president began to sway with her, flexing tummy muscles, clamping his buttocks, shifting taut balance from one foot to the other, then, oops, she's gone. Okay, like a dolphin she swims, but her surfing is not yet top-class. Maybe she'll let me coach her.

The vice-president pushed his binoculars into a drawer, returned his glass to the cocktail cabinet complete with stainless steel sink and fridge, pressed the button that concealed it behind walnut veneer. Then he pressed another button.

"I'll see Annenburg now." Digital Man, he added under his breath, Uncle Gadget.

Matt Annenburg was all brisk confidence, carried a plastic-bound report.

"Well, Mr. Vice-President, I think we are now about wrapped up on Operation Weedkiller. It's been a long haul, some shit hit the fan, but nothing we couldn't sanitise, and all just within budget. I have here for you personally, no one else has seen it bar my own personal staff, the latest update on the situation as of now."

"Fine Matt. Just leave it there."

"I think I should say sir, once we had the Tenerife situation figured out, we were able to move quite quickly and contain it."

"Oh sure Matt. But I can read, you know?"

There was a pause. Almost long enough for it to seem to register Annenburg's surprise that this should be so.

"Then sir, I'll leave you . . . with it."

"Fine Matt. Fine. And stay close, won't you?"

"Of course, sir."

Close? What did he mean? Not go away or not tell anyone else? Annenburg took no chances if he could help it. He returned to his own section of Core One, declared to his staff that he was out to all but the vice-president, and settled in to playing out his latest computer game. The blurb suggested four weeks for an ace. After ten days he reckoned he had damn near cracked it.

The vice-president leafed through the folder. He saw that nothing in the first sixteen pages was new. He took up the story that far in.

Miller sustained quite serious injuries in his fall. He dislocated his left shoulder, broke his left collarbone, and the bone in his upper arm. Yet again he demonstrated how well he was adapted for the assignment for which I had had him recruited. Only fitness and a trained resistance to pain got him back to Sant'Simon. Francisco Franco also showed commendable initiative. He arrived there early in the morning although the rendezvous had not been kept the previous afternoon. He drove Miller to the Central Hospital, Parque Carillo, San José. There Miller underwent minor bone-setting surgery and was put under sedation.

Esther Somers made a rational guess, went to the hospital where she used guile and charm at the Casualty Department Reception to obtain Miller's admission card for just long enough to ascertain Miller's name and address at the Fortuna Hotel. She learned that he would not be able to move for twenty-four hours, and would be asked to remain hospitalized for much longer.

Somers then went back to Carter's apartment, cleaned herself up, collected money and checks and credit cards which she held jointly with Carter. She also took personal articles for herself and her infant. She also collected the telephone answering-machine cassette on which was recorded Portillo's last message to Carter.

Next she went to Everton's apartment. The police had sealed it. Nevertheless, continuing to use the resource which has made her a formidable nuisance, she sweet-talked her way into the next-door apartment on the pretext that she was an old friend of Everton's. She climbed the partition between the two balconies, broke a window, and recovered Everton's Microwriter, whose memory may still hold the rough draft of Everton's report on *Zea diploperennis talamanca*. She then booked into the Fortuna Hotel and obtained a room close to Miller's.

Miller discharged himself from the Central Hospital on Sunday, Easter Sunday, April seventh, and returned to the Fortuna. Somers overheard him asking the desk clerk to book him first-class on the earliest route to Tenerife Sud. She booked herself on the same flight but traveled economy. She returned to Carter's apartment where she collected a large suitcase which she filled with clothes and bedding and placed the Smith and Wesson .38 in the middle. Ballistic tests have since confirmed that this belonged to Charles Darwin, Junior; the gun itself remains unrecovered. Somers consigned this suitcase to baggage where it escaped close examination.

It was now a simple-enough matter for Somers to follow Miller through Miami, Madrid, and so to Tenerife. It seems from accounts I have at hand of her appearance in Costa Rica (source: Francisco Franco), and from the police mug shot in Santa Cruz, that somewhere along the line she contrived an important change in her appearance which may have left Miller off guard regarding her.

On arrival in Tenerife Miller went directly to the apartment that had been reserved for him and deposited the money Francisco Franco had paid him, and other effects, in a small hotel-style safe. This presented no difficulties, and the money and other documentary evidence that might link him to us are now in-house.

Miller, in spite of his injuries, now went out on the town. He was followed by Somers. Their movements become a matter of conjecture. But Miller certainly propositioned and picked up a local whore called María Victoria de los Angeles with whom

Somers had probably already struck up an acquaintance. At two o'clock on the afternoon of Tuesday, April ninth, Miller took María Victoria de los Angeles to his apartment in Paraíso del Mar. The girl helped Miller who was the worse for drink compounded with powerful dysilgesics on to a sun-lounger on his balcony. She then brought him a strong rum and Coke of which he drank half very quickly. The girl sat with him in hot sunlight on the balcony for twenty minutes. She then withdrew and three minutes later Somers appeared on the balcony. Miller now appeared to be asleep. Somers slapped him into wakefulness and then shot him three times in the head with Darwin's Smith and Wesson.

All this was observed by two tourists who had been sunbathing on the next balcony. They reported what they had seen to the police, who arrested Somers at Tenerife Sud airport. Later they also arrested María Victoria de los Angeles on suspicion of being an accessory. Both girls were remanded in custody and are now at La Familia Sagrada Casa de Corrección para Las Mujeres, Santa Cruz, Tenerife, pending full committal proceedings.

They are represented by Licenciado Don Jesús Batista y Galdós, a local lawyer with a reputation for quixotry and civil rights agitation. He is also very able. We believe he is attempting to put together a defense of justifiable homicide and to this end he has persuaded Somers to tape a full account of why she killed Miller. Batista is incorruptible but one of his clerks is not, and we have a transcript of this tape, a copy of which is appended as Appendix A.

It is clear from this transcript that Somers must be treated as a hostile with topmost rating, and effectively neutralised. Three courses of action present themselves.

(1) Termination. This is not as of now, considering her whereabouts, a viable option. There is also the question of the telephone answering-machine cassette, Everton's notes and specimen of *Zea diploperennis talamanca*, and Everton's Microwriter. None of these has come to light. Clearly if they enter the public domain following Somers's demise, they could cause us considerable damage.

(2) Somers is, however, vulnerable through the infant Zena Carter Somers. Her possessive attitude to this infant is clearly expressed in her deposition to Batista at several points. If a credible threat to remove the infant is mounted, it is our opinion Somers will be induced to reveal the whereabouts of the missing articles and alter her plea.

(3) Pressure can be exercised in Costa Rica to ensure that the

242

deaths of Portillo, Everton, Carter, and even Darwin, and the subsequent murder of Miller are presented as the outcome of a sordid sexual entanglement. No connection will be made with Sant'Simon, or Bullburger Costaricense, SA.

I have to report options two and three are being implemented as of now. Francisco Franco reports considerable progress in San José. In Santa Cruz there have been difficulties, mainly the result of the nimble legal footwork of Batista, but I see light at the end of the tunnel. Infant Zena remains the Joker in our pack and the threat to have her put in state care or handed over to Somers's British foster-parents looks likely to pay off. If, as above, this all works out we might bring option one off the backburner though I do foresee that a Spanish court, influenced by reports from San José along the lines suggested, might well convict Somers for premeditated murder and sentence accordingly. This would be, in my view, the most satisfactory outcome.

I should like to close this interim report with an update UNAFO-wise. Here, I have to say, everything has gone well. Roberto González has retired prematurely to his sanatorium, where he is comfortable. Hedborg provisionally sits at the Middle America Desk, but the appointment will not be confirmed until the Board of Governors, on which we are represented not only de facto but through the State Department, meets in December.

Hedborg accepts the San José police reconstruction regarding the deaths of Carter, Portillo, and Everton. Apparently he reacted quite badly to Somers's out-of-order behavior when he dined with Somers and Carter at the Playboy, and is ready to accept that version of events. Later, at Greenfinger Cay, he expressed the opinion that Carter had "gone a little off his rocker over Sant'Simon," and since then he has ascribed this personality imbalance to the emotional strain of holding his corner in the Portillo/Somers/Everton affair. We are giving him maximum publicity and cooperation over the Belize Project, and while this may be a loss-making operation for some time, it will have its spin-offs, not least in continuing the process of peripheralizing the British. In that of course we have the fullest support of the State Department and even, I believe, of the White House itself.

The vice-president pushed the report away. From the other side of his desk he pulled in a sheaf of telex print-out. Then he reopened the cocktail cabinet, poured himself another three fingers of scotch, and spent five minutes watching the tall, dark, but white-haired girl in the surf. At last she wrapped a large red towel round herself and disappeared beneath the cement coping of the sea wall.

He pressed a button. "I'll have Annenburg again."

When Annenburg came in the vice-president was looking not at the surf but across to Core Two where one of the tinted windows reflected the AFI logo, the "I" a corncob, slowly turning against a sky flawed only by a vapour trail.

"I like your report, Matt. It's most thorough."

"Why, Mr. Vice-President, that is really most—"

"One thing though."

"Sir?"

"It's dated four days ago."

"Well, yes. I finished my own draft just five days ago. My secretary tidied up—"

"Where you been for four days, Matt?"

"Well, sir, I had some leave due me. Actually, because of this business I missed my Easter break and—"

"You've not been in the office for four days."

"That is not quite correct, sir. This is the fourth day. . . ." His voice died.

The vice-president let the AFI logo turn three times, finished his drink. He turned.

"Matt, take a look at that telex stuff. No. Skip it. I'll tell you." He leant on the desk, thrust his large round head forward, let spittle form on his over-pronounced bottom lip. Annenburg, tall, thin, in immaculate, genuinely London-tailored suit, flinched back, grabbed for his spectacles and handkerchief.

The spittle flew. "That telex stuff is from Santa Cruz, Tenerife. Neither Somers nor that brat either, for that matter, are on Tenerife any longer. The whore had a pimp. A skilful operator. He got them out of the Casa de Corrección, got them false passports, and got them on a plane. To Lisbon in the first instance and no one knows where the fuck since. It's just possible that nimble-footed asshole of a lawyer had a hand in it. And they did it night of Friday. No one knew they were gone until Saturday morning. And no one thought of sending us that telex until yesterday P.M. Today is Thursday. They have been running for damn near a week. Annenburg, you can stuff your options one, two and three—"

244

"Sir. This is terrible. I should have been told. I'll get straight—"

"Annenburg. Piss off. When I got that, when I found you were AWOL, I took you off Operation Weedkiller. Jethro has been in charge as of this A.M. Now get out before you shit yourself."

Heart pounding, the vice-president freshened his glass, lit a cigar. It took a long time for his pulse to come back to normal. He waited, and looked down the wide boulevard that separated hotels, condominiums and office blocks from the ocean, looking for that white head. At last, he said, aloud, "That I enjoyed." He slapped his thick thigh. "Shee-it! I enjoyed that. Digital Man has had his digit well and truly returned to where it belongs."

Half an hour later his own lift took him down to his own bay in the basement car park. He got into his metallic purple Rolls Bentley. Three barriers rose for him in response to signals from the car itself, and a ramp decanted him into the bright sunlight. A fourth barrier rose and fell, and as it did an open Lincoln slid across the slipway in front of him. A cassette blasted from its stereo speakers.

We're living in the heart of the common people
Smile from the heart of a family man
Daddy's going to buy you a dream to cling to
And Mama's going to love you as much as she can
And she can. . . .

Two girls. One, with swags of black hair, wearing shades, olive skin, sat in the back with a coffee-coloured baby who wore a tasselled leather waistcoat. The other, very dark skin set off by silvery short hair and a mini-skirted red dress, snapped off the audio, left the driving seat, and came towards him. She was carrying a small, soft leather bag. Across the sudden silence the baby shouted, "Di, di, di, dah, daah!"

The vice-president's blood began to pound again. Shee-it, she's a nigger. It's five years since I had a black ass. Tight, black pussy. His window slid down. He half put his head out.

The girl stooped. She was very tall.

"I'm Esther Somers," she said, and she shot him three times in the head. Some of the debris came back on her forearm. She

245

dropped the empty Smith and Wesson .38 on the car floor at his feet.

She returned to the Lincoln. "Mama's going to love you just as much as she can / And she can . . ." receded as the big car slipped away.

Half a minute passed before the Rolls Bentley stalled. High up and behind it the AFI logo continued to turn, and the green and gold corncob flashed back in the sun.